Dear Reader,

For many years Harlequ
supporting and promoti
to women, and celebrati
extraordinary difference.
The Harlequin More Than Words program honors
three women each year for their compassionate
dedication to those who need it most, and donates
$15,000 to each of their chosen causes.

Within these pages you will find stories written by
Sherryl Woods, Christina Skye and Pamela Morsi.
These stories are beautiful tributes to the Harlequin
More Than Words award recipients and we hope they
will touch your heart and inspire the real-life heroine
in you.

Thank you for your support. Net proceeds from the
sale of this book will be reinvested into the Harlequin
More Than Words program so we can continue to
support more causes of concern to women. And you
can help even more by learning about and getting
involved with the charities highlighted by Harlequin
More Than Words, or even nominating an outstanding
individual in *your* life for a future award. Together we
can make a difference!

Sincerely,

Donna Hayes
Publisher and CEO
Harlequin Enterprises Ltd.

NEW YORK TIMES BESTSELLING AUTHOR

SHERRYL WOODS

BESTSELLING AUTHORS
Christina Skye
Pamela Morsi

HARLEQUIN
MORE THAN WORDS

Where Dreams Begin

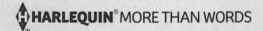

HARLEQUIN® MORE THAN WORDS

Recycling programs
for this product may
not exist in your area.

ISBN-13: 978-0-373-83784-7

MORE THAN WORDS: WHERE DREAMS BEGIN

Copyright © 2013 by Harlequin Books S.A.

Sherryl Woods is acknowledged as the author of *Black Tie and Promises*
Christina Skye is acknowledged as the author of *Safely Home*
Pamela Morsi is acknowledged as the author of *Daffodils in Spring*

Printed in U.S.A.

www.Harlequin.com

CONTENTS

Stories Inspired by Real-Life Heroines

RUTH RENWICK
∽—Inside the Dream—∽

Imagine you're a seventeen-year-old high school student. You've worked hard, done well and now you're about to graduate. Your classmates are looking forward to the graduation festivities, but for you the prospects do not look promising. In fact, it's unlikely you will be able to go. There's nothing in your closet remotely suitable to wear for the occasion, and no money to buy what you need.

It may come as a surprise to some to learn how many students face this dilemma. One of the most important occasions in their young lives is looming, and they're actually dreading it because they're probably going to have to miss it. Too many quietly withdraw rather than face the misery and embarrassment of showing up without a dress or tuxedo suitable for the occasion.

Ten years ago Ruth Renwick decided to do something about this. A social worker in the Greater Toronto Area's Peel Region, she was accustomed to helping people in all sorts of troubling situations, so when a fellow worker, Tracey Ciccarelli, called to ask for help for a single mother whose daughter could not afford to attend her graduation, Ruth went home and ransacked her closets for something suitable. She also provided a corsage, shawl, jewelry and a disposable camera so the girl could take pictures of her graduation.

Helping that girl was the beginning of Inside the Dream, a not-for-profit organization that Ruth set up to assist high school graduates in straitened circumstances. Since that day, she has so far helped 1,803 students realize their dreams of graduating alongside their peers.

At a special Boutique Day held once a year in May, the students—who have all been referred by a social worker or counselor—turn up to select gowns (from a minimum of three to five choices for each student, "to give them options"), tuxedos, shoes and accessories. Last year, about 267 students in the area benefited from this service.

Ruth is touched by their stories. Some of the recipients have such low self-esteem that they're barely able to make eye contact. One girl who was shown a beautiful dress told Ruth, "I don't deserve that dress," and eventually selected the plainest one she could find. Ruth put the beautiful dress in a bag and gave it to her social worker for her. Another girl, verbally abused at home, arrived early at a Boutique Day on her way to her part-time job. "We weren't ready, but she didn't have much time, so we let her come and choose what she needed," Ruth says. As she left, the girl told Ruth, "I never had a reason to smile until today." That girl has now graduated from university.

It's students like that—"smart kids in need, kids with great potential"—who inspire Ruth to redouble her efforts. She is constantly on the lookout for people who can help her with donations of clothing and accessories, and isn't the least bit shy about approaching a beautifully dressed woman at a charity event and persuading her to contribute a gown—and to get her friends involved, as well.

As a social worker, Ruth sees all kinds of people in need—so why this particular cause? "I'm a mother," she says simply. "I know what it means to young people to want to celebrate something they have accomplished. It's one of the first big events in your life. I want to help them create memories." And so, with meticulous care, she creates the opportunity for each one of them to be a prince or princess for the day.

Originally from Peru, Ruth had trouble at first believing that there could be such a need in Canada. One mother cried when Ruth took a picture of her with her daughter on graduation day. "She had never had her picture taken with her daughter."

Janace King-Watson, a social worker who worked closely with Ruth for three years, calls her an "incredible blessing" to families. "She makes the young people feel really special and treats them with such dignity," she says. She remembers the beaming face of a boy she had never seen smile, who was transformed by his graduation formal wear. "Something happened that day that made all the difference," she says, noting that many more of the students are now attending their proms as well as graduation, something they were reluctant to do before because they didn't want to embarrass themselves.

The students who come to the Boutique Day are comfortable because they know all their information is confidential. They are each accompanied by a volunteer "godmother" (for girls) or "godfather" (for boys) to help and advise them. The volunteers take tremendous pride in the successful outcomes for the students, Ruth says. "Look what happened to my boy" or "my girl" is a typical reaction.

Volunteers are a big part of the enterprise. They include the hairdresser who styles each girl's hair before her big event, the person who does makeup, a professional photographer and a seamstress who does the alterations, as well as the many individuals who run errands and donate clothing, and corporate sponsors who provide everything from snacks and dinners to cosmetics and tickets to various events for the students. A school in the area recently held a drive and donated almost three hundred dresses, and boxes of tuxedos were sent from a boutique in New Jersey that was closing. Ruth uses her website to solicit donations, but also to provide help and advice to other communities interested in setting up a similar program.

By persistence and persuasion, Ruth is helping to build precious memories for young people who would otherwise be deprived of a pleasure others take for granted. She wants everyone she meets to become involved. "If you can't give me anything yourself," she tells people, "you have friends who might be able to."

It's not just a request for help—it's an invitation to come Inside the Dream.

For more information visit www.insidethedream.org or write to Inside the Dream Formal Attire Program, 3326 Martins Pine Crescent, Mississauga, Ontario L5L 1G4, Canada.

SHERRYL WOODS

∽―Black Tie and Promises―∽

∿—SHERRYL WOODS—∿

With her roots firmly planted in the South, Sherryl Woods has written many of her more than 100 books in that distinctive setting, whether in her home state of Virginia, her adopted state, Florida, or her much-adored South Carolina.

She is the *New York Times* and *USA TODAY* bestselling author of the Sweet Magnolias series and is best known for her ability to create endearing small-town communities and families. She divides her time between her childhood summer home overlooking the Potomac River in Colonial Beach, Virginia, and her oceanfront home with its lighthouse view in Key Biscayne, Florida. Visit her at SherrylWoods.com.

CHAPTER
~ONE~

Jodie Fletcher leaned across her desk and studied the earnest expression on Laurie Winston's face. Though beautiful and popular, Laurie was one of those high school seniors who actually thought more about others than she did about herself. Perhaps it was simply her upbringing, or maybe losing her mother at fifteen had turned Laurie into a more compassionate person. Whatever the explanation, Jodie tended to give more credence to Laurie's heartfelt pleas than she did to those of the teenager's self-absorbed classmates.

Okay, there was more to it than that, Jodie admitted to herself. She paid attention because Laurie was Trent Winston's daughter. A lifetime ago Jodie and Trent had been in a relationship that had been doomed from the start. She'd seen that, even if Trent hadn't.

Trent had ambitions to make it big in high-end residential construction, and he'd needed a woman by his side who could help him make the climb to the top. Jodie hadn't been that woman. She'd had zero self-confidence after years of being the less-than-perfect daughter, the less-than-perfect student, the less-than-perfect younger sister. Back then, she hadn't considered herself an ideal match for anyone, despite Trent's obvious feelings for her.

In what might have been the most unselfish gesture of her life, she'd ended the relationship, setting Trent free to find someone better suited to help him build his empire than a woman still struggling to find herself. He'd fought for her for a while, but in the end he must have seen the wisdom in her decision because he'd finally stopped calling. A couple of years after the breakup, she'd read about his marriage to Megan Davis, the socialite daughter of multimillionaire Warren Davis, a gorgeous, delicate woman with all the right connections. Only then had Jodie truly moved on.

When she'd joined the staff at Rockingham High School last year, she'd been taken aback when she'd gone through the student records and discovered that Laurie

Winston was Trent's daughter and that he owed for two years. Every time she encountered she avidly looked for traces of Trent in Laurie's features. Obviously, though, Laurie had inherited her coloring and looks from her mother's side of the family. Jodie did see a tiny hint of Trent in Laurie's persistence and in the way she spoke so passionately when she cared about something, like now.

"There has to be something we can do, Ms. Fletcher," Laurie repeated. "There just has to be. It's not fair that so many kids miss the prom and all the other graduation activities just because they don't have anything to wear. It happens every year and it's wrong."

Jodie had often thought much the same thing at her old school in a neighboring district, but until this past summer she'd been at a loss as to what could be done. Now she actually had a few ideas, thanks to a friend she'd visited in Canada who was familiar with a program called Inside the Dream that provided clothing, accessories and everything else that was needed to kids who might otherwise have to miss those important senior-year events.

Longtime staff at Rockingham High School told Jodie that as the prom had become more elaborate and expensive, it was no longer within reach for many of the students. More and more young people pretended not to care that they were missing their senior prom. Girls with stars in their eyes, who'd been dreaming of that night ever since they'd started high school, suddenly claimed to have better things to do. The boys, rigid with pride, made their own plans for a guys' night out and swore it was better than any dumb old dance could ever be.

As a counselor, Jodie had seen the same unspoken heartbreak many times at her previous school, but she was curious about what had made Laurie aware of the dilemma faced by many of her classmates.

"Why is this so important to you?" she asked the teen.

With her pale complexion, there was no mistaking the blush that spread across Laurie's cheeks. She brushed a strand of silky blond hair back from her face. A diamond tennis bracelet winked on her wrist. "Actually it's because of Mike," she admitted. "You know Mike Brentwood, right?"

Since Rockingham High only had a few hundred students, Jodie knew most of them, at least by name. She knew Mike better than most. She nodded. "You and Mike have been dating for a while now, haven't you?"

"Since we were juniors," Laurie said.

"So you know his family?"

Laurie nodded.

"Then you've known for some time that the expense

of a big dance might be more than he could handle," Jodie suggested.

Mike was one of four kids being raised in a mostly affluent community by a struggling single mom who earned minimum wage. Money was always tight. Jodie knew more than she intended to share with Laurie. She'd already helped to get Mike's younger sisters and brother free school breakfasts and lunches because they were coming to school hungry too often. Mike had refused any similar help for himself, claiming he got to eat at his after-school job as a busboy at a local restaurant.

"I've known from the beginning that it's tough for his family," Laurie said. "Last year we skipped prom. We talked about doing that again this year, and to be honest, I'd be okay with it, but I can tell Mike feels really, really bad about it, like he's letting me down or something. And then, when we were setting up the organizing committee, I was talking to a couple of girls in my class and they admitted they didn't have the money for dresses and getting their hair done and all that stuff, so I started asking around. There must be at least a dozen girls, probably more, who can't afford to do any of the things that the rest of us can. I didn't ask the boys, but I'll bet there's just as many of them who don't have extra cash. They shouldn't be left out, Ms. Fletcher. Like I said before, it's wrong."

Jodie nodded, impressed by her compassion. "Okay, then, if you've done all this research, I'm sure you have some thoughts about what needs to happen."

Laurie grinned. "Actually, that's why I came to you. You're in the business of fixing things. I only had one idea and basically it sucked."

Jodie laughed at her candid assessment. "What idea was that?"

"To cancel prom and do something different that everyone could afford." Laurie shrugged. "That didn't seem fair, either. In fact, I'd probably get run out of school for even suggesting it."

"You could be right," Jodie agreed. There were some traditions that no one wanted to tamper with. The prom was one of those rites of passage.

"So?" Laurie asked, that earnest expression back on her face. "Do you have any ideas?"

"Actually, I do," Jodie admitted. "But it's only a few months until prom. It would take a lot of work to pull off my plan in time, but I'm willing to give it a try if you'll agree to work with me."

"Tell me," Laurie said eagerly. "I'm sure I can get

more people to help if it means everyone will be able to participate this year."

Jodie pulled up the Inside the Dream Web site on her computer and turned the screen so that Laurie could see it. "A friend I was visiting last summer told me about this organization," she explained. "They find donations of dresses, suits, tuxedos, shoes, you name it. Some tuxedo rental businesses donate gift certificates. The organizers get volunteer seamstresses to make alterations. They find hairstylists and makeup artists who can help out."

Laurie's eyes lit up. "That is so awesome. I'll bet we could do that here. A lot of moms give tons of business to the boutiques in the area. I'll bet they could persuade some of them to donate gowns. And there must be a lot of dads who buy or rent tuxedos all the time, too. They might be able to arrange for some rentals or give us their old tuxes."

"Some of your classmates might view getting a free gown or a tuxedo as charity," Jodie cautioned. "They still might not want to go to prom."

"But at least it'll be their choice, then. It won't be because it's impossible."

"What about tickets, Laurie?" Jodie asked. "Have you considered that? The cost of the tickets alone can be prohibitive for some of these students. Unless you're willing to cut costs dramatically and do a smaller event, all of the rest might not matter."

Laurie sat back. "Oh, my gosh, I hadn't even thought about that. We've barely started with all arrangements, but I already know how expensive the hotel and food are going to be. We tried to get good deals, but I don't see any way to cut those costs."

"Unless you did the prom here," Jodie suggested. "That's what lots of high schools do."

Laurie looked skeptical. "I could suggest it, I suppose, but I know the committee would hate it."

"Any other ideas, then?" Jodie asked.

Suddenly Laurie's expression brightened. "I remember some of the moms talking about a fund-raiser they were doing. They found businesses to underwrite a lot of the costs. Do you think we could do that, maybe have a program with ads in it? I'll bet if we explained that this was something kids were going to save and look at again and again and show their parents, too, a lot of stores would see it as good advertising. Then we could cut ticket prices. I think everyone should pay something, though, don't you?"

"I do," Jodie agreed. She had to admire Laurie's enthusiasm and her wisdom. "Okay, then, once you know your hotel and food costs, do a mock-up of the program and figure out possible ad sizes and costs. You could even pitch the hotel to see if they'd give you a bit of a break in return for a full-page ad. I'd suggest you have a separate committee to handle all this, since it's going to be time-consuming."

Laurie started scribbling notes like mad. "We have a committee meeting tomorrow. I'll bring this up then."

"And let's make a list of the donations and volunteers we'll need," Jodie suggested, reaching for her own pad and pen and starting to jot down notes.

"You're the best, Ms. Fletcher. This is going to be the best prom ever."

Not the best, Jodie thought, but if she could make a difference for just a few teens, give them memories she'd never had, it would be worth all the extra time she'd have to put in over the next few months. It would also give her a chance to spend some time with Trent's daughter and get to know her a little better. And maybe find out just what kind of man Trent had become.

Trent Winston shrugged out of his tuxedo jacket, jerked off the annoying bow tie he'd struggled with earlier, and then went to work on the studs in the overly starched shirt.

"I am never, ever going to another black-tie event,"

he declared to the empty room as he tossed the offending garments onto his king-size bed. To lend emphasis to
the statement, he entered his walk-in closet and pulled
out two more custom-tailored tuxedos and threw them
onto the bed as well.

He looked up to see his daughter in the doorway, staring at him with a bewildered expression.

"What are you doing?" Laurie asked, her gaze on the
discarded formal wear.

"I've just made a decision," he announced. "I have at-
tended my last black-tie event."

"Really?"

To his surprise, she didn't seem the least bit upset.
For years she'd loved to sit quietly and watch while he
and her mother got ready for all of the fancy charity auc-
tions, dinners and dances that Megan insisted they attend if his company was to grow. Megan had considered
these extravagant bashes to be an investment in their
future. Laurie had always acted as if her parents were
leading some elaborate fairy-tale existence—the dark-
haired prince taking his blond princess off to the ball.

Since Megan's death, he'd continued to pay the ex-
orbitant prices for these mostly boring functions out of
habit, but the reality was that Winston Construction no
longer needed the same exposure that it had in its early

days. He'd been custom-building luxury homes in the far western suburbs of northern Virginia for more than a dozen years now. His reputation was solid, and word-of-mouth gave him more opportunities than he could ever accept without sacrificing his hands-on approach which included overseeing every detail from framing the house to installing the kitchen cabinets. These days he could just as easily write a check and satisfy the company's commitment to various charities. It would leave his nights free to spend time with his daughter, who was growing up too darn fast.

Tonight she was wearing wrinkled pajamas that to his eye didn't look all that different from the casual pants and tank tops she wore to the mall, though these pants did have some kind of kitty design she probably wouldn't be caught dead wearing out in public. With her face scrubbed clean of makeup, he was able to forget for a moment that she was seventeen, almost an adult. It always caught him off guard when he realized that next year she'd be away at college. Right now, she still looked like his little girl.

"Okay, what's on your mind?" he asked, expecting the lecture Megan would have given him about the importance of networking. In some ways, Laurie was her mother's daughter, savvy about getting ahead. She'd already chosen her college major—investment banking. In other ways, she'd inherited his down-to-earth attitude and total lack of pretensions.

"What are you going to do with those tuxes?" she asked, surprising him.

"Give them to a thrift shop, I suppose. Why?"

"Can I have them?"

He stared at her blankly. "Why would you want three tuxedos?"

She grinned. "Prom's coming up, and yesterday Ms. Fletcher and I came up with this totally awesome idea to make sure that everybody gets to go. Did you know there are kids at school who stay home every year because they can't afford the tickets or the clothes?"

"I had no idea," he said. "And frankly, I'm a little surprised that it matters so much to you."

"Dad, you know why," she said impatiently. "Mike."

The single word was enough to have him grinding his teeth. Mike Brentwood was a good kid. He was polite, hard-working and seemed smart enough, but Trent thought Laurie was way too young to be so serious about a boy. Any boy.

Every time he tried to broach the subject, though, she looked at him as if he'd just arrived from Mars and was speaking some incomprehensible language. Or worse, as if he were some prejudiced jerk who hated the kid for being poor. Trent hadn't always had money. He knew what it was to struggle to make ends meet. He also knew that a serious relationship could be a distraction that a kid like Mike didn't need. He wasn't just thinking of his daughter, he told himself nobly. He was also thinking of Mike and his future.

He decided now was not the time to rehash that particular sore subject.

"If Mike needs to borrow a tuxedo, all you have to do is ask," he told Laurie.

"You're missing the point, Dad. He's not the only one. And Mike would never accept charity from you. He'd be totally humiliated."

Trent could understand that. To be honest, he would have felt the same way at eighteen. Borrowing clothes from his girlfriend's dad would have been too embarrassing. He'd had a tough-enough time swallowing his pride as an adult and letting Megan's father back him when he'd started up his business. Even though the deal had been handled in a totally businesslike fashion and he'd paid back every dime of that money with interest, it had put their relationship on an uneven footing from the beginning. He doubted they'd have had any contact at all now if it weren't for Laurie. Warren Davis adored his granddaughter as he had his own daughter. Trent would never get in the way of that bond, especially with Megan gone.

He sat down on the edge of his bed and patted a place beside him. "Tell me about this plan of yours."

Laurie sat cross-legged beside him and explained that so many kids missed out on activities because they couldn't afford the right clothes or even the tickets. "So, I spoke to Ms. Fletcher and she told me about Inside the Dream, an organization that helps kids get to the prom. We looked at the Web site and decided that even though we only have a few months, we could do the same thing here. The prom committee met today and everyone agreed. In fact, they're really jazzed about the whole idea. I'm in charge of finding clothing donations and accessories. Dave Henderson and Marcy Tennyson said they'd try to get underwriting and sell ads in the program. Sue McNally is contacting hairstylists and manicurists." She rolled her eyes. "With the money she and her mom spend in salons, I'm sure they won't have any trouble guilting people into helping. Ms. Fletcher said she'd try to find a seamstress who could make alterations. And she's in charge of identifying all the kids who might need clothes for that night. I gave her a list, but she'll finalize it. She thinks some are going to be pretty hard to sell on the idea."

"She could be right," Trent warned. He thought of the teenage sons of some of his employees. Their families were struggling to remain in homes they'd had for years and were resentful of the wealthy newcomers who'd moved into the area, even as they accepted that their income was dependent on those same people.

"The boys might have an especially hard time with it. Have you spoken to Mike to see what he thinks?"

She shook her head. "But I'm not worried. I'm leaving that to Ms. Fletcher. She can talk anybody into anything. She's great!"

"Still, it sounds like a lot to be accomplished in a short period of time. It's already January and prom is when? May?"

Laurie nodded.

"Sounds like you have your work cut out for you. What do you need from me besides the clothes off my back?"

Laurie giggled. "Dad, you said yourself you weren't ever going to wear those tuxedos again. If you change your mind, you can buy a new one."

"I won't change my mind," he said adamantly.

Laurie's expression sobered. "It's because of Mom, huh? You don't like going to those parties without her."

"That's part of it," he conceded. "But I never liked going in the first place. Your mom thought they were important for business and she enjoyed them. She'd grown up going to all sorts of fancy events. Me, I feel dressed up if my blue jeans have a crease in them."

Because he didn't want to talk about all the differences between him and Megan, differences that had started to grate before she'd been diagnosed with cancer, he changed the subject. He never wanted to disillusion Laurie with the knowledge that her parents' marriage had been anything but idyllic right up until the end. Her mom was gone. There was no reason to spoil the memories.

"Come on, kiddo, what else can I do to help?"

"After the committee meeting today, Ms. Fletcher and I talked again. We were thinking that it might be fun if we had a big place where all the girls could spend the day together going through the dresses and shoes and stuff, sort of like a real shopping spree. The guys, too. Not in the same room, of course, just the same place, so shopping would be part of the fun. Maybe we could even use the place again on prom night, so the girls could get their hair done, fix their makeup. Did I tell you that

Molly Williams is going to ask her mom to see if the department store where she works at Tyson's Corner will donate makeup samples?"

Trent grinned at her enthusiasm. "You're really excited about this, aren't you? It's not all about Mike, either, is it?"

"No, it's not," she said, her expression thoughtful. "I mean, it started that way, but then it got bigger. And when I talked to Ms. Fletcher and she said she thought there was a real need for this, too, then I knew it was something worth doing. Everyone I've spoken to has been willing to pitch in." She wrapped her arms around his neck. "I'm so lucky, Dad. I take way too much stuff for granted, you know. Since Mom died, I guess I've started to realize that things can change in an instant and we should never take anything for granted."

He gave her a hug, this seventeen-going-on-thirty-year-old kid of his. "I'm so proud of you. And I have an idea about that place you want for your shopping extravaganza."

Her eyes lit up. "Really? At first I was thinking about the gym at school, but that's really boring and it mostly smells like sweat, you know what I mean?"

"I do, indeed," Trent said. "Why don't you call your granddad and ask him if he'd let you use the ballroom at Oak Haven? It's been years since he's thrown a party in there, so I'm not sure what shape it's in, but it's certainly big enough."

"And it has that really fabulous chandelier," Laurie said excitedly. "Oh, Dad, it would be perfect. Do you think Granddad would agree?"

"I think he'd like being a part of this project of yours. And I think he would do just about anything for his favorite girl. Heck, if you go back there on prom night to get ready, he might even spring for a few limos to take all of you to the dance." He winked at her. "Just make sure you tell him that was your idea, not mine."

"And it's a great idea!" She bounced off the bed. "I'm going to call him right now."

Trent snagged her hand. "Hold on, kiddo. It's after midnight. You might want to wait till morning."

"Right," she said at once. "I'll call first thing." She started from the room, her arms loaded with the tuxedos he'd tossed aside. When she turned back there was a glint in her eyes that should have been a warning. "There is one thing you could do, Dad."

"Oh?" he asked warily.

"Three tuxedos are a really good start, but we need at least ten. Or gift certificates for rentals."

"I'll make some calls," he promised.

"And one more thing…"

"What?"

"Maybe you could help out with the guys on shopping day and on prom night. Ms. Fletcher's going to be there to coordinate things for the girls. You'd have to come to a couple of committee meetings, probably, but it won't take a lot of time other than that."

"I could do that," he said. "I hope you remember that I'm lousy at tying a bow tie, though."

"Believe me, you're an expert compared to the guys at school."

Again, she started from the room, then paused. "Would you do *one* more thing?"

"If I can."

"Ms. Fletcher has to chaperone at the dance and she always does it alone. There are other teachers there, but mostly couples. I thought maybe you'd come with her. I mean, she's doing all this work, so she deserves to have a good time, too, right?"

Trent's stomach did one of those nosedives it always did when his daughter had just bamboozled him. "Maybe Ms. Fletcher would prefer to get her own date," he suggested mildly.

Laurie shook her head. "She never does, at least not at last year's prom or for Homecoming last fall. I checked.

I guess she takes her chaperoning duties seriously. But this time is different. You'll be on the committee, too, so it won't be like a big deal or anything."

"Does she know you're asking me to do this?"

Laurie flushed, a sure sign that there was at least one more surprise in store. "Not exactly. I thought maybe you could ask her yourself, so she won't think it's like some pity thing that I set up." She ran back, dropped the clothes and threw her arms around him. "You'll do it, won't you? Please."

"You just absconded with all my tuxedos," he reminded her.

"I'll give you one back," she offered. "Or you can buy a new one. That'll give you leverage to persuade the store owner to give us some free."

Trent mentally cursed the fact that he'd been blessed with a daughter, rather than a son. A son would never try to manipulate him into something like this. A son wouldn't have him twisted around his finger.

"Can I at least meet Ms. Fletcher first?" he asked, a plaintive note in his voice.

"You'll have plenty of time to get to know her," Laurie promised. "She's totally awesome, Dad. You're going to love her. Now, promise me you'll do this. No excuses, okay?"

Since Trent had never been able to deny his daughter anything, he nodded reluctantly. "I promise."

But as his daughter's enthusiastic words sank in, Trent finally grasped that this was about a whole lot more than one night and one dance. His daughter—God help him—was matchmaking.

CHAPTER
✦TWO✦

Mike Brentwood slouched down in the chair across from Jodie, his expression filled with annoyance. Slim and wiry, he was blessed with a quickness that had made him an outstanding receiver on the football team. In addition, he had dimples, wavy brown hair with golden highlights that most girls would envy, and blue eyes that were like chips of ice when filled with the kind of disdain he was obviously feeling now.

"This was Laurie's idea, wasn't it?" he grumbled. "She wants to go to prom and she knows I can't rent a tux, so now she's made this whole big thing out of it. Come on, Ms. Fletcher, give me a break. I don't want to wear some hand-me-down tuxedo that won't even fit right. I'll feel like a jerk."

"Maybe you should think about Laurie's feelings," she suggested. "She's going to a lot of trouble, not just for you, but for your classmates. She really wants this night to be special for everyone."

"It's a dance," Mike said disparagingly. "It's not going to bring about world peace. I don't see why it's such a big deal. She didn't raise this much fuss about the Homecoming dance last fall or prom last year."

"I imagine she was trying to spare your feelings," Jodie told him. "Besides, neither of those was the very last dance you'll ever attend in high school."

Mike frowned at her. "Okay, maybe, but I don't see why Laurie didn't just ask me herself, instead of having you get on my case. We talked about this. In fact, she told me just a couple of weeks ago she didn't even care about going to prom this year."

"And I'm sure she meant it at the time, but then she started getting involved with the committee and she realized how many kids were feeling left out." She gave him a wry look. "Now she's really excited about making sure everyone gets to go this year. I imagine she didn't want to tell you herself that she'd changed her mind."

"Yeah, well, she should have. I would have told her this whole clothing drive of hers is a dumb idea."

Jodie winced at his depiction of the project. If that's how these kids were looking at it, it was going to be a tough sell.

"I was actually hoping you'd help me to convince some of the other guys that it's an okay thing to do," she said, trying a new tactic. "I need someone the other students respect to pave the way on this. You're a big football star. You're going to college next year on a scholarship. You're the perfect role model for a lot of these young men."

He rolled his eyes at the unabashed flattery. "How many different ways do I have to say I'm not interested?"

"Come on, Mike," she coaxed. "Help me out here."

"Why would I do that?"

"How about because I'm the one who convinced you that you could be accepted by a good college. I'm the one who helped you fill out all those scholarship applications. Let's face it, your future is brighter because of me."

He groaned. "If I'd known I was going to hear about that for the rest of my life, I might not have accepted your help. You didn't say it came with strings."

"It didn't. I was doing my job." She gave him a chagrined look. "I was just hoping you'd be so grateful,

you'd want to help. Forget that and think about Laurie.
I know it would make her really happy if you agreed to
this, not just for her sake, but for yours. She wants you
to have this night to remember, too." She watched his
face intently. She could tell from his wavering expression that she finally had him. For all of his bluster, Mike
didn't really want Laurie to miss out on prom. Jodie sat
silently and waited while he weighed the alternatives—a
hit to his pride or a miserable, disappointed girlfriend.

"You really don't play fair," he mumbled at last.

She grinned. "But I'm effective, don't you agree?"

"You really think we can convince some of these hard-
asses to accept a freebie tux so they can go to a dance?"

Her smile spread. "I convinced you, didn't I? If we
work together, who'll be able to resist us?"

Trent was running a half-hour late when he slipped
into the classroom where the latest prom committee
meeting was being held. Though there had been others, this was the first he'd been able to attend. Laurie
beamed at him as he sat down quickly in the closest
seat. One of the other girls was giving a report. Since
she had perfectly highlighted blond hair, he had to assume this was Sue McNally, who was in charge of getting volunteer stylists for the big night. Apparently she

and her mother—Candace McNally, if he remembered correctly from a few encounters at charity functions—had lined up five hairdressers, two makeup experts, but only one manicurist.

"Don't worry, though," she told the committee confidently. "My mom says once she talks to Henri, all of his manicurists will pitch in. He'll make sure of it."

"Very good, Sue—that's excellent work in just a month," someone behind him said, most likely the awesome Ms. Fletcher.

Oddly, her voice sounded familiar, tugging at a distant memory. A scent, so faint he wasn't sure he hadn't imagined it, teased his memory as well. Trent wanted to shift around for a look, but another student stepped to the front of the room to give a report on corsages.

The whole discussion took him back to his own senior year, when the most important things in life seemed to be prom and graduation festivities. He could recall standing in a florist shop, his palms sweaty, little more than twenty hard-earned bucks in his pocket, trying to decide if three tiny pink rosebuds clustered together with a bit of lace would impress Jean Kerrigan or convince her that he was the biggest loser in the class. The florist—grandmotherly Norma Gates—had apparently sensed his uncertainty and assured him he wouldn't be embarrassed. She'd been right. Jean had been thrilled, right up until he'd jabbed her with a pin while trying to help her put on the corsage without accidentally grazing her breast. Oh, the pitfalls of being an awkward adolescent. He didn't envy his daughter or any of the rest of them the next few months.

He listened to half a dozen enthusiastic reports from those on the committee, impressed with the amount of work they'd accomplished since last month. When asked, he chimed in with his own report on the tuxedos he'd managed to secure. Bottom line, there were already enough dresses and tuxedos for the teens who needed them.

"Do you think we should stop now and be content with our success for this first year?" Ms. Fletcher asked. "You all have done an amazing job, as it is."

Across from him, Laurie shook her head. "I think there are a few more kids we can talk into going if we take another shot at it. I just know they'll regret it later if they say no. Turning us down was, like, some gut instinct. They didn't even think about it."

"I'm not sure I have another argument left in me," Ms. Fletcher responded, sounding weary. "Mike tried, too, with the boys, but some of them were adamant. Neither of us felt we could push any harder."

"They're just being stubborn," Laurie insisted.

"A trait I'm sure you recognize, Laurie," Ms. Fletcher said wryly. "Okay, I'll try one more time."

Trent heard her stand up behind him and watched curiously as she stepped briskly to the front of the room. She was wearing a pair of navy-blue linen slacks, a sweater in a paler shade of blue. Dark brown hair with just enough curl to make it unmanageable sprang into ringlets at the nape of her neck. Her low-heeled shoes made a staccato sound as she walked, but it was the subtle, very feminine sway of her hips that held his attention.

When she reached the front of the room and turned to look at him directly for the first time, it took every bit of his well-developed control not to let his mouth gape. Jodie? Jodie Jameson? Memories flooded through his mind in such a rush that he didn't realize at first that she was speaking to him.

Trying to gather his composure, he stared at her blankly. "What?"

He glanced sideways and saw Laurie regarding him with a confused expression. He forced a smile. "Sorry. I got sidetracked for a second. What did you say, um…" He caught himself just before calling her Jodie and added, "Ms. Fletcher?"

"I asked if you thought it would be possible to round

up a few more tuxes?" she said, barely hiding a smile, well aware that she'd completely thrown him and quite pleased with herself about it.

"I'll do my best," he promised.

First, though, he needed to get out of this room and far, far away from the woman who'd walked out of his life twenty years ago with virtually no explanation.

They'd met on a summer job, dated all through college. He'd planned on asking her to marry him right after graduation, but before he could get the carefully rehearsed words out of his mouth, she'd told him she was sorry, but she didn't think they were going to work out, after all. Worse, before he could recover from that stunning announcement, she had whirled around and walked away.

For weeks he'd called and stopped by her apartment, ready to plead for an explanation, but she'd refused to take his calls and pretended she wasn't home. It was as if she'd severed him from her life with one quick, unrepentant slash, leaving behind a wound that simply wouldn't heal.

His heart broken and his self-confidence shattered, he'd been a mess when Megan had literally waltzed into his life at a party one night. He'd been working for a developer of cookie-cutter housing projects and was at the party to network with prospective clients, when Megan had twirled by in another man's arms. Somehow she'd wrangled a switch in partners on the dance floor and that had been that. She was the joy and laughter that had been missing from his life since Jodie's abrupt departure. Her determination to catch him had been a much-needed balm to his bruised ego.

Once again, he dared to meet Jodie's gaze. There was a bit less certainty in her eyes now, as if she understood that this wasn't quite the happy surprise reunion she'd been envisioning. They were two adults in a roomful of impressionable teenagers, including his daughter, so clearly she knew there wouldn't be an explosion of temper, either.

Trent wanted out. Not just out of this room, but out of the whole prom thing. Twenty years ago he'd wanted to confront Jodie and demand answers, but those answers were no longer relevant. *She* was no longer relevant. Life moved on. He hadn't thought about Jodie in years, or if he had, he'd squelched the memory before it could start to nag.

Around him, the meeting began to break up. Suddenly Laurie was beside him, her expression quizzical.

"Dad, are you okay? You look kind of funny, like you've seen a ghost or something."

Yes, that was it, he thought. A ghost. That's all Jodie was. He'd gotten over her years ago. He had a full life, a wonderful daughter. He didn't need to be taking any unexpected strolls down memory lane. He swore to himself it wasn't bitterness he felt when he looked at Jodie. He felt nothing. Less than nothing. She simply didn't matter. He wouldn't allow her to matter ever again, because she couldn't be trusted.

"Sweetie, I have to run. I just remembered an important meeting and I'm late already. We'll talk tonight, okay?"

He gave Laurie a glancing kiss on the cheek and bolted from the room with its scent of chalk and floor polish and lily of the valley, suddenly desperate for fresh air. Lily of the valley, for heaven's sake. How could he have shoved Jodie from his mind for all these years, but still remember her favorite perfume? When Megan had brought home the same scent, probably a more expensive version of it, he'd accidentally-on-purpose broken the bottle the first time she'd worn it. Thankfully, she'd never replaced it.

He filled his lungs with fresh air, then headed for his car. Inside he sat behind the wheel and stared straight ahead, trying to figure out what he was supposed to do now. He supposed he could suck it up and pretend everything was just fine. Or he could come up with an excuse that would get him out of town until prom was over and the "awesome" Ms. Fletcher was no more a factor in Laurie's life than she had been in his for more than twenty years. Personally, he liked option number two, but he knew his daughter. The odds that he could get away with a vanishing act were slim to none.

Besides, as Laurie was bound to remind him, he'd promised to take Ms. Fletcher to the prom, and the one thing Trent had vowed never to do was break a promise to his daughter the way he'd broken so many he'd made to his wife.

"Dad, you were acting really weird today, like something had freaked you out," Laurie said as she dished up spaghetti for their dinner that night.

Ever since Megan's death, Laurie had taken over responsibility for dinner. When she was fourteen, that hadn't amounted to much more than setting the table and warming the meals left by a housekeeper, but for the past year or so, she'd been cooking. She wasn't half bad at it, either.

"Sorry," Trent said. "I just remembered that meeting at the last minute and I got distracted after that." Determined to shift the subject, he asked, "Have you spoken to your grandfather yet?"

Laurie's eyes lit up. "I talked to him a few days ago and then I went by there after school today. I'd forgotten how cool that ballroom is. It's amazing, Dad. The floor has all this inlaid wood. It must have cost a fortune. And the windows go from the floor all the way up to the ceiling, so there's all this light shining in, or there would be if someone washed them. The ceiling must be fifteen feet high, maybe more. I wish I'd seen it just once when it was filled with people dancing and that amazing chandelier was all lit up."

She frowned. "Of course, it's kind of a mess now. Granddad's been using it for storage. He says he hasn't gone in there since Grandma died. In fact, he says the last time anyone was in there was when Mom dropped off some of our stuff that she wanted out of the attic here. He said if the kids will help clean the place up and if I'll sort through all the old junk and either give it away to charity or decide if I might want it someday, we can use the ballroom for our shopping day. I've already called Mike and he says he can get some of the guys to haul stuff away. A couple of his friends have pickups. And if a bunch of us go after school one day, we can polish the floor and mop up all the dust. Granddad said he'd have a service do the windows and the chandelier, 'cause he doesn't want us climbing on ladders."

"I hadn't realized it was in such bad shape," Trent commented. "Given how little time you all have with planning the prom, studying for finals and so on, maybe it would be better to find someplace that won't require so much work."

"No, please, there's lots of time," Laurie said. "Between Mike and me, we'll find enough kids who'll be willing to help and it won't take that long. It's just a bunch of dusty boxes and some old, broken-down furniture."

Trent winced. "I suspect some of that broken-down furniture, as you call it, could qualify as priceless antiques. Don't go giving any of it away without checking with your grandfather."

"But he said—"

"Trust me," Trent insisted. After growing up in a house filled with furniture from secondhand shops, he had a healthy appreciation for antiques, not just for the value, but for the history. "If he doesn't want those things and you're absolutely certain you'll never want them, then get an appraiser from one of the antique shops to come by and see if they want to take the pieces on consignment."

She gave him an odd look. "Granddad doesn't need the money."

And, truth be told, Warren didn't have a sentimental bone in his body, either, Trent thought, but he hated the idea of carelessly tossing family heirlooms aside. Someday Laurie might come to appreciate them. He should probably go through the boxes Megan had stored there, too, in case there was anything important.

"Why don't you and I do a quick survey before everyone else gets in there to clean?" he suggested. "That way something valuable won't get tossed by mistake."

She shrugged. "Okay, whatever." Her gaze narrowed as she studied him thoughtfully. "So, Dad, what did you think of Ms. Fletcher?"

"She seems okay," he said neutrally.

"That's it? That's the best you can do?"

"Sweetie, we barely spoke."

"Because you took off out of there as if the room was on fire." She regarded him suspiciously. "Did you really have a meeting?"

"Do you think I'd make that up?"

She gave him a knowing grin. "That's what you do whenever you want to get out of something without offending anybody. Besides, I saw you sitting in the parking lot for a whole half hour after you took off."

"You think you're smart, don't you?" he mumbled.

"I *am* smart, and I have the grades to prove it," she responded. "So, what was really going on, Dad? Did you take an instant dislike to Ms. Fletcher or something?"

"Not exactly."

"What then?"

"Nothing. It's not a big deal."

"If it's not a big deal, then it's a little one, but it's still a deal. That means something did happen."

He shook his head. "Your logic astounds me."

"But I'm right," she insisted. "I know I am. Come on, Dad, tell me why seeing Ms. Fletcher freaked you out."

Trent wondered if he could explain his previous relationship with Jodie in a way that would minimize its importance. He had to try. This was no time to start keeping secrets from his daughter, or to let her imagination run wild and magnify things out of all proportion to their importance.

"Okay, here it is in a nutshell. I recognized Ms. Fletcher from a very long time ago. Her name wasn't Fletcher back then, so I had no idea your guidance counselor was someone I actually knew. It just caught me off guard, you know, the way it surprised you that time we ran into one of your school friends when we were on vacation in Maine."

"You know Ms. Fletcher?" Laurie repeated, looking almost as stunned as he'd felt in that classroom this afternoon. "Wow! How cool is that?"

It was so far from cool, it was in another climate zone, Trent thought, but didn't say so. He shrugged, feigning complete indifference. "Like I said, no big deal. It was just unexpected."

Laurie studied him thoughtfully, clearly not convinced. "How long ago?"

"Years," he said. "Way before I met your mother and obviously before Jodie—I mean, Ms. Fletcher—married whoever she was married to. What happened to her husband, by the way? If she needs a date for the prom, then obviously she's no longer married."

"I think he died in an accident a couple of years ago, before she moved here. At least that's the rumor I heard when she came last year." Laurie gave him another of those disconcertingly direct looks. "Were you in college when you knew each other?"

"Around that time, yes."

"Oh, my gosh," she said, her expression filling with excitement. "Mom told me once you had this major thing going with a girl in college, but that it ended before she met you. Was that Ms. Fletcher? Was she like the big love of your life before Mom?"

Her tone scared the daylights out of him. He envisioned her matchmaking escalating to whole new heights. "Laurie, please, don't try to make this into something it isn't. Don't romanticize it. It was years and years ago. We were just a couple of kids."

She stared at him with utter fascination. "Why'd you break up? Did you fall out of love with her or was it because you met Mom?"

Trent was flattered that his daughter thought he must have been the one to break things off. Of course, he wasn't all that eager to disillusion her. In fact, he was pretty tired of the whole topic. He'd rather listen to Laurie spend a half hour discussing the latest fashion trends, a subject that usually sent him into a near-catatonic state of boredom.

"Sweetie, I am not going to discuss any of this with you. It's ancient history and doesn't matter now, but I'm sure you can see why it would be awkward for me to stay on your committee and especially awkward for me to ask Ms. Fletcher to the dance."

"But you just said yourself that what happened wasn't a big deal and it was years and years ago, so why are you backing out now?"

"Please, let it go. Take my word for it. It would be awkward." Make that a disaster, he thought grimly.

"But you promised," Laurie reminded him. "And this makes it even better, because it won't be like two strangers going together. You'll have stuff to talk about. You can reminisce about old times and catch up on everything that's happened since then."

Sure, they could reminisce, Trent thought with an uncharacteristic edge of sarcasm. Jodie could explain why she'd dumped him all those years ago. That was a conversation he could get really excited about.

"Not going to happen, Laurie. Look, your committee is in really good shape. It sounded today as if everything's under control. You don't need me."

"But you made a commitment, Dad, and you always tell me that once you make a commitment, you should never, ever back out of it. Even if it's only something you agreed to do verbally, it's as good as a written contract."

Trent winced at hearing his words thrown back in his face with such earnest faith. He knew when he was beat.

"Okay, fine. I'll stay on the committee and I'll do whatever I can to help."

"And you'll take Ms. Fletcher to the prom," she added as if there were no longer any question about that, either.

"I seriously doubt that Ms. Fletcher will agree to go with me," he hedged.

"But you'll at least ask her, right?"

Once again, Trent wished he'd had a son who never listened to a word he said, much less took it to heart. "Yes, I'll ask," he said grudgingly.

He'd just erect a steel barricade around his heart in case Jodie Fletcher wanted to stomp all over it yet again.

CHAPTER
~THREE~

Jodie lay awake for half the night. Trent had taken one look at her and fled the classroom practically midsentence. The encounter hadn't gone at all the way she'd anticipated. She'd expected surprise, maybe even a faint touch of dismay, but not the genuine hostility she thought she'd seen just below the polite facade he'd put on in front of the kids.

Sure, she'd dumped him without any warning, but it had been twenty years ago, for heaven's sake. And though their relationship had been heading in a serious direction, they hadn't actually been engaged. They hadn't even discussed marriage, for that matter. She'd broken up with him before things got that far.

She sighed. Okay, she was a big, fat liar. The relationship had been serious. That's why she'd been so scared. That's why she'd called it off. She'd known that sooner or later Trent would see their differences and break up with her, maybe after they'd gotten engaged or even married. There'd been nothing noble about what she'd done. All these years she'd been lying to herself about that. She'd walked away to save herself inevitable heartache.

Still, even though the breakup was all on her shoulders, she'd honestly expected him to have forgiven her by now. They'd both gone on to live happy, fulfilled lives with other people. At least she had. She could only assume Trent had, as well. He'd married a far more suitable woman. He was successful and rich. He had an amazing daughter. She'd never imagined him holding a grudge about something that had happened so long ago, something that had paved the way for everything good in his life that had followed.

She wondered if Laurie had picked up on the tension. She was a smart girl, and Jodie had a hunch she'd involved her father in this project specifically in the hope that he and Jodie would hit it off. She'd seen the anticipatory gleam in Laurie's eyes the second her dad had entered the classroom, almost as if she were expecting sparks to fly. Well, they had, just not in the way Laurie could possibly have been expecting. Jodie, either, for that matter.

Annoyed that Trent's reaction even mattered, she punched her pillow a few times, settled onto her side and tried once again to fall asleep. If she didn't get at least a couple of hours of decent rest, it would be a very long day. She simply wasn't one of those people who bounced out of bed on a few hours of sleep, ready to take on the world.

Unfortunately, even as she tried to count sheep, images of Trent kept appearing. He'd looked good. Really good. His face was a bit weathered from working outdoors, his shoulders thicker, his waist still trim. All the changes had been good ones. Trent was still the most attractive man she'd ever known, pure male, from his thick black hair to his muddy work boots.

"I have to stop this," she muttered, and determinedly resumed counting sheep.

Around the time she counted her five hundredth little lamb, she gave up in disgust. Trent simply wouldn't get out of her head, sheep or no sheep. She concluded that the only thing to do was to call him and face this whole thing head-on. Even if he did harbor some residual and justifiable resentment, surely he could put it aside for a few weeks for the sake of Laurie and the other kids. If he couldn't, he wasn't half the man she remembered.

Come to think of it, she didn't remember a man at all, but a boy, really. As mature as they'd thought themselves at twenty-one, it was only with twenty years' hindsight that she saw how ridiculously idealistic and naive they'd been. For a couple of years they'd convinced themselves that love—okay, passion—was all that mattered. They'd built a future on the quicksand of dreams, not on the rock-solid foundation of reality. She'd just recognized their folly before Trent had. He would have figured it out himself sooner or later, but by then things could have been a whole lot messier.

A glance at the clock told her it was still an hour before dawn, but it was evident she wasn't going to get any sleep. She might as well shower, stop somewhere for a decent breakfast and get to her desk early. She had a couple of tense meetings on today's calendar. Explaining to parents why their children would be attending summer school rather than graduating with their classmates in June was never at the top of her list of favorite things to do. Maybe if she was stuffed with pancakes and plenty of maple syrup, the uncomfortable conversations she was facing would be easier to handle.

And after those were behind her, maybe she could

work up the nerve to call Trent and straighten things out, at least enough to make these weeks before prom bearable for both of them. She wasn't hoping to pick up where they'd left off years ago—she was far too realistic for that—but it would be nice to have him back in her life as a friend. That was another sign of maturity, she thought. She'd learned to value friendship.

Unfortunately, something told her it was going to take more than pancakes to work up the arguments necessary to convince Trent of the same thing. In fact, she thought as she sat up and flipped on the harsh light of her bedside lamp, what if she'd misinterpreted his reaction yesterday? What on earth made her think that what happened twenty years ago was so important to him that he might still be angry or hurt about it? He'd probably forgotten all about it and she was the one who'd be dredging up the past for no good reason. She'd wind up looking pathetic. Talk about humiliating.

That thought gave her pause, but she refused to back down. They had to talk, find some way to make peace for the sake of Laurie and this project that mattered so much to her. In person would be better than on the phone, she decided. She could tell from his expression just what he was thinking.

That resolved, she took the time to add a little more

mascara to her lashes and a faint hint of blush to her cheeks, something she rarely bothered with. If she was going to make an idiot out of herself with Trent later, then she was going to look darn good doing it.

Trent had been having breakfast at Dinah's Diner every morning for years. It was the local hangout for long-time residents, and he could get a healthy serving of up-to-the-minute gossip along with his meal. He'd met clients for coffee at the red Formica-topped tables, haggled with subcontractors at the counter. Over the years he'd gotten to know the owner, Dinah Lowery, her two white-haired waitresses—Gloria and Hazel— and the steady rotation of kids who held summer jobs and learned responsibility under Dinah's firm tutelage. He might be comfortable enough in places with white linen tablecloths and fancy wine lists, but Dinah's was where he felt totally at ease.

With a set of blueprints under his arm, he waved to Dinah, then headed for a booth in the corner, his regular spot, only to see that it was occupied, and not by just anyone. He'd know that explosion of dark brown curls anywhere. Jodie. Again.

This time the annoyance that zinged through him had as much to do with his booth being taken as it did with the occupant herself. Some habits were hard to break and his morning ritual was one of them.

As he stood there debating with himself, Jodie looked up and a smile broke across her face, then slowly faded at his lack of a responding greeting, verbal or silent.

"Join me," she said, her tone turning the words into a command, not a request.

Trent bristled, but since Dinah had just appeared with his coffee and a questioning look, he opted to sit. If he'd refused the invitation, word of the incident would have been all over town by noon. The interpretations would range from a lover's tiff to outright rudeness on his part.

"I'll be right back with your breakfast," Dinah assured him, then cast a glance at Jodie. "You need more coffee, hon? I'll bring that, too. You look like you need it."

"Thanks," Jodie said as if she'd been promised much-needed salvation. Her tired gaze shifted to meet his. "I'm in your usual spot, aren't I?"

He shrugged as if it were of no consequence.

"Sorry. There wasn't a reserved sign on it," she said, a mocking note in her voice.

"People who come here regularly pretty much know." He skimmed a glance over her. "I haven't seen you in here before. Or anywhere else in town, for that matter."

"Weekdays, I usually eat a banana on the way to work,

but I come in here occasionally on the weekends when I have time to splurge on a big breakfast. A couple of my students work here and they recommended the pancakes."

He gave her a pointed look. "It's a weekday."

She shrugged. "I got out of the house earlier than usual." She gestured toward her plate, which was stacked high with pancakes. "This morning I'm on a carb binge."

Trent chuckled despite himself because he recalled exactly what had driven her to such splurges, at least in the past. "You planning to have a bad day? I seem to recall that the number of carbs you required during final exams was extraordinary."

"Oh, yeah," she said between bites of pancakes dripping with syrup. "Two conferences with parents who were expecting their kids to graduate. I have to inform them the diplomas will be delayed till after summer school."

"Sounds grim."

"Not half as grim as the conversation I planned to have after that."

"Oh?"

"I was going to stop by your office to speak to you."

Trent wasn't at all sure how he felt about being on her to-do list, especially in the category of something she was dreading. Then, again, he didn't much look forward to dealing with her, either, even though the past few minutes had been reasonably civilized.

"I don't see we have that much to talk about," he said tightly.

"You made that pretty obvious yesterday," she said. "Seeing me threw you, didn't it?"

He hadn't expected her to be so direct. "Let's just say you had the element of surprise on your side. Seems to me that gave you a pretty unfair advantage."

She studied him, her dark brown eyes filled with some emotion he couldn't quite read. It bothered him, because there'd been a time when he'd known all her moods, when he'd been able to know at a glance what she was thinking.

"Trent, what's this about? Surely you can't still be angry about what happened twenty years ago. People grow apart. It happens. They move on. I did. So did you. We're different people now. Adults. Surely we can spend a little time in each other's company without old news getting in the way."

Trent wanted to explode at her simplistic view of their past. Obviously she wasn't the one who'd had her heart ripped out. Knowing that it had all meant so little to her made him want to break things. If he hadn't had a healthy respect for Dinah, the ceramic mug he was clutching in both hands would have been history.

Then, again, such a move would also have told Jodie way more than he was willing to admit about how much the past ate at him even after all this time. It was a truth he'd only recently discovered—yesterday, in fact—and he was still trying to figure out what to make of it. He'd reacted to seeing her on some gut-deep level that had completely thrown him, even as it had apparently mystified her.

Fortunately, Dinah returned just then with his breakfast—two eggs over easy, bacon, whole-wheat toast. It never varied. Today it might as well have been sawdust. His appetite had fled, along with his good humor.

"Heard about what you're doing for prom," Dinah said to Jodie, while casting glances in his direction as if she was trying to figure out the source of the tension at the table. "It's a great thing. A couple of the kids who work for me weren't going to go, but now it's all they talk about."

Jodie beamed. "That's exactly why we're doing it, so everyone can share in the experience. Thanks for telling me that."

Dinah nudged Trent's shoulder with her hip. "Heard Laurie was behind it. You've raised a real decent girl."

"That was Megan's doing," he said, though he was pleased by the compliment.

"Hey, don't sell yourself short," Dinah scolded. "You've been on your own since Laurie was barely fifteen. These past couple of years are some of the most critical for a girl." She turned to Jodie. "Isn't that right?"

"I've always thought so," Jodie agreed. "I know what a mess I was in my teens."

"Me, too," Dinah concurred. She set the carafe of coffee on the table. "Might as well leave this here. It'll save me running back and forth."

After she was gone, Trent felt Jodie's gaze on him.

"She's right. You have done a wonderful job with Laurie. She's never in trouble, she has a great support system at home—that would be you—so I don't know her as well as I know some of the problem students. Even so, just in the past few weeks of working with her, I've come to realize that she's an amazingly compassionate young woman."

"Thanks."

She leaned forward, her gaze locked with his. "A father who gave his daughter such solid values surely wouldn't let her down by walking out on a project that's so important to her, would he?"

He blinked at her sneaky tactic. "Boy, you really do

know how to go straight for a man's Achilles' heel, don't you?"

She grinned and sat back. "The kids think I have a knack for it."

"You don't have to sound so blasted pleased with yourself," he grumbled.

"In my line of work, you develop survival skills early on, or you get out," she said. "Figuring out what makes people tick and how to use that is a survival skill." She stared straight at him. "So, Trent, are you in or are you out for the whole prom thing?"

He didn't know why she bothered asking since they both knew it was a foregone conclusion. "I'm in," he said grudgingly.

"Good. Then you'll line up a few more tuxedos?"

"Once you've gotten a few more boys to agree to go," he challenged.

She sighed dramatically. "I've got to tell you, I'm fresh out of ideas on how to accomplish that. Mike was supposed to help but he's thrown in the towel, too. Frankly, if it weren't for Laurie, I don't think he'd participate at all."

Trent wasn't entirely sure whether to buy her claim that she had no strategy. He had a feeling there was something more behind it. He couldn't resist challenging her. "Really? I never took you for a quitter. Then again, you did walk out on the two of us."

She winced slightly but ignored the jab about the past. "I'm not quitting, I'm regrouping," she insisted.

He ignored the alarms going off in his head, telling him not to get any more involved with this project—or with her—than he already was. "Ever thought about asking for help?"

Her gaze narrowed. "From you?"

"I am a guy," he reminded her.

"Yes, I'm aware of that."

"I do get how the male mind works in a way that might elude you, or even the less-experienced Mike." He pushed aside his plate and tossed his napkin on the table. "Let's start with why they're objecting to going in the first place. Any ideas?"

"They say it's not their thing," she said, then shook her head. "I know that's not it, though. These kids act tough and disinterested, but they want to fit in, maybe even more than most. They're just afraid they'll get it wrong, that they'll look foolish in front of their friends. Some of them simply don't want to admit that they don't have the funds to rent their own tuxes. It's a matter of pride. Young male pride is quite a force."

"How did you convince Mike to go along with this?" he asked. "I'm sure he had the same reservations."

"I mentioned that he needed to think about Laurie's feelings. Believe me, that was the only thing that resonated with him."

Trent grinned. "Exactly. Female power. Are most of these guys dating girls at school?"

He watched as understanding dawned. Her expression brightened.

"You're absolutely right. I can't imagine why I didn't try the same thing with them that I did with Mike. I suppose I know him better than I know the others, and how important Laurie is to him. I'll get right on this as soon as I get to school."

"Hold it," he said, not entirely certain why he was pushing this. Maybe it was because of Laurie. More likely, it was because he wanted to prove something to Jodie. He had no idea what. That he was better at persuasion than she was? How idiotic was that? Or maybe that being around her didn't bother him as much as she probably thought it did? Whatever it was, he couldn't seem to back down. "I'm thinking these guys might be more easily persuaded in a man-to-man conversation."

"You want to handle it?"

Her surprise was unmistakable. In fact, he thought

it might be just the tiniest bit excessive. Once again, he had the feeling that she had an agenda. Regarding her suspiciously, he shrugged. "Unless you don't think I'm up to the task."

Suddenly she looked just a little too pleased with herself, confirming his suspicion that this had been her plan from the beginning. She'd reeled him in neatly, the hook firmly embedded in his own stupid ego.

"Fine," she said too cheerfully. "You want the job of persuading these boys to go to the prom, be at school at three o'clock. Most of them will be in detention, I'm sure. It should be quite a conversation."

Trent found her attitude slightly disconcerting. Maybe he'd got it wrong, after all. Maybe it hadn't been about tricking him into doing exactly what she'd wanted him to do all along or maybe she was looking forward to seeing him fail. He wasn't overjoyed by either alternative. Worse, he had a hunch that the mention of detention had been deliberate, a warning that she didn't expect him to make much progress with this particular group of young men.

"I'll be there," he said grimly.

And those boys would go to prom, if he had to bribe them to do it. He reminded himself to stop by the bank for a few twenties on his way to the school.

* * *

Jodie had the uncomfortable feeling that Laurie knew all about her past with Trent. The teenager had appeared in Jodie's office fifteen minutes ago clutching a pass from her study hall teacher. She claimed she wanted to go over some new developments with their project, but so far the conversation had been pretty rambling and her eyes hadn't left Jodie's face, as if she was trying to learn something from her expression.

"Laurie, I thought you wanted to talk about prom," Jodie said when the scrutiny had gone on a little too long.

Laurie sat up a little straighter. "Sorry, I was just thinking about something else for a minute. I really do need to talk to you about prom." She launched into the arrangements she'd made with her grandfather about using Oak Haven. "We'd probably need eight or ten kids for the cleanup. Should I get the kids on the committee or some of the kids who are going to benefit from all this? Maybe if they helped, they wouldn't feel as if they were getting something for nothing."

"Sort of the way sweat equity works in the Habitat for Humanity program," Jodie said enthusiastically. "I like that. I think the kids will appreciate what's being done for them more if they have to work for it. We won't make it a requirement, because some of them have after-school jobs, but I think most of them can be persuaded to pitch in. When did you want to clean the place up?"

"I think it has to be no later than the last Saturday in March," Laurie said, her expression thoughtful. "We probably need to do the whole shopping thing a week or two later, so there's time for any alterations to be done, and prom is the first weekend in May."

Jodie looked at her calendar. "That makes sense. I'll mark it down." She hesitated, then asked, "Are you counting on your father to be there?"

"I know he wants to go through the place with me ahead of time to make sure there's nothing valuable that should be saved, but we didn't talk about him helping." She gave Jodie an oddly knowing look. "Why? Do you want him to be there?"

"I was just wondering. He didn't mention anything when I ran into him earlier today."

Laurie looked taken aback. "You've seen my dad today?"

"I saw him at the diner." She grinned. "I accidentally sat at *his* table."

Laurie laughed. "I'll bet that got to him. All the regulars at Dinah's have their special tables and heaven help anyone who sits at one of them by mistake. They go all territorial."

"I noticed," Jodie said. "I haven't run into that problem on the few Saturdays I've been in. It's usually packed with families and everyone just fends for themselves. I often wind up at the counter."

"So, did he sit with you or just get huffy?"

"He sat. We talked. Actually, he's going to come by the school this afternoon."

She didn't like the excitement that flashed in Laurie's eyes. She recognized that look. It confirmed her suspicions that Laurie had her own agenda for her father and Jodie.

"Then you two have, like, a date or something?" Laurie asked, clearly struggling to keep her tone neutral, when she looked as if she'd like to leap up and do a little victory dance.

"Hardly. He's coming to talk to some of the holdouts, to see if he can convince them to participate in the whole prom thing."

"Oh," the teenager said, sounding deflated.

"Laurie, did your father mention that he and I knew each other years ago?"

She nodded but revealed nothing about what Trent had said.

Jodie pressed on. "So, you can understand that the two of us working together might be a little awkward."

"Yeah, he said the same thing," Laurie admitted. Her expression turned earnest. "But I don't get why. I mean, I don't know what happened or anything, or if there was some big love affair or whatever, but it was a long, long time ago. You've both been married to other people, so you moved on, right?"

"Right," Jodie agreed. "It just makes things a bit more complicated, that's all, but I'm sure we'll work through it, at least enough to pull off a successful prom night."

"In other words, I shouldn't get my hopes up," Laurie said, then blushed. "About you two becoming friends, I mean."

"No, you shouldn't."

Rather than looking disappointed, Laurie brightened. "You know, Ms. Fletcher, I figured you getting together with my dad was a long shot, but what with this whole thing from the past and the way you're both acting all weird about it, I'm beginning to think this might be the best idea I ever had."

She bounced up before Jodie could think of a single thing to say.

On her way out, Laurie stopped in the doorway. "Oh, since you're seeing my dad this afternoon, maybe you can tell him about what's happening at my granddad's. He might help if you ask him to. Bye, now. I've got to get back to study hall. I still have math homework to do before next period."

And then she was gone, leaving Jodie to wonder how her attempt to caution Laurie about the danger of false hope had gone so dreadfully awry.

CHAPTER
⚬⟩ FOUR ⟨⚬

Half-a-dozen sullen young men, a culturally diverse mix of Hispanic, Anglo and African-American, stared at Trent with suspicion. He'd deliberately chosen to come straight from the construction site, dressed in jeans, a T-shirt and work boots that were filthy thanks to a drenching March storm that had turned the site into a sea of mud. He'd expected Jodie to regard him with disapproval for not being more professionally attired, but she smiled slightly as she took in his appearance.

"Smart move, coming here dressed like that," she murmured as she patted his arm. "It's a very man-of-the-people, I'm-one-of-you look. Good luck."

She made a brief introduction, then turned and left, leaving him alone with an obviously hostile audience. Trent had a hunch, though, that she hadn't gone far. She was probably ready to step in the second he lost control.

"Why don't you gentlemen introduce yourselves?" he suggested, sitting on the corner of the desk at the front of the room. "Tell me a little about yourselves, while you're at it."

"What is this? Some kind of afternoon tea party, man?" one boy demanded.

Trent grinned. "Last time I checked, this was detention. Think of it this way, at least talking to me will kill the time." He stared pointedly at the boy who'd challenged him. "Let's start with you. Your name is?"

"Marvin," the boy said grudgingly.

"Anything else you'd like to add, Marvin?"

"Not especially."

"Do you like school, Marvin? Have a girlfriend? A job?"

The boy gave him a hard look. "Whoa! You looking for workers, dude, count me out. I ain't into breaking my back for no man." He turned and high-fived the boy seated next to him, thrilled with his little show of rebellion.

Trent looked him in the eye. "Unless you clean up

that grammar, son, back-breaking work may be all you can get," he commented wryly.

The boy gave him a hard stare. "Say what?"

"I think you understood me just fine," Trent responded.

"I know what this is," Marvin's friend said. "You're one of those do-gooder volunteers who's here to motivate us." He drew quotation marks in the air to emphasize *motivate*.

Trent chuckled at the description. "Do you get a lot of those?"

"Man, all the time," Marvin said with disgust. "If that's why you're here, save your breath."

"That's not why I'm here," Trent assured them. "I understand there's a big dance coming up in May, the junior-senior prom."

"Why do you care about that?" Marvin's pal asked.

"What's your name?" Trent asked him.

"Ramon."

"Well, Ramon, to be honest, I'm with you guys. Dressing up in a fancy suit is just about the last thing I'd ever want to do." He gestured toward his own clothes. "Do I look like a guy who'd put on a tuxedo willingly?"

"I hear you, brother," Marvin said, suddenly more congenial.

The other boys murmured agreement.

"There's just one thing," Trent warned. "You boys all have girlfriends, right?"

All but one, a slender kid with thick glasses and a defeated expression, nodded.

"How do they feel about missing prom?"

One of the Hispanic youths, who identified himself as Miguel, gave him a resigned look. "I have heard about nothing else for a week now, ever since Mariana found a way to get a dress to wear."

"So, the dance means a lot to the girls," Trent said.

All of them grunted in the affirmative.

"I've got to tell you, I don't get it," Marvin added. "I take Devonia dancing all the time—you know, to places where you can look like a normal dude."

Trent grinned. "That's the problem. Your high school prom is a special occasion, especially to women. I guarantee if you guys bite the bullet and get into those fancy duds for one night, it will make your women very, very happy, you know what I mean?"

They looked intrigued.

"I still don't understand why this matters," Ramon said.

Miguel nodded. "It's like Marvin said, Mariana and

me, we go to parties. We go to clubs. Why is that not enough?"

Trent regarded him with sympathy. "Because this is arguably the biggest event of all your years in high school. Your girlfriends deserve this kind of memory, right? They deserve a night they can discuss with their friends, instead of having to sit on the sidelines while everyone around them talks about the big dance." He looked each of them in the eye. "Sometimes a man has to step up and do something he doesn't want to do just to make the woman in his life happy. It's one night, right? How painful can it be?"

He leaned forward. "You know what I said about hating the whole tux thing? Absolutely true, but for fifteen years I put one on at least once a month, sometimes more often, just because it made my wife happy. That's what men do. They try to please women, to show them they care about their feelings."

All six young men exchanged looks.

"Dude, you're laying it on kinda thick, aren't you?" Marvin asked.

Trent shrugged. "I'm on a mission. I promised a young woman I'd handle this."

"You mean Ms. Fletcher?"

"Her, too, but I was talking mostly about my daughter, Laurie. You all know her, right? Laurie Winston?" He watched as their faces registered surprise. "This whole thing is really important to her. She wants everyone to have a good time at the dance this year, to not feel left out."

"You really think we won't look like total dorks?" the boy with blond hair and huge glasses asked.

"Jason, dude, you gonna look like a dork forever," Marvin taunted. "What's one more night?"

Trent stepped in. "No, I don't think you'll look like dorks. In fact, I think you'll be surprised at how handsome you'll look."

"Jason, dude, why are you so worried?" Marvin asked. "Can you even find a date for this thing? Or am I going to have to do it for you?"

Though Marvin's tone was taunting, there was a hint of compassion in his eyes. Jason gave him a surprisingly cocky smile. "I can get my own date," he retorted. "That was never the problem." He shook his head. "The whole tuxedo thing, though. I just don't know."

"Same here," Marvin agreed.

Trent seized on the tiny opening he thought he heard in Marvin's comment. "Does that mean you're in, Marvin? You'll consider going if we can get you a tuxedo?"

"These tuxedos you're talking about, they're not

going to cost us anything?" Marvin inquired worriedly. "I have to give all the money I make to my mom to pay the rent. With her bad back she hasn't been able to work for a couple of months now. I can't be wasting money on some fancy clothes to wear for one night."

"We have quite a few tuxedos that have been donated, and we also have gift certificates for rentals," Trent assured him. "One way or another, none of you will have to pay for the tux you wear that night."

"Either way, they'll be borrowed, which means the sleeves will be too long and the pants will drag on the floor," Jason said, sounding resigned.

"No way," Trent assured him. "You'll get to try them on ahead of time and someone will alter them so they fit perfectly. I'm telling you, you guys won't recognize yourselves when you look in the mirror. Better yet, you'll impress the heck out of your girlfriends." He turned once again to Marvin. "So, are you in?"

For a moment, Marvin looked as if he were struggling with himself. Trent simply waited.

"What about the tickets?" Marvin asked. "Last year they cost as much as I make in a week. I can't blow that kind of money on a dance."

"Laurie has the committee working on that. They're doing a program with advertising to help underwrite the costs of the hotel and the food. That'll bring the ticket prices way down. They won't be free, but I think they'll be within your budget, certainly no more than a night at some club." He looked straight at Marvin. "How about it? Any other roadblocks?"

"I guess not," Marvin conceded grudgingly.

"Then you'll go?"

"Okay, sure. Why not?" The boy gave an exaggerated shrug. "No point in ticking off Devonia if there's a way around it."

One by one the others nodded.

"You're not going to regret this," Trent told them as he stood up to leave.

"Hold it, dude," Marvin commanded.

Trent settled back on the edge of the desk and studied the surprising uncertainty in the boy's eyes. "What is it, Marvin?"

"I just thought of something else. You know there's more to this prom than buying the tickets and getting dressed up in some fancy clothes. The girls usually get flowers. I checked on that once. Those things are expensive."

"It's being handled," Trent assured him. "Once the girls have their dresses picked out, you can tell the florist what color flowers you want."

Jason raised his hand tentatively. "I've never tied a bow tie before."

"Me, neither," Ramon admitted.

Next to him, Marvin rolled his eyes. Before Trent could chastise him, Ramon scowled at him.

"Oh, like you have," he muttered to Marvin.

"Well, I can figure it out," Marvin retorted.

"Not to worry," Trent promised. "I'm no expert, but I'll be there prom night to help any of you who need it." He looked at each of the boys in turn. "Any other questions?"

"I have one," said a boy who'd been silent all afternoon. "Why are you guys doing this for us?"

Trent tried to explain it as he thought Laurie or Jodie would. "Because prom and graduation are really big deals in a person's life. Skipping them because you don't want to go is one thing, but you shouldn't miss those things just because money's tight in your family. You should be able to have the same experiences and memories of prom that your classmates will have."

He looked each of the boys in the eye. "The fact that some of you work to help out at home, that's a good thing, something you should be proud of. And no one wants you to have to shortchange your family or yourselves to participate in these special senior-year activities. Maybe someday you'll come across a young man or woman in need of a little help. If you do, I hope you'll remember this and do what you can to give them the same opportunity."

A bell rang. "End of detention?" he asked.

All of the boys were instantly on their feet and heading for the door, which was answer enough. Marvin slowed, then came back.

"Thanks, dude. I'm going straight to Devonia's to tell her about this. Maybe she'll stop looking at me like I've let her down."

"Good luck," Trent told him. "And if you ever change your mind about wanting the kind of work I can offer on one of my construction jobs, come to see me. I can always use a responsible young man."

Trent wasn't sure, but he thought Marvin stood a little taller at his words.

"You never know, dude. I'll see you around."

As Marvin left, Jodie stepped into the room. Trent grinned at her.

"Listening at the door?" he teased.

"Of course," she said, a twinkle in her eyes. "I had to be sure you weren't going to bribe them into going, didn't I?"

Trent thought of the fistful of twenties he had in his pocket. "That was my next tactic," he admitted.

"Well, thank goodness you didn't need to resort to that," she said, regarding him with something that looked an awful lot like admiration. "You were good with them, Trent. Something tells me you had to be persuaded to put on your first tux, too. I certainly never saw you in one."

"Megan's doing," he admitted. "And believe me, I fought it just as hard as these boys did. Harder, maybe." He smiled at the memory of the first ill-fitting tux she'd coaxed him into wearing, one of her dad's cast-offs, though she hadn't told him that at the time. "Megan had a way of talking me into doing a lot of things I didn't want to do."

"Then it was a good marriage?" Jodie asked, studying him intently.

Trent froze at the question, at the hint of worry behind it. "You looking for absolution, Jodie? You trying to find out if dumping me turned out all right in the end?"

She frowned at him. "What if I am?"

"It's a little late to be worrying about that," he told her. "You made a decision. You refused to discuss it. I just had to live with it, so that's exactly what I did. I lived with it. I met someone. I got married. I had a child.

My wife died. Maybe the exact same thing would have happened if you hadn't walked out. Maybe we would have broken up, anyway. Maybe that was just my fate." He knew he sounded harsh, but it was too late to stop. "I have to tell you, at the time, it felt a whole lot like you'd single-handedly grabbed our future and ripped it to shreds right in front of me."

She blanched. "I'm sorry. I thought I was doing the right thing."

"For you or for me?"

"You, damn it. It was all about you."

He stared at her incredulously. "You actually believe that, don't you? You think you did me a favor."

"I did," she said, though she sounded less confident.

"Well, just a piece of advice, Jodie. In the future if you want to do someone a favor, maybe you should ask them what *they* want first."

Because he couldn't stand here and talk about this for one more second, he walked past her and out the door. Unfortunately, leaving her behind was a whole lot easier than leaving behind the anger and the memories. And until this prom was over, it looked as if the past was going to keep right on nagging at him.

Jodie arrived at Warren Davis's estate on the last Saturday in March filled with trepidation. Trent had been so angry when he'd walked out on her at school and she hadn't seen any sign of him in the past two weeks, even though they'd had a committee meeting. She hadn't been prepared for him to question her motives. Couldn't he see that she'd been hurt as deeply as he had, that doing the right thing had cost her as much as it had him? Obviously not. She wasn't looking forward to round two, now that the gloves were off.

As she parked on the far side of the circular driveway in front of the huge brick Colonial house, she noted there were plenty of cars and pickups ahead of her. At least she wouldn't be alone with Trent, and he certainly wouldn't cause a scene in front of his daughter. Maybe they could get through the day like civilized adults, after all.

When she rang the doorbell, it was Laurie who answered, her face flushed with excitement. "At least twenty kids showed up, Ms. Fletcher. Isn't that fantastic? We've already made a lot of progress. Wait till you see."

She grabbed Jodie's hand and dragged her through a huge foyer filled with priceless art and an antique Chinese vase that probably cost a fortune. Jodie had to stop herself from gawking.

As soon as she walked into the cluttered, dusty ballroom, her gaze immediately landed on Trent. He'd dressed in a pair of well-worn jeans that hugged his backside and a faded T-shirt that was molded to his chest. She had to stop herself from gaping.

"Dad came," Laurie said, stating the obvious. "Even though you forgot to tell him about it."

"I didn't really have a chance," Jodie responded defensively. She wasn't about to mention that Trent had been in no mood to listen to anything she had to say when she'd seen him.

"Hey, Ms. Fletcher." Marvin walked by carrying two huge boxes as if they weighed next to nothing.

Once again, Jodie was left speechless. She hadn't expected to find Marvin here or Ramon or any of the other boys Trent had met with, but every one of them appeared to be working industriously. Was this more evidence of Trent's powers of persuasion? Or had Laurie worked her magic with them as she had with so many others, her dad and Jodie included?

"What do you need me to do?" she asked Laurie.

"Actually, Dad and I didn't get to go through all the boxes. Last night was the first chance we had to come over and there were more boxes than we expected. There are still a couple that need to be checked before we haul them to the dump. Over here," she said, leading the way to the far side of the ballroom. "Could you go through these and put anything that looks important in that empty box next to them? Someone will take the rest of the junk out in a little while."

"How am I supposed to know what's important?" Jodie asked, but Laurie was already gone.

Jodie sat down on the floor and opened the first box. A college yearbook sat on top. From *her* college. From *her* senior year. She glanced in Laurie's direction, suddenly guessing why this particular task had been left to her. Unfortunately she didn't have a clue which of these mementos Trent would want to save.

Still, it wouldn't hurt just to glance through a few things before she turned the task over to Trent. She flipped through the yearbook to the pictures of the senior class. It had been years since she'd seen that awful photo of herself with her hair curling wildly like Little Orphan Annie's. She rolled her eyes, then turned the pages until she came to the *W*'s.

Trent's picture stared back at her, solemn, yet ridiculously masculine. Even then he'd exuded a confidence in his own masculinity, unlike the other male students in their class. Maybe that had fooled her into thinking he wouldn't be affected by the decision she'd made. She told herself that a man as sure of himself as Trent wouldn't be shaken by her walking away from the relationship. Had she misjudged things so badly?

Under the yearbook, there was more college mem-
orabilia, a banner that had been on the wall in Trent's
dorm room, his diploma still in its leather binder, match-
books from campus-area bars, a couple of T-shirts with
fraternity insignia.

Beneath these odds and ends was a framed photo,
turned upside down. Before flipping it over, Jodie knew
instinctively what it was—a picture of the two of them,
taken on a windy day at Ocean City. The waves high behind them, their faces tanned by a week at the shore,
they looked very much in love. She couldn't seem to tear
her gaze away. Seeing herself with Trent like that, she
wondered how she'd ever convinced herself to leave.

"Hey, Ms. Fletcher, is that you?" Marvin hunkered
down beside her, looking over her shoulder.

Jodie wanted to hide the picture, but it was too late.
"Yes," she admitted softly. "It's from a long time ago."

"Who's that with you?" he asked, then whirled around
and looked straight at Trent. "Mr. Winston? That's the
dude in the picture?"

She nodded, unable to stop the tears that sprang to
her eyes. She swiped at them ineffectively, seeing the
sudden dismay in Marvin's expression. "Sorry."

"Did the dude break your heart or something? He

seems like an okay guy, but I can get down with him, if you need me to."

She smiled at his willingness to fight her battle. "No need, Marvin. It was the other way around."

"You're not gonna sit here and bawl your eyes out, are you?" he asked worriedly.

"No," she said, though a part of her wanted to do just that. "I am most certainly not going to cry."

"You want to blow this scene, I can cover for you," he offered.

"No, I'm fine. Just a little nostalgic, that's all."

He cast a hard look across the room at Trent. "You change your mind, just say the word, okay?"

"Thanks, Marvin. It's very sweet of you to offer." Who knew the kid had a gallant streak in him?

"How about a soda? Can I bring you a soda?"

"Now, that I will accept," she said, forcing a bright smile. "Thank you."

As soon as he'd set off on his mission, she shoved everything back into the box. Not sure why she wanted to torture herself with the memories, she made a hasty decision. Standing up, she glanced around to make sure that Trent wasn't close by, then hurried from the ballroom. She wanted a few private moments at home with these mementos. She carried the box straight to her car and stuffed it in the trunk, vowing to return it before it was missed. When she turned to go back, Trent was standing right behind her.

"Taking off with family treasures?" he inquired mildly.

"Just packing some stuff up for a trip to the dump," she said.

He shook his head. "I don't think so, Jodie. I know exactly what was in that box. I packed it myself twenty years ago."

"And saved it," she reminded him.

His features darkened. "I wasn't the one who said those days didn't matter." The silence built between them, heavy with nostalgia and regrets. "Oh, Jodie," he murmured sorrowfully. "What were you thinking? How could you give up on what we had?"

To her surprise, he tucked a finger under her chin, then leaned down and touched his lips to hers.

Although she sensed his reluctance, he deepened the kiss until her senses were reeling. Knees weak, she clung to his shoulders, then very nearly stumbled when he jerked away.

"Sorry, my mistake," he said. "I guess some feelings aren't quite as far in the past as I'd hoped. Keep the box, Jodie. Maybe it will help you recall what you gave up on."

She didn't need the stupid box or anything in it to do

that, Jodie thought as he walked away. She already knew what she'd lost. What she didn't know was whether it was possible to get it back.

CHAPTER
∞FIVE∞

Trent stood in Warren's driveway and watched Jodie drive off. He tried not to think about the hurt he'd seen in her eyes, the pain he'd caused. He told himself she deserved it, that it was nothing compared with the anguish she'd caused him.

Dark clouds rolled across the sun, promising an early spring storm and cooling the air. He shivered and turned to go back inside, only to see Laurie heading his way, her blond hair whipping around her face in the sudden breeze.

"You were out here with Ms. Fletcher, weren't you? And now she's gone." A frown creased her brow. "What did you say to make her leave, Dad?"

"I didn't say anything," he said defensively. "She was already leaving when I came out here."

"I don't think so." Laurie held up a purse. "She left this inside."

Trent winced. Apparently he'd rattled Jodie even more than he'd realized.

Laurie gave him another accusing look. "Marvin said she was really upset and that you had something to do with it."

"Okay, you want to know what happened?" Trent said mildly. "Your little scheme backfired. I know you deliberately gave her that old box of my stuff from college to go through, hoping it would spark some sort of nostalgic reaction."

"So what if I did?" she asked with a touch of defiance. "Somebody needs to push you two back together."

Trent sighed. "Maybe you haven't noticed, but both Ms. Fletcher and I are adults. We're perfectly capable of deciding whether we want to spend time together without any help from you."

Laurie studied him quizzically. "Do you want to spend time with her?"

"Sweetie, I told you before, it's complicated."

"No, Dad," Laurie insisted stubbornly. "It's only complicated if you *make* it complicated. Either you do want to see her or you don't. Which is it?"

"It's a bad idea."

"That's not a no," she said.

"It's not a yes, either," he emphasized. "It's not an opening for you to keep meddling. You need to stay out of this, sweetie. I mean it. Leave it alone."

She didn't try to hide her disappointment, but she clearly wasn't ready to let go of her plan despite his direct order. "But you'll at least take her to the prom, won't you?" she cajoled. "You promised, and you've always said you would never break a promise to me, and you haven't."

Trent winced. She had quite a knack for inducing guilt, this daughter of his. "I might have to this time," he told her. "I'm sorry."

"Dad, no!" she protested. "This is the most important promise you've ever made to me."

Trent was startled by her vehemence. "Why?"

"Just because I said it is."

It was the kind of logic he'd once tried when disciplining her. He wasn't crazy about being on the receiving end of it.

When he remained silent, Laurie pressed him. "Come

on, Dad. Have you even talked to her about going to the prom?"

"No."

"No, you won't take her, or no, you haven't asked her yet?"

Trent smiled despite his sour mood. "You are your mother's daughter, you know that, don't you? Once you get an idea in your head, you don't let up."

She grinned unrepentantly. "Granddad says that's a good thing."

"Your grandfather doesn't have to live with you," Trent said wryly.

"You haven't answered me yet, Dad," she reminded him.

"This is really that important to you?" he asked, already resigned to giving in. Maybe part of him even *wanted* to give in, but he wasn't telling Laurie that. Not ever. Who knew what she'd do with the knowledge?

Her expression brightened as she sensed victory. "Really, really important," she told him.

"Okay, fine, but it's one date. You do understand that, don't you? This is just about the prom and the promise I made to you. Nothing more. It is not about me getting together with Ms. Fletcher."

"Whatever," she said, making it clear that she was only humoring him.

"I don't want to hear another word about me and Ms. Fletcher after that night, understood?" He was determined to get her agreement. Otherwise she'd pester him till he found himself watching Jodie walk down the aisle in his direction.

"I said okay, didn't I?" Laurie grumbled.

"No, as a matter of fact, you said 'whatever,' which usually means you're trying to pacify me now but intend to fight again another day."

Rather than answering him, she turned to walk away. "It's starting to rain. I need to get back inside. Are you coming?"

Trent decided against making an issue of her failure to agree to his terms. Better to let her go and prepare his own battle plan for another day. "No, there's something I need to take care of. I'll check in with you in a couple of hours to see if you need more help." Knowing he was opening himself up to more speculation, he added, "Give me Ms. Fletcher's purse. I'll see that she gets it."

Laurie's expression brightened. "Really?" She looked as if she wanted to say more, but apparently thought better of it. "Great. See you later. Love you."

"You, too."

He shook his head as she ran across the driveway and went inside. He'd always grasped the concept that a parent would—and *should*—do anything possible for a child. He just hadn't expected his daughter to be so adept at turning that to her advantage.

An hour later Trent had tracked down Jodie's address and driven across the county to the town house subdivision where she was living. He told himself he was doing it because he might bear some responsibility for her running off without her purse. He was also going because he'd made a promise to Laurie and there was no point in postponing the inevitable. Deep inside, though, he knew neither of those was the real reason. On some level he felt the need to check on her, to make sure he hadn't wounded her too deeply with his cutting remarks. She might deserve every harsh word, but he was too much of a gentleman to feel good about lashing out at her. In fact, he'd surprised himself with some of the words that had poured out of his mouth. They'd been way too revealing.

The kiss hadn't been such a smart move, either, but he'd been drawn to her in a way he hadn't been able to control. The way her mouth had felt beneath his had stirred all sorts of memories, good ones this time. The kind best left dead and buried.

When he reached the entrance to her development, he had to hold back a sigh of dismay. The developer of Fox Run Estates had leveled the land before building, leaving very few of the old oaks and maples. Each tiny front lawn had been freshly planted with something barely taller than a twig. He doubted the current residents would remain long enough to see those twigs grow into mature trees, assuming they weren't destroyed by the first heavy snowfall.

At least the construction of the town houses looked solid enough, he thought as he wove through the twisting layout of dead-end streets and cul-de-sacs until he found Laurel Lane and Jodie's street number. He pulled into the driveway behind her car.

He didn't allow himself to wonder what the devil he was doing here in a driving rainstorm. He just bolted for the front steps and rang the bell, then rang it again since he doubted Jodie could hear it over the sound of the symphony she had playing on the stereo.

Finally he heard the tap of her shoes as she crossed the entryway—tile from the sound of it—to the door. When the door swung open, she stared at him with surprise, and perhaps just a hint of wariness.

"I came to apologize," he said, hoping that would get him in out of the storm. "And to return this." He held out her purse.

She accepted the purse, then stepped aside and, without a word, gestured toward the living room.

"Maybe I should go drip all over your kitchen floor instead," he said, gazing at her pale beige carpet with concern.

She finally looked directly at him, surveying him from head to toe. "You have a point. It's this way. I'll make a pot of coffee. You look as if you could use something warm." She hesitated. "Or would you rather have something stronger?"

"Coffee's good." He was going to need all his wits about him to negotiate his way through this minefield of his daughter's making.

Jodie paused en route to turn down the volume on the stereo, then went straight to a cupboard and took out coffee beans. Trent sat at the table and watched her brisk, competent movements, looking for even the faintest sign of nervousness, but unlike him she seemed perfectly at ease. For some reason, that annoyed him. He felt as if he'd been off kilter and on the defensive since the day he'd walked into that classroom and discovered that Jodie—*his* Jodie—was Laurie's awesome guidance counselor and the object of her matchmaking scheme.

When she turned around at last and set a cup of steaming, fragrant coffee in front of him, he decided to turn the tables. "My daughter has plans for us, you know," he blurted.

"I suspected as much," she said.

"And that doesn't bother you?"

Her lips quirked up. "Apparently not as much as it bothers you," she told him. "She's a teenager and she has all these romantic notions in her head. That doesn't mean we have to go along with them, especially given our history."

"You can actually look at it that rationally?" he asked, incredulous.

She regarded him with tolerant amusement. "Is there another choice?"

Before Trent could reply, she held up her hand. "Look, I know you and I regard the past very differently. I hurt you back then, even though I thought I was doing the right thing. I was hurt, too, you know. Walking away was a huge sacrifice for me." She met his gaze. "I loved you, Trent, but I did what seemed to make sense at the time. And since it was my decision, I suppose it makes it easier for me to see you again without quite so many conflicting emotions."

"There you go again, being all calm and rational."

"You say that as if it's a bad thing."

"It is. We were all about heat and passion, Jodie. At least that's how I remember it. You sound as cool and analytical as if you were talking about the price of coffee beans then and now."

She flushed at the accusation. "Maybe I've just grown up," she lashed back. "Maybe I don't put my emotions out there anymore."

"Oh, you mean the way I do? I'm not supposed to be angry about how you threw everything away?"

"Not after twenty years," she retorted. Suddenly she paused and bright patches of color appeared in her cheeks. "Unless... Did you have feelings for me all this time, Trent?"

"Absolutely not," he said, knowing that he was lying. He had, and he'd hated himself for it every single day that those feelings had affected the life he was trying to build with Megan.

Sometimes he'd go for weeks, even months, without thinking of Jodie, but then memories would flood over him and he'd pull away from the woman he'd married. It was little wonder Megan had mentioned ending their marriage on more than one occasion. Her illness had taken that option away from them. He would never have agreed to let her go through cancer treatment alone.

Jodie gave him an odd look. "Tell me about your wife."

"No," he said fiercely. He'd betrayed Megan enough, if only in his thoughts. He wouldn't diminish what they'd had for Jodie's benefit.

"You must miss her," she prodded.

The comment, common enough from friends for months after Megan's death, caught him by surprise now. Or maybe it was his reaction that caught him off guard. For the first time, he acknowledged that he did miss Megan. Saying so wouldn't be just words, the expected reaction of a grieving husband. For so long, through so many heated exchanges, he'd convinced himself that their marriage had no future.

Then she'd fallen ill, and during those long, devastating months, he'd come to see his wife in a whole new way. Time—and the grace with which Megan had handled her illness—had faded all the bad memories of their endless disagreements and left him at last with mostly good ones, plus a ton of admiration for her bravery.

"Yes, I do miss her," he said. He met Jodie's compassionate gaze head-on. "You lost your husband even more recently. How are you coping?"

"After Adam died, it was hard at first. That's why I changed jobs after it happened and moved here a couple years ago. I needed to start fresh. The change has been good for me."

"I didn't have that option," he said. "Because of Laurie. She needed the stability of her home, of her friends, and being close to her grandfather."

"So, you understand something about making sacrifices for someone you love," she said.

Trent knew the point she was trying to make, but he didn't want to acknowledge it, so he looked straight into her eyes. "What are we going to do about prom? Laurie wants me to escort you and I promised I would. It's important to her that you have a date and enjoy yourself."

Jodie flushed, clearly embarrassed. "It's not necessary. I always go alone, and believe it or not, I do enjoy myself."

For some reason, her rejection of the idea made him more determined to accompany her to the dance, and it was no longer all about pleasing Laurie. He was supposedly masterful at charm and persuasion, and he could tell from the stubborn jut of Jodie's chin that he was going to need all of that skill right now. "But you wouldn't want to deprive me of the chance to see how our project turns out, would you? I can hardly go without a date."

Her gaze narrowed. "You actually care about going to a high-school prom?"

He started to insist that he did, but doubted he could sound convincing. "Okay, it's mostly about making Laurie happy. Would it be so awful if we went together?"

"Not awful, just awkward," she said. "I'm sure Laurie will understand that it was a bad idea." She stood up. "Thanks for stopping by and bringing my purse, Trent, but perhaps you should go now."

He snagged her hand. "Hold on, Jodie. Nothing's settled."

"Trent, this is crazy. You're still angry with me. You're only asking me because your daughter wants you to. Why put ourselves through an entire night of misery?"

With each rejection, Trent grew more determined. He scrambled for a more persuasive argument.

"I know you heard every word I said to those boys the other day. All that matters when it comes to prom is that a man do whatever he can to make sure his woman is happy."

She immediately bristled. "I am not *your* woman."

His lips twitched. "Who said I was referring to you? Laurie's the only woman in my life these days."

Her cheeks flushed with embarrassment. Trent took pity on her.

"And it is at least a little bit about you," he admitted. "Prom matters to you, Jodie. I've seen it in your eyes when you talk about that night and how important it is that these kids get to participate. You look, I don't know, almost wistful. Something tells me that expression isn't just about making the night special for the kids, either. Maybe if we can find some way to trust each other again, you'll open up and tell me why that is."

He saw instantly that his insight had startled her, and that she immediately wanted to shut down his curiosity. Before she could utter the refusal that was clearly on the tip of her tongue, he added, "Let me start this whole discussion over again. Forget everything I said. Forget that this was my daughter's idea. Would you please do me the honor of letting me escort you to the prom, Jodie?"

Several emotions seemed to be warring inside her. He could see the battle in her eyes. Finally coming to a decision, she tilted her head, her expression thoughtful as she met his gaze.

"Will you bring me a corsage?"

The unexpected request made him laugh. "If that's

what it takes to get you to say yes, then you can have any kind of flowers you want."

A smile spread slowly across her face. "I'll think it over and get back to you about the flowers."

"Don't take too long. I understand the florists are going to be especially busy this year."

She looked away, then lifted her coffee cup and took a slow, deliberate sip. When she looked back, her face was composed, betraying none of her earlier emotions. "Trent, do you realize that you never once asked me to dance when we were in college? I always assumed you had two left feet. Or that you thought I might."

"Neither one. As I recall, we had too many other things to do," he responded. "That just makes this night long overdue."

And maybe forgiveness was long overdue as well.

Jodie couldn't seem to keep her hands from shaking every time she thought about going on a date—to the prom of all things—with Trent. How many years had she dreamed of the prom night she'd missed during her own senior year in high school and envisioned it turning out differently? How many times had she seen herself on the dance floor, in the arms of the handsomest boy in the senior class? She didn't like thinking about the accident that had robbed her of her special night and so much more.

As a guidance counselor at Rockingham, she'd been nudged into taking on the prom as one of her extracurricular duties and had had to face those regrets all over again. She'd done it stoically, standing on the sidelines at last year's dance, keeping watch over the punch bowl to be sure no one got the bright idea to spike it. She'd envied the other chaperones who danced in the arms of their husbands or wives.

She wasn't bitter, she told herself at least a hundred times during the planning sessions for the big night. She was happy to be part of an event that these young people were bound to remember fondly for the rest of their lives.

Now, with Trent's invitation still echoing in her mind, she knew just how badly she'd lied to herself. Only now, as excitement stirred inside her, along with a healthy dose of nerves, did she truly understand the magic of prom night.

"If you don't set that cup down, all the coffee is going to splash out of it," Carmen Nogales commented as she entered the staff room and regarded her friend with amusement. "What's going on with you, Jodie? You've been jittery for the past couple of weeks. Everyone's commented on it."

Jodie winced. She'd had no idea her nervousness was that obvious. "Just thinking about prom," she said, making the answer evasive enough that the teacher might assume it had to do with the event itself.

"Really? I know for a fact that you could run that dance with both hands tied behind your back and have it turn out perfectly, so what's different about this year? Does it have something to do with this project that you and Laurie Winston are working on? Fill me in on that. I know the basics, but none of the details."

Unwilling to admit to her own personal insecurities, she told Carmen how the committee was making the event accessible to students who normally couldn't afford to go.

Carmen nodded. "It's all I've been hearing about lately. Marvin is in my first-period history class. He's been grumbling about wearing a monkey suit for a couple of weeks now." She grinned. "You know what, though? I think he's really excited about it. And Devonia is absolutely glowing. Whenever he grumbles, she tells him he's going to be the handsomest boy at the prom. I swear he sits up straighter when she says it. This idea of yours and Laurie's is really making a difference for these kids.

For once I don't have the feeling that there's a big group of students who feel left out. I think it's going to be a huge boost to their self-image, too."

"That's the goal," Jodie said.

Carmen gave her a more intense survey, then shook her head. "That's not it, though. You're agitated about something else. Tell me." Her expression turned knowing. "It wouldn't have anything to do with the fact that Laurie's dad is escorting you to the dance, would it?"

Jodie stared at her in dismay. "You know about that?"

"Sweetie, the whole school knows about it. Laurie is practically bursting at the seams with excitement. She might be proud of opening the prom up to more kids, but getting you and her dad together seems to be her crowning achievement."

"Oh, no. I was afraid of that," Jodie moaned. "He just asked to be polite."

"Really? Then why are you so flustered?"

"Do you know Trent?"

"I've seen him. He's gorgeous, single and rich. A pretty incredible combination, if you ask me."

"Exactly, and I haven't been on a date in years, not since I met my husband eighteen years ago." She wasn't about to bring up her past history with Trent and how that was contributing to her bad case of nerves. "The man looks as if he was born to wear a tux and I look exactly like the wallflower I am, who's worn the exact same dress to every school dance since I started as a counselor years ago."

"You're worried about a dress?" Carmen asked incredulously.

"And my hair and my makeup and shoes," Jodie told her, overwhelmed by the magnitude of the transformation she needed to keep up with a man like Trent. "I know it sounds ridiculous. I counsel these girls all the time that all that matters is what's on the inside of a person, but suddenly I get why the right clothes are so important."

"Well, stop your worrying right now," Carmen said decisively. "The students have you and Laurie as their fairy godmothers, but trust me, neither of you can hold a candle to me. Be ready tomorrow by nine-thirty. I'm picking you up and we're going shopping."

"I can't do it tomorrow. We're having the shopping day for all the kids."

"Already? It's only the middle of April and prom's not for a few more weeks."

"We need to allow enough time for clothes to be altered," Jodie explained. "And if we have anyone who's hard to fit, we need to find out now so we can scramble for a new dress or tux."

"So, forget tomorrow. We'll go Sunday." Carmen clearly wasn't going to back down. "We can go at noon."

"I can do that." Despite herself, Jodie felt a stirring of very feminine excitement. It was years since she'd gone shopping for something special. Still, she cautioned, "Just remember that my budget doesn't allow me to splurge on a dress I'll wear only once. It needs to be practical."

Carmen rolled her eyes. "Fairy godmothers don't do practical. Don't you know anything?"

"The state of my bank balance," Jodie commented.

"Give me a figure and we'll work with it," Carmen promised. "Bargain-hunting is my favorite hobby. Trust me, Cinderella won't have anything on you."

"Just as long as I don't have to add scrubbing floors to my duties once the clock strikes midnight."

CHAPTER
∽SIX∽

Trent drove Laurie over to her grandfather's practically at dawn on Saturday. Her excitement was palpable, but he detected a hint of worry under the enthusiasm.

"What's wrong, kiddo? Something bothering you?"

"Mike's still not into this," she admitted. "I'm not even sure if he'll show up today. He said he had to work, but I think he deliberately asked for extra hours just to avoid coming over to Granddad's."

Trent thought he knew the boy pretty well and that didn't sound like something Mike would do. He was unfailingly considerate, especially of Laurie. "I think you're making too much of this. If his boss asked him to work some overtime, you know he can't afford to turn down extra pay. We can always make arrangements to fit his tux tonight or even tomorrow."

She turned to him, her eyes clouded with dismay. "Dad, I think he might break up with me over all this. He said something to me the other night about having my priorities all messed up and being more worried about a stupid dance than about him."

Trent glanced at her quickly. "Any chance he's right about that?"

"No," she said indignantly. "From the beginning all I wanted was for him to be able to enjoy the prom like everyone else. That's what I wanted for all these kids. I thought Ms. Fletcher made him understand that."

"Maybe you should have explained it yourself. Talk to him, sweetie. Don't let this issue get blown all out of proportion. Mike adores you. He only agreed to this in the first place because of how much he cares about your feelings. Now you need to listen when he tells you what *he's* feeling, okay?"

Laurie sighed. "I'll try."

Rather than the optimism Trent expected from his daughter now that she had a concrete plan of action, he heard dejection. "Is there something more on your mind?"

"A lot, actually." She turned to him, her expression earnest. "What if everyone hates the dresses or the sizes are all wrong and the seamstresses can't fix them in time? And the shoes. Dad, there are, like, a zillion things that could go wrong with the shoes. Do you know how hard it is to get shoes that fit right, especially if you have to keep them on all evening and dance in them?"

"How many pairs of shoes were donated?" he asked, determined not to show even a hint of amusement at what to her were major worries. Her concern about Mike, he understood, but shoes and dress sizes?

"Two dozen, I guess."

"Lots of sizes?"

"Yes."

"And there are a handful of gift certificates for shoes, too, right?"

"Yes."

He recalled an earlier conversation they'd had, though he'd only had half his attention focused on it. "And wasn't one of the requests for the donated shoes that they go with any color of dress, so some girl in purple wouldn't be stuck with red shoes?"

Beside him, Laurie sighed. "Okay, I'm acting a little crazy, huh?"

"Just a little," he conceded. "But one of the things I

love about you is how much every detail about today matters to you. You want these kids to have the best experience of their lives, and I think that's fantastic."

"It's just that I know how girls think. Even the ones who don't have much money want to look as fashionable as they possibly can."

"You don't seem nearly as concerned about the boys," he noted.

She shrugged. "There's only so much that can go wrong with a tux and a pair of black shoes."

"Not according to your mom," he said, remembering the many objections Megan had had when he told her to just go pick out anything and he'd wear it. Then, again, these boys were no doubt as clueless as he'd once been. As long as the clothes and shoes fit, they'd be okay.

As soon as Trent parked the car and they'd started up the walk, the front door swung open and Warren Davis stood waiting for them, a smile on his face as Lauric bounded up the steps to give him a hug. Even on a Saturday morning at dawn, he was already shaved, and every silver hair on his head fell neatly into place, thanks to the stylist who came to the house at least once a week to keep his hair trimmed. He was wearing dress slacks and a silk-blend shirt, though he did have the sleeves rolled up and the collar open. Still, there was no mistaking him for anything other than a man of sophistication and wealth.

"Thanks again for doing this, Granddad," Laurie said. "You're the best."

Warren winked at Trent. "Hey, I got that old ballroom cleaned up for free. Seems like a good deal to me. You two want a little breakfast before the hordes descend? I've got the cook on standby to do eggs, waffles or whatever else you'd like. The coffee's made, too. Trent, you look as if you need to be fortified with a little caffeine."

"Absolutely," Trent said.

Laurie had started through the foyer, but at the mention of waffles—her very favorite breakfast treat—her step slowed. "Any blueberries?"

Warren grinned. "Of course."

"Give me two seconds to make sure everything's set up okay and I'll meet you guys in the dining room," she said. "Tell Sarah I'd like one blueberry waffle with blueberry syrup if she has it. And lots of butter." Her order placed, she darted off in the direction of the ballroom.

Warren watched her go, then turned to Trent. "She's an admirable young lady, isn't she? Megan would be proud. I certainly am."

"Me, too," Trent said.

"So, besides that coffee, what can I get you? Eggs? Bacon?"

"Are those on your diet?" Trent asked, concerned. Warren had had a heart scare this past year. Though he hadn't required surgery and had recovered quickly, he'd been told to change his diet and lifestyle. "I thought you were watching your cholesterol."

"I am. I have a bran muffin with my name on it. I was just hoping I could live vicariously by watching you eat."

"Then, by all means, have Sarah fix me a couple of eggs and some bacon," Trent said, settling himself at the massive dining room table that had been set for four.

"Who else are you expecting?" he asked when Warren returned from speaking to his cook.

"I thought maybe that Ms. Fletcher that Laurie's so crazy about would get here early, too." He studied Trent intently. "Pretty woman. Have you noticed that?"

Trent had a feeling that his former father-in-law was playing a cat-and-mouse game with him, that he knew more than he was letting on. "She is attractive," he agreed.

Warren's lips twitched at the bland response. "Hear she's your date for the prom."

"Your granddaughter has a big mouth," Trent commented.

"Laurie seems real happy about it. Are you finally getting serious about somebody new?"

"No," Trent said at once, then sighed. "Look, Jodie's not exactly new in my life. I knew her years ago, back in college. We met again by chance when Laurie started putting this whole prom committee together. Our history wasn't all sweetness and light, but we're trying to get along for Laurie's sake. That's it."

Warren gave him a searching look. "Too bad," he said eventually. "You deserve to find happiness, son. I know you and Megan had some rough patches...."

When Trent would have interrupted, Warren held up his hand. "I'm not blind. I could see you were both unhappy, but I admired the way you stuck by her when she got sick. No one could have been more caring during that awful illness and I will be forever grateful to you for that. Now, though, it's time to move on. You're still a young man. You could start a new family."

"The old one's tricky enough," Trent commented dryly. "Laurie's a handful."

"She's your daughter, but you need a wife," Warren said.

"And you think I should let my daughter handpick the woman to fill that position?"

Warren chuckled. "Her taste can't be all that bad,

since you chose the same woman yourself years ago. Look, I know you don't need my blessing, but maybe you'll feel better if you have it. I'm telling you here and now that there's nothing wrong with moving on."

"You never did," Trent pointed out.

"Different situation. Grace was the love of my life. We had a good marriage. I don't harbor one single regret beyond wishing she'd been with me longer. And at my age, what kind of woman can I expect to find? Some gold digger after my fortune?"

"You have better judgment than to let that happen," Trent said.

Warren shrugged. "You know what they say—there's no fool like an old fool. No, Trent, I'm content with the way things are. I have female friends. Widows I've known for years who are good company, play a decent hand of cards and can carry on an intelligent conversation over dinner. I don't need more than that. You, however, are too young to be settling for nothing more than companionship."

Just then the doorbell rang and Warren was on his feet. "Think about what I've said," he advised as he left to answer the door. "Take another look at this Jodie and consider what might be, instead of what was."

Only after Warren had left the room did Trent feel a

smile tugging at his lips. Never in a million years had he expected to be getting relationship advice from a tough old man who had an international reputation for chewing up business rivals and spitting them out without the slightest hesitation. Since Warren hadn't steered him too far wrong all those years ago when Trent had been setting up his business, maybe there was some wisdom in what he had to say about Jodie as well.

Devonia was near tears. Jodie saw the expression on the girl's face and rushed over to her.

"What's wrong?" she asked, handing her a tissue.

"None of these dresses are right for me," Devonia said with a resigned sigh. "Either my chest's popping out or they won't even zip up. I'm not going to be able to go to prom after all."

"I don't want to hear that kind of defeatist attitude," Jodie scolded. "Let's take another look. What size do you wear?"

"Fourteen," Devonia said. "All these gowns were made for the rest of these skinny little things."

"Not so," Jodie insisted. "We got a range of sizes. Come with me. Did you try this rack over here?"

Granted, there were only three dresses left hanging on it, but surely one of them would work. She and

Laurie had been very careful to make sure that each girl had at least a couple of choices in the right size. They'd wanted to avoid a moment just like this, when someone who wasn't a perfect size six or eight felt humiliated.

Jodie checked the tags and found two size fourteen dresses and one size sixteen.

"I tried those two on," Devonia said, her discouragement plain.

"What was wrong with them?"

"The blue one was cut too low. My mama would never let me out the front door in that. I know I'll be getting dressed here and she won't know, but I just can't wear it."

"And the red?"

"Too tight across my hips."

Jodie nodded. "Did you try on the sixteen?"

Devonia immediately looked insulted. "I am not a size sixteen."

"Of course not," Jodie said hurriedly. "But if you like the dress and it's too big, we can have a seamstress cut it down so that it does fit. Want to give it a try? It's a beautiful dress. I think the color would look amazing on you."

The shimmering copper satin was only a few shades lighter than Devonia's skin. She held the dress up as they stood side by side in front of a mirror. "See what I mean?" Jodie encouraged. "The color's fantastic."

Devonia's expression brightened slightly. "It's not bad, is it?"

"Try it on. Let's see if we can make it work."

A few minutes later Devonia emerged from behind a curtain that cordoned off a dressing room area. Jodie saw the trepidation in her eyes as she walked toward the mirror.

"It's amazing," Jodie reassured her. "Come on, Devonia, see for yourself."

The teenager finally lifted her gaze to the mirror. Her mouth gaped. "Wow!"

Jodie grinned. "I'll say. Marvin is going to swallow his tongue when he sees you. It needs a little nipping and tucking here and there, but it's perfect for you. Don't you think so?"

For the second time, Devonia's eyes swam with tears. "I never…" She swallowed hard. "I never thought I could look like this. I'm almost beautiful."

"Not almost. You *are* beautiful. Shall I get the seamstress over here?"

Devonia couldn't seem to tear her gaze away from the mirror. She merely nodded.

Jodie barely contained a smile as she went off to find

someone to make the necessary alterations. The moment Devonia had seen herself as beautiful for the very first time—one of many such moments Jodie had witnessed throughout the day—was what this entire project was about. First thing tomorrow she was going to sit down and e-mail the founder of Inside the Dream and thank her for the inspiration. Because of it, these kids were going to have a whole new image of themselves and the possibilities that stretched out in front of them.

Two hours later, the ballroom was deserted except for Jodie, Laurie and, on the other side of the dividing curtain, Trent. Jodie suspected Warren Davis was lurking about somewhere as well. When they'd all grabbed a quick cup of coffee together before the day got started, he'd seemed as excited as she and Laurie. Trent was the only one who'd been oddly subdued.

"This was totally awesome, wasn't it?" Laurie said, her arms filled with the dresses that hadn't been chosen. They'd be packed away for next year, giving the seniors a head start if they chose to continue with the project.

"It couldn't have gone better," Jodie agreed.

"Did you see the way Mariana looked when she tried on that white gown with the gold thread woven through it?" Laurie asked. "She looked like a delicate fairy. It was as if that dress was made for her." Impulsively, she dumped the dresses on a chair and gave Jodie a fierce hug. "Thank you for making this happen."

"You're the one who made it happen, you and the other kids on the committee who worked so hard," Jodie corrected. "The day you came into my office, you started the ball rolling. I hope you know how proud I am of you. Your grandfather and dad must be, too."

Laurie shrugged. "They'd be proud no matter what I did. It's in the job description."

"No, you really earned their admiration this time," Jodie insisted. "I wonder how things went with the boys?"

"Let's get Dad and go out on the patio out back. It should be warm enough. Granddad said he'd have something for us to eat whenever we were ready. I'll let him know we're starving, at least I am."

"Me, too," Jodie admitted. She hadn't noticed missing lunch in the mad rush to get all the girls outfitted, but now she heard her stomach growl.

"If you go through the dining room, there are French doors that lead outside," Laurie told her. "Think you can find your way?"

"Is there a restroom on that route?"

"Just two doors down from here," Laurie directed her. "I'll get Dad and the food and meet you outside."

"Sounds good," Jodie said.

After she'd freshened up, she found her way back to the dining room and then onto the brick patio outside. She was the first one there and sank eagerly onto a comfortable chaise longue in the sun, relieved to be off her feet. The April afternoon was balmy. Enjoying the lingering scent of the last, fading lilacs, she closed her eyes. She couldn't think of the last time she'd felt this kind of exhaustion, one that came from working hard at something so rewarding.

"You sleeping?"

Trent's teasing voice jerked her back from the edge of sleep. She blinked up at him.

"Nope. Just resting my eyes. It's been a long day."

He studied her intently as he sat down beside her. "A good one, though?"

"It was on my side of the curtain. How about yours?"

He handed her a glass of lemonade from a tray. "You know, I expected it to be all grumbling and complaining, but it wasn't like that. It almost felt as if these boys were transformed right in front of my eyes to young men."

Jodie grinned. "Exactly. The same with the girls. It was a good feeling, wasn't it?"

"It was. Just one problem on my side and I'm not sure what to do about it. Mike didn't show up."

Jodie sat up. "Laurie's Mike?"

He nodded. "She was afraid he wouldn't. He told her he had to work, but she thinks he was just making an excuse."

"I don't think so," Jodie said. "That wouldn't be like him at all."

"That's what I told her. And there are tuxedos and one gift certificate left, so he can be fitted whenever he has the time. Now, the question is, do I tell her now or wait?"

"Don't you think she already knows that he wasn't here? I'm sure she was keeping an eye out for him, despite how busy we were. Maybe you should just wait and see if she brings it up."

Trent looked relieved. "Good idea. Now, tell me, did everything go smoothly with the girls?"

"We had one or two crises, but the problems were resolved pretty quickly." She turned to him. "This might sound silly, but I think I'm almost as excited about the prom this year as the girls are."

"Something tells me that doesn't have anything to do with your date with me, either," he commented.

"Sorry if that hurts your ego, but no, it doesn't. It's

about these kids. I can't wait till they're all dressed and see themselves for the first time. It'll be like a glimpse of what they can be if they strive for it."

"You're expecting a lot from a fancy dress or a tuxedo," he said.

She sat up straighter. "No, Trent, really, didn't you see how proud they looked when they tried on these clothes? Oh, I'm not saying they're all going to suddenly find a way to go to college and become CEOs. But when people have only seen themselves one way all their lives, struggling just to get by, something like this can show them they can fit into that other world, that the only thing holding them back is their own self-image. They might start to believe they can work hard and accomplish anything, that they're not that different from all those kids who don't need our help."

His gaze warmed. "You must be an incredible guidance counselor. How could any kid not want to reach for the moon with you in his corner?"

Tears stung her eyes. "That may be the nicest thing you've said to me since we first saw each other again. Are you having a change of heart about the kind of person I am?"

"In a way," he replied, glancing over at her. "A very

wise man said something to me recently about letting go of the past."

Jodie wasn't sure how she felt about that. "Even the good memories?"

"I don't think he was talking about tossing everything out the window, just the things that keep you from moving on."

"Then he is a wise man," she said, looking straight at him. "You going to take his advice?"

He smiled slowly. "I'm thinking about it."

"Good to know I still have a little influence around here," Warren Davis announced, joining them with a tray loaded down with thick sandwiches and slices of decadent-looking chocolate cake. Laurie was right behind him with a bowl of salad.

Jodie flushed at the realization that he was the one who'd been giving Trent advice, apparently about her. Still, she was grateful to have another person—someone Trent obviously respected—in her corner.

She wasn't sure it was possible to recapture what the two of them once had. There was too much water under the bridge. But maybe they could find something new together. She knew she wanted to try.

Because from the minute she'd laid eyes on Trent in that classroom a couple of months ago, she'd known that she was still very much in love with him. She hadn't been willing to admit it, even to herself, until now. The thought that he might not love her back was too scary.

But if there was a chance—even a very slim one—that she could have him back in her life, she wanted that chance more than she'd wanted anything in a very long time.

CHAPTER
❧ SEVEN ❧

Trent didn't mean to eavesdrop, but he couldn't help himself when he heard Mike's voice rise in anger. He didn't intend to step in unless things got out of hand, but he wasn't happy hearing anyone speak to Laurie in that tone of voice. Then he listened to the point Mike was trying to make and that his daughter apparently wasn't hearing. It was difficult to stand by and listen to them struggling to reach an understanding on something so complex that many adults couldn't manage it. Both of them had valid viewpoints, and finding the middle ground seemed all but impossible.

"I did not blow off today," Mike told her heatedly. "Come on, Laurie. Don't you know me better than that?"

"I thought I did," Laurie responded just as angrily. "But when you didn't show up at Granddad's today, I felt like it was a slap in the face. You know how hard I've worked to make this happen and you couldn't even be bothered to be there."

"Because I was *working*," he retorted impatiently. "I told you I had to work. What part of that don't you understand? I need to work as many hours as they'll give me. My family needs every dime I can earn and I have to start putting away some money for college next year. The scholarship won't cover all of my expenses."

"I know that," Laurie said, sounding somewhat apologetic. "But today was really important to me. It should have mattered to you."

Mike sighed heavily. "What's happened to you, Laurie? If things don't go exactly the way you want them to, then I'm disrespecting you? You never used to be like that. You never used to act like a spoiled brat."

Trent heard Laurie's gasp, then silence. He could feel her anguish, but he could also understand Mike's frustration. When Laurie finally spoke, her voice was thick with tears.

"I had no idea you felt that way," she whispered. "Do you want to break up? Is that what this is about?"

"Are you crazy?"

To Trent's relief, Mike sounded incredulous, as if nothing could be further from the truth.

"Laurie, if you and I are going to stay together, we have to be able to work through stuff like this. We come from very different backgrounds, that's just a fact. You take things for granted that are out of reach for me."

"I was just trying to put them within reach," she told him. "Just for prom, not for anything else. You're fine the way you are. In fact, I love who you are. You're smart and you care so much about your family. You work hard and still keep your grades up and find time for sports and for me. You're terrific. Don't you know how much I admire you?"

"I wish you'd said all that a few weeks ago," Mike told her. "I thought you were ashamed of me."

"Never!" she said fiercely.

"You know, if you'd just said that prom was important to you, I would have found some way for us to go," he told her wearily. "You said it didn't matter, and then, all of a sudden, there's this huge production to make sure all the poor kids like me get to go. And to top it off, you got Ms. Fletcher on my case about it. Do you know how that made me feel?"

"I just meant for you to feel included," she whispered.

"Well, I didn't. I felt embarrassed and humiliated, and

worse, I got drafted to talk the other guys into it. It's not that I don't appreciate your motives, but did you ever stop to think about how it would make me feel to have to take all this free stuff from somebody? I was brought up to pay my own way, and if I couldn't, then I did without. The only time I've broken that rule is when I asked Ms. Fletcher to help me get free school breakfasts and lunches for my brothers and sister. It about killed me to ask for that. I only did it because my mom was too proud to, and they were going to school hungry."

"I'm sorry. I guess I didn't think this through. Do you think the others feel the same way?"

"No, and if I can shove my pride aside, I get that you're doing a really nice thing. And prom is going to be great this year, because almost everyone will be there. It's just hard, you know, feeling like I can't provide everything you want."

"I just want you," she told him softly. "Just you."

Silence fell then and Trent didn't want to think about any making up that might be going on, so he slipped away and went down the hall into his office. As he sat at his desk, he thought about what Mike had said, that he and Laurie had to work through things, not make assumptions and run off to lick their wounds.

Was that what he had done years ago with Jodie? Had

he been so hurt by her decision to break up that he'd failed to fight hard enough for what he believed they had? Oh, sure, he'd made plenty of calls. He'd even gone by her place a few times, but he could have done more and he knew it. He'd been afraid to push too hard for answers because he thought he already knew what they would be—that she'd tired of him, that she no longer loved him. He hadn't wanted to hear those words spelled out any more clearly than they already had been. He'd made assumptions rather than having faith in what he *knew* they had between them.

Before he could change his mind, he picked up the phone and dialed the number he'd written down when he'd looked up her address a few weeks before.

"Hello," she said cheerily, with yet another symphony booming in the background. "Hang on a sec. The music's too loud."

Once it was muted, she came back on the line. "Sorry. I always thought Beethoven was meant to be heard at full volume."

"You never liked classical music when we were together," Trent commented.

"Trent?" She sounded surprised.

"It's me," he said. "When did you develop this fondness for Beethoven and the rest of the classics?"

"When I was married. Adam liked it and I developed an appreciation for it, too, though to be honest my preference is for Mozart's pieces for the flute. What about you? Have your musical tastes changed at all?"

"Sorry, no. I'm still a little bit country, a little bit rock 'n' roll."

She laughed. "Like the Osmonds."

"Pretty much."

"I assume you didn't call to talk about music," she said. "Is there something in particular on your mind?"

"I was sitting here thinking about some things," he began, not entirely sure what to say now that he had her on the phone. He just knew that everything that had happened wasn't entirely her fault, after all.

"The past?" she asked.

"Mostly," he acknowledged. "I owe you an apology."

"Oh?"

"I still don't like what you did all those years ago, the unilateral decision you made that affected our future."

"Yes, you've made that clear enough," she said dryly. "I'm not quite hearing that apology yet."

"Hold on. I'm getting to it." His lips curved slightly, but the smile faded as he formed the rest of his thoughts. "You made that decision, Jodie, but I'm the one who let you get away with it. I should have owned up to my part a long time ago, but it was easier to blame you. I could have fought harder, made you talk to me about why you decided to end it, instead of just running off with my tail between my legs. Maybe if I'd forced things and we'd really sat down and talked it all through, things would have turned out differently."

"Oh, Trent, I don't know about that. I was pretty stubborn and pretty darn certain I was right. I spent my entire childhood being told by my parents that I wasn't as pretty or as smart or as clever as my sister. When I was in that car accident—remember, I told you about that when we first met—things went from bad to worse. Oh, my folks were there for me, but they couldn't seem to help reminding me afterward that I was less than perfect. When I met you, I was still pretty much convinced that I could never measure up. You were going places and I didn't think I could keep up. Even my folks commented one time that I would probably hold you back."

"That's ridiculous," he said heatedly.

She sighed. "I know that now, but I didn't have the kind of self-confidence and strength then that I do today. That comes with maturity and getting away from all that nonstop negativity."

"I wish you'd explained all this back then," he told her. "I could have told you how wrong you were."

"I wouldn't have believed you. After all, the message had been ingrained in me for a very long time, if not with overt criticism then with comparisons in which I always fell just a little short of my sister."

"But I could be awfully persuasive when I set my mind to it, or have you forgotten that?" He chuckled as a memory came to him. "I got you to go parasailing at Ocean City despite your fear of heights, didn't I?"

She groaned. "I have definitely tried to forget that. Maybe that was when I saw we didn't have a real future. I wasn't sure I was prepared for a lifetime of taking outrageous risks. I'd always pictured myself as a sedate schoolteacher, setting a proper example for her students."

"You could have done both," he said.

"I'm not so sure about that."

"Let me prove it to you, starting with prom."

"I've already agreed to go with you," she reminded him.

"I know, but I'm not sure when I asked and you agreed to go that either one of us was doing it for the right reason."

"And what is the right reason?"

"Because I want to hold you in my arms and dance with you," he told her, his voice low and seductive. "I want to start over, Jodie, see what's left of what we once were or maybe find something new altogether. How about it? Just take the first step on the long road toward a future with me."

She was silent for so long, he thought maybe she wasn't anywhere near as ready as he was.

"One step," she agreed at last. "And then we'll see."

"That's all I ask," he said. "Good night, Jodie."

"Good night, Trent."

He held the phone after she'd disconnected, not ready to break that fragile tie with the woman he'd once loved with all his heart… and just might love again.

The May evening couldn't have been more perfect. The sky was littered with stars, the temperature balmy. Inside Oak Haven, the ballroom quite literally took Jodie's breath away. It looked different than it had when they'd held their shopping spree there a few weeks earlier. The massive chandelier sparkled like diamonds and spilled light over polished oak floors inlaid with elaborate designs. The part of her that had once dreamed impossible dreams could imagine a full orchestra at one end of the huge room, music soaring to the rafters and mingling with excited chatter and high-pitched laughter. That was the world to which Trent was accustomed. She tried not to let that intimidate her. Instead, she focused on the chatter and laughter around her tonight.

A dozen girls were at the center of a beehive of activity, their dresses nipped and tucked one last time until they fit perfectly, their hair in giant rollers as they awaited a turn with one of the four stylists who had volunteered to help. They jockeyed for position in front of the half-dozen full-length mirrors that had been brought in for the occasion, their eyes bright with wonder as they saw themselves transformed. Several moms had come along for the special night and they sat on the sidelines, smiling at the joy on their daughters' faces.

Laurie darted among the girls, her own pastel-pink dress a fairy-tale confection of tulle and silk and glittering rhinestones. She was a never-ending font of helpful tips, of glowing compliments that kept the other girls beaming with pride.

"I had no idea I could ever look like this," Mariana Padrone whispered to Jodie as she stared at the image in the mirror in front of her. In the white dress threaded with gold, she looked like a delicate princess.

A shy girl with decent but not extraordinary grades, Mariana was destined for community college classes that could fit around her work schedule. Tonight was giving her a little bit of the magic that had been missing from her life.

"You look beautiful," Jodie told her. "Miguel is going to be blown away when he sees you."

"I am so grateful to Mr. Winston for talking him into this," Mariana said, glancing toward the portable dividers that separated the girls' dressing area from the boys'. "He is going to look so handsome in his tuxedo. I wish I had a camera to take pictures so we can always remember tonight."

"Done," Jodie said, grinning at her and pulling a disposable camera from a bag filled with two dozen of them. "There's one for each of you. Allow me to take the first picture."

She snapped it, capturing Mariana's beaming smile forever.

Over the next hour, she took dozens of photos of the girls alone in their finery and then of the couples as they prepared to ride in one of the limos that Warren Davis had arranged to take them from his home to the hotel. The drivers would wait and deliver the students to one of several parent-supervised after-prom parties that would last until dawn.

When the final limo rode away, Jodie turned to find Trent behind her. She'd found him attractive enough in his work clothes, but in a tuxedo he was devastatingly handsome. He looked as if he'd been born to wear one. All those years ago, she had known that his life was meant to be like this, from the fancy clothes to the extravagant events.

Then she reminded herself that this was a high school prom they were about to attend, an event from her world, and he looked as if it were as important as any big-dollar charity event.

"Unlike the boys, you look very comfortable in that tux," she commented. "You must have had it specially tailored."

"I had to," he said. "Laurie took all my old ones for this project."

He pulled his hand from behind his back and held out a florist's box. "You never did say what kind of flowers you wanted, so I had to rely on a tip from my daughter." He glanced from her shimmering sheath of cream silk, which Carmen had talked her into paying way too much for, to the ivory camellia resting against delicate lace and waxy, dark green leaves.

Jodi regarded the corsage with amazement. He'd gotten it exactly right, simple and classy, just like Trent himself.

He grinned at her. "Trust me to pin it on, or would you rather do it yourself?"

She had to swallow against the tide of emotion clogging her throat. "You do it, please," she said softly.

When his knuckles grazed bare skin, she trembled, but she kept her gaze level with his, felt the heat stir between them. The once-familiar sensation was exactly the way she'd remembered it. For the second time in her life, she felt as if her prince had come along.

She'd just never expected to have to wait so very long for him to find his way back to her.

Trent stood at the edge of the dance floor, Jodie beside him, and felt an unexpected swell of pride that his daughter had turned this night into something special for so many people. Sure, some of the students here were having the night they'd anticipated, taken for granted, in fact, but he could pick out those for whom it was an unexpected blessing. There was an air of bemusement about them, a sense of wonder that was lacking in the other kids.

Even Marvin and his oh-so-resistant cohorts were standing taller, gazing with genuine amazement and appreciation at the girls on their arms. And Mike had finally relaxed and let himself enjoy the party. He and

Laurie couldn't seem to take their eyes off each other. Trent couldn't help rooting just a little bit for the two of them. He was impressed more and more with Mike's maturity.

Jodie said something he couldn't hear over the music so he leaned closer, breathing in the scent of the camellia that he'd noticed her touching from time to time as if it were a talisman.

"What?" he asked.

"I said I haven't heard Marvin refer to a single person tonight as a dude," she said, grinning. "That alone is miracle enough for me." She glanced across the room. "Laurie and Mike look happy. Did they settle their disagreement or is this just detente?"

"They talked and settled things, I think," Trent said. "At least for now. Who knows what's in store for those two, but I have to say my respect for Mike has increased lately. He's got a good head on his shoulders. Maybe they can make it, after all."

Jodi studied him quizzically. "Will you mind that very much?"

"I never objected to Laurie dating Mike," he said. "At least not for the reason you're thinking. I thought it was too soon, that Mike especially had a tough road ahead of him and shouldn't add a serious relationship to the mix." He glanced at her. "Sounds like the same mistake you made about me, misjudging what I could handle."

"Okay, okay, I get it," she said. "I thought we'd settled the fact that I'd been an idiot and you were, too."

"I don't recall the word *idiot* ever crossing my lips," he commented.

"Implied," she said. "It was definitely implied."

"We're communicating now, though, and that's what counts," he told her. "We'll never make that same mistake again."

"Never," she promised.

Trent looked around the dance floor and chuckled as he saw Marvin trying to do a sedate slow dance with Devonia. He looked as if he wanted to break loose and speed up the beat. Ramon and his girl were wrapped tight in each other's arms. Miguel's gaze on Mariana was bewildered, almost as if he'd never seen her before and didn't know quite what to make of this precious, lovely creature. Even Jason, small for his age, his eyes too big behind his thick glasses, was talking intently to a girl wearing braces and whose hair was as uncontrolled as Jodie's. Even though she was inches taller than Jason, she was gazing at him raptly and seemed to be hanging on the boy's every word.

Trent looked into Jodie's eyes. "You and my daughter did a good thing tonight," he said. "A very good thing."

"Does that mean you'll help us again next year, even if Laurie's away at college?"

"If you need my help, you've got it," he said at once. "On one condition."

"Oh?"

"Dance with me, Jodie. That was part of our deal for tonight, but every time I've asked, you've suddenly found something requiring your attention. Even the most dutiful chaperone doesn't need to check the punch bowl that many times, especially since we've been standing right next to it for most of the night."

She winced. "You noticed that?"

"I notice a lot of things about you," he said, brushing a wayward curl from her cheek. It was a futile exercise, since more sprang free from the delicate, sparkling combs meant to hold her hair in place.

"Name one."

He laughed. "You did it again. You tried to divert me. Come on, Jodie, it's time to pay the piper. I'm claiming this dance."

She backed up a step. "I can't."

He paused, struck by the genuine fear he saw in her

eyes. "What do you mean, you can't? Do you really have two left feet, the way you said the other day?"

"I don't know," she confessed.

He was more confused than ever. "How can you not know?"

"The truth is that I never learned to dance."

Trent didn't even try to hide his disbelief. "But the way you got involved with this, the fact that it's so important to you…" He didn't know what to make of any of it.

"I know it must not make sense to you," she said.

"Explain," he pleaded.

Her cheeks turned pink. Carefully avoiding his gaze, she finally blurted, "You remember that when I was just starting my senior year of high school, I was in an accident, a bad one. Broken legs, broken pelvis."

Trent nodded. "You told me about that and you mentioned it again the other day. What does that have to do with you not dancing?"

"I finished the year in rehab and at home. For a while they thought I would never walk again, but I proved them wrong." She met his eyes straight on. "Don't you remember that when we met our junior year I still had a little bit of a limp? I was so self-conscious about it."

He shook his head. "All I noticed was that you were

the most beautiful woman I'd ever seen and that your laugh made me happy. Beyond mentioning the accident, you never made a big deal about it. I had no idea it was so serious."

"I didn't want you to feel sorry for me and I was trying to forget what had been a very painful time in my life, not just physically, but emotionally. I was grateful that I could walk. I really was, but I missed so much, things I can never get back."

He regarded her with sudden understanding. "Like your prom."

She nodded.

"But you came to this one," he said. "Did you go to the prom at your old school, too?"

She nodded. "As a chaperone. I've done it for years. I kept hoping it would make up for what I'd missed, but it's not the same. It couldn't possibly be." Again, she touched the camellia fleetingly. "At least until tonight."

Trent's heart turned over in his chest as he tried to imagine how it must have hurt each year to see young people celebrating the end of their high school days, while she had only memories of pain and heartache from hers.

Not only had her revelation given him a deeper insight into this amazing woman, it also reassured him that even if they spent a lifetime together, there would still be new discoveries to make. The prospect excited him.

"You know," he said, "dancing's not that difficult."

"Maybe not for you," she said. "You've had lots of practice."

"Come on," he insisted, tugging her onto the floor and then into his arms. "Just hold on to me, Jodie. Trust me."

Her body swayed into his and he gave her a moment to relax before he began to move. "Listen to the music—feel it," he encouraged her, wishing he could feel it himself over the beating of his heart and the sweet sensation of her body pressed against him.

"Don't even think about dancing," he said. "Look around you. See what you've done for these kids. You gave them magic, Jodie. You gave them memories they'll treasure for a lifetime, rather than living with the regret of missing this night the way you had to."

A smile spread across her face as she looked around. He could tell the precise moment when she forgot about her fears, her awkwardness. Satisfied that he'd accomplished one goal, he went for another and spun her around and around till she was laughing, her feet off the ground. The kids around them stood back and applauded.

Seeing Jodie let go, listening to the laughter that had once brought him such joy, Trent knew he'd captured a little magic tonight, too.

And this time, he wouldn't let it go. He'd do whatever it took to make sure it lasted forever.

* * * * *

Dear Reader,

How many times in your life have you opened your closet door before an evening out and murmured, "I have absolutely nothing to wear," even though the closet is crammed with clothes? It's one thing to face such a dilemma as an adult, but in the fashion-conscious world of teenagers, it's quite another, especially if the lack of appropriate clothes is real. At no time does the absence of something special to wear seem quite as important as it does for all of the activities associated with high school graduation and, most especially, the prom.

Ruth Renwick, a Canadian social worker, encountered that need firsthand when she learned of a girl who was going to miss her high school prom because she simply couldn't afford a dress to wear. The first dress Ruth took by was too big. With time running out, Ruth searched her own closet, found more options and took them to the girl's home. It seemed such a little thing to her at the time, but the delight she saw on the girl's face, the transformation that took place, led Ruth to think about all the other young girls and young men in similar circumstances. With her huge heart, the glimmer of an idea and the help of her family and others such as social workers Tracey Ciccarelli and Janace King-Watson, Ruth began

Inside the Dream. You can read much more about the organization on the website www.insidethedream.org. If you're able to help, please do. If there's a need for a similar organization in your community, start one. It takes only one person with a dream and a vision to make a huge difference in someone's life.

With all good wishes for your dreams to come true,

Sheryl Woods

BARBARA HUSTON
⮞PARTNERS IN CARE MARYLAND⮜

I magine waking up one morning so old and frail that a simple run to the corner store to pick up milk, bread and soup takes over three hours. Imagine constantly fretting that your bedroom light bulb will burn out and go unchanged for weeks because there's no easy way to reach it. Imagine what it's like to boast a sharp mind, an independent spirit and a true desire to live at home, but not have the funds to periodically pay the fifteen to twenty dollars an hour for services to help make that happen.

But there is another way. It's called Partners In Care Maryland, a vital, niche resource for older people and their families and friends living in Maryland—and a dream come true for Barbara Huston, the organization's CEO.

"Most older adults want to stay in the community,

but that doesn't mean having something done for them necessarily. It's about participating in that community," she says, explaining the nonprofit's "service-exchange" philosophy.

Put simply, the service-exchange concept is based on the idea that everyone has something to contribute to their community. People give their time and talents, and that time is logged into the "bank," so when they need to draw from it, they can. For example, a seventy-five-year-old woman with 20/20 vision could read letters to a sight-impaired member and then ask yet another member for a ride to the doctor's office or help repairing a leaky faucet. This network of care helps older adults feel as if they're part of the solution rather than the problem or, worse, a charity case, says Barbara.

No wonder that if anyone uses the word volunteer around Barbara, she quickly changes it to member.

A bunch of nice ladies

In some ways Barbara can't believe she has been running Partners In Care Maryland since 1993. Back then the kitchen table served as a boardroom, and her sister and friend, both with gerontology degrees, helped run the show. Barbara had just left a career as a navy budget analyst working in the Pentagon after starting her family. That background, she says, certainly helped her learn how to burn the midnight oil to get a job done.

"You really can't find anything that's more high-pressure than that. It just cooks all the time," she says.

Her tenacity paid off. That first year they transported twelve people to medical appointments and convinced the local hospital to donate one room to work out of. She's the first to admit, almost cheerfully, that nepotism helped her get through the door.

"Our partner's neighbor was the hospital's new head, so he couldn't really say, 'Don't come see me.' When we pitched the idea we were just so sincere he gave us space," she says.

Others were equally impressed with the "bunch of nice ladies" writing grants and knocking on doors, so eventually a foundation in Baltimore decided to fund them, as long as Partners In Care Maryland found a fiscal agent to handle the money until they landed their nonprofit status.

Today, Barbara still hits the ground running every morning, overseeing a budget of $900,000 per year, eight full-time staff, nine part-time staff and about twenty-four office volunteers as they help to coordinate about 175 rides and hundreds of other matches per week at four sites and the thrift store—not to mention offering a growing number of other services for the whopping 2,600 members now signed up.

For instance, Partners In Care Maryland offers emergency kits containing food, water, a radio (with large buttons so everyone can see them), whistles and glow sticks. The organization also runs Repairs with Care to help with handyman-type chores, and networking programs that assist isolated and lonely seniors in reaching out to find friends. Recently Barbara collaborated with the CEO of the local hospice, which acquired a property to build a community campus of care. In exchange for engaging contractors and member handymen to rehab one of the buildings on site, Partners In Care was able to move their offices to rent-free space and to enlarge the thrift store so that it will be able to offer even more financial support to the program, a very important step in difficult economic times. The first organization on site, PIC will be part of a continuum of care campuses for older adults and those with chronic illnesses. Another PIC program will help in this new arena. The Mobility-Bus was started in 2012 with a grant from the state to support members who no longer can get into a volunteer driver's car or who may need a caregiver or family member to travel with them. "This new option makes sure that we can continue to help our members as they age in the homes they love," says Barbara.

"People have really taken to this idea," she says. "We are still amazed and giddy that people wanted to belong and that it's been so effective."

Good for all

Beyond Barbara's unyielding energy and kindness, one of the reasons for the nonprofit's success is its far-reaching benefits. Not only do frail older people win, so do their families, particularly those who live too far away to help with ongoing, day-to-day care.

As families become more mobile, spreading out across the state to be where the jobs are, seniors are often left behind without a support system in place. Meanwhile, even a short drive of forty miles can quickly add up to hours on the road if an elderly mother needs a ride to the doctor's office in town and there's no one local to take her.

"It really takes the whole day. And it's not that you don't love your mother   it's if she has to do that two times a week, that's really going to upset your work-life balance," says Barbara.

It's little wonder, then, that many businesses are also seeing the advantage of organizations like Partners In Care Maryland. If it can locate local drivers for errands and medical visits, family members need less personal time off to care for their elderly loved ones. When it comes down to it, people all over the world are learning about Partners In Care. For example, in 2010 Barbara was invited to speak at an international conference in Northern Ireland, as government leaders were interested in showcasing Partners In Care as a model for helping their own aging population.

Running itself

Ask Barbara what she is proud of, however, and she's quick to answer that she's amazed and thrilled that Partners In Care Maryland can now run itself. People know their jobs and do them well, she says.

Not that Barbara has been made redundant. She discovered this just recently when Partners In Care Maryland conducted an operations report that revealed staff and volunteers still say they turn to her for ideas and insight. Barbara remains at the helm, inspiring others to do good work.

"They said I'm still the head mother," she says, laughing.

For instance, when Barbara went away on vacation not long ago, she arrived back to a sign on the desk that simply read "WWBD," or "What Would Barbara Do?"

Here's part of that answer: she pitches in. When staff

members have a difficult time trying to coordinate a ride for a member and no one else is available, Barbara hops into the car and does the job herself. Or if she's at the office after five o'clock and everyone else has gone home, she makes it a point to answer the telephone. It's a rare CEO who is willing to wear the hat of receptionist in a pinch.

Even when her husband developed multiple sclerosis and cancer five years ago, Barbara did double duty, caring for him and still running Partners In Care Maryland with her usual patience and grace.

With that dedication and hard work behind her, no one can blame Barbara for wanting to kick back and enjoy a little R & R someday. So what will she do when that day comes?

"I don't know. I never grew up—or at least I never knew what I wanted to be when I grew up. I might not be finished yet," she says.

After a moment's pause, though, she answers, her voice taking on a softer, almost dreamy tone. A lover of books and a voracious reader, Barbara talks about opening a bookstore near the small beach house her family owns.

"I could read all day, wear flip-flops to work and I wouldn't have to make apologies for that!" Barbara says.

Until then, she'll do everything she can to make her

members' lives easier, more fulfilling and less lonely, working with like-minded people who come to Partners In Care Maryland with good intentions and an open heart.

"Every day is a good day," she says. "That just gives me joy."

For more information, visit www.partnersincare.org or write to Partners In Care Maryland, 90-B Ritchie Highway, Pasadena, MD 21122.

CHRISTINA SKYE
~Safely Home~

❧─CHRISTINA SKYE─❧

Christina Skye loves living in Arizona, where she hasn't met a sunset she didn't like. The night she finished this story, three owls gathered outside her window, calling back and forth until dawn.

Readers can find excerpts of her books, knitting and crochet patterns (yes, she loves both!) and special reader contests at www.christinaskye.com.

To my mother,
who taught me about optimism and about
remembering what is important.

CHAPTER
~ONE~

There was something sad and lost about the big dog sitting by the side of the road. Looking confused and worried, it watched Sara drive past. Or was that only her imagination?

Sara Winslow pressed one hand against the center of her chest, in the empty part that had never been filled. She had wanted a dog desperately when she was six.

And then when she was nine.

And again at eleven and thirteen.

Something had always made it impossible. Moves. Job changes.

Death...

She glared out the window. No point in dredging

up the past. Her parents were gone, barely memories now. After the plane crash that had taken their lives, her grandparents had stepped in. They had been wonderful to Sara and her younger sister, even though taking charge of two lively teenagers had been a serious challenge.

Those memories were warm and secure. Sara had skipped a generation of caregivers growing up, and when her grandparents began to fail, she and her sister, Hannah, had stepped in to take care of them.

Now all she had was Hannah.

Loneliness was a shadow always waiting at the corner of her eye, assuming she let herself see it. And sometimes in the stillness of night Sara yearned to feel her mother's touch or hear her father's booming laugh. She still dreamed about a dog whose soft fur could warm her hands on long spring walks.

Stupid.

She didn't have time to stop on a deserted road in the middle of nowhere. No, she couldn't take in a stray dog—no matter how tired or sad he looked.

Sara frowned at the mountain road in front of her. Probably he wasn't really sick or lost. Besides, she had her own worries, and miles to go before she could rest. She rubbed her tired eyes and peered back through the twilight. Maybe it was all in her imagination. After days of driving you started to see things that weren't there.

Slowing her dusty Wrangler, Sara craned her neck and glanced back. The big chocolate Lab was still sitting beside the road. His fur looked thick and soft and his eyes shimmered against the purple twilight. She could have sworn he was staring after her, looking sad and a little wistful—just the way she felt.

Frowning, she glanced down at the rough hand-drawn map that Hannah had sent her a month before, in preparation for Sara's vacation visit.

West on I-80. Connect to I-76 and pick up I-25 in Colorado. Watch for 40 in Albuquerque. South on 17 in Flagstaff.

Then watch for the red—

More roads followed a streaky area where the words became mottled as if Hannah had dropped something on them. Why did the thought of tears jump into Sara's mind?

Impossible. Sara's sister never cried. She was a spur-of-the-moment free spirit, with a good heart and a short attention span. Hannah never stayed anywhere long. She was the life of the party, the toast of a string of boyfriends, but she vanished before you knew it, off in search of new adventures.

Something burned at Sara's throat. She swallowed hard, forcing away her uneasiness, the same way she'd done in Iowa. And Nebraska. And Colorado. She told herself she was overreacting. She hadn't heard from her sister for almost a week now, not by phone or e-mail, but there was probably a perfectly good reason. Maybe Hannah had taken a spontaneous road trip to Las Vegas or L.A. She had a habit of getting restless. There was no reason to keep conjuring up grim images of danger. Sara would soon see that for herself when she reached the town of Sedona, nestled in the rugged red-rock country several hours north of Phoenix.

She leaned forward, squinting until she recognized the name of a road on Hannah's map. With the full moon somewhere over her right shoulder, she turned west onto a winding two-lane drive below the first sprinkling of stars. She couldn't shake the feeling that her life was about to change in ways she couldn't imagine. The feeling left her uneasy rather than excited.

When she looked back at the trees beside the road, the big dog was gone.

As twilight faded into full darkness, Sara twisted through silent canyons filled with whispering cotton-wood trees. The moon was high overhead when she saw the welcome glow of lights in the distance.

She frowned at the unbroken darkness stretching away on either side of the road. Who could live in an isolated place like this? It felt unnatural to be so far from other people. Hers had been the only car on the road for the past ten miles. Back in Chicago, every corner had a deli or a coffee shop. The Chicago L ran all night, and many bookstores stayed open until eleven.

Here there was only darkness and silence. Arizona was not what Sara had expected. The huge sky that stretched away forever had touched the photographer in her, making her yearn to pull over for her camera, but that same rugged terrain left her with a heavy sense of isolation. You had to be self-reliant in a place like this. You could walk into a high canyon and never be seen again, leaving no clues and no witnesses.

Had her sister vanished that way?

She rubbed her neck and felt a wave of relief when she saw the little café and gem shop nestled beneath dark cliffs. Only a few cars were parked outside, but it would be a good place to get directions, since the last road Hannah had mentioned didn't appear on the map.

When she pushed open the carved blue door, a bell chimed a cheerful two-note welcome. Nine heads looked up from a long oak table in the corner. Two men were playing Scrabble. Three more men were hunched over neat piles of poker chips. Three women—and one man—were knitting beside the poker group. The man who was knitting looked familiar.

Sara realized he was an ex-astronaut, in the news a

few years earlier after he bought a microbrewery. After that he'd written some kind of cookbook.

A few of the people glanced up at her, but almost immediately went back to their quiet conversations. The feeling of easy camaraderie between everyone was almost tangible.

Sara felt a keen sense of being the outsider, covertly assessed and measured. That feeling faded as a short man with powerful shoulders came out from behind the counter, wiping his hands on a clean but well-used apron that said "Grateful Dead Revival Tour."

"Welcome to Sedona, ma'am. You're the first new customer I've had in two hours, so the first cup's on me. What will it be? Coffee or tea?"

"Or me," the astronaut muttered slyly from his seat near the wall, without looking up from his knitting.

"Just ignore Charly over there. He's already had one too many tonight."

"Too many root beer floats?" the astronaut countered. "Not a chance, Emmett."

The two men continued to argue as Sara sat down at the counter and rubbed the tense muscles in her neck. "A tall coffee with just a splash of milk would be perfect." She eyed the array of pies along the counter. All of them looked homemade. Calorie laden, but delicious, she decided. "A piece of pecan pie, too."

"Good call. Fresh this evening, courtesy of Charly over there."

The astronaut? He was cooking in a tiny café outside Sedona now? But it was none of Sara's business. She swallowed a yawn, grateful for the deliciously scented coffee and rich pecan pie the owner set in front of her. She was surprised that she was hungry when she'd had an apple and an energy bar only an hour earlier.

The pie vanished in record time.

"You vacationing at the new golf resort, on your way up to Flagstaff or are you lost?" the café owner asked as she finished the last bite.

Sara hesitated, then pulled a commercial map out of her pocket. "I'm looking for Navajo Ridge Road. I don't think I went past it."

The room went silent. Tension seemed to grow as she felt the force of searching gazes behind her.

"No, you didn't miss it. Three miles ahead, ma'am. Make a left after the grocery and psychic healer." The man studied her just a little longer. "Pretty rugged country up there. No hotels or resorts anywhere close. You sure you have the address right?"

For some reason Sara didn't want to give him any more details. Not until she knew if her sister was in some kind of trouble. Instead, she gave a friendly smile, counted out change and laid it by her plate. "No, I'm just visiting. Thanks for the directions." At the door anxiety made her turn. "About three miles down the road there was a big chocolate Lab. He looked lost."

The man named Charly stood up and stretched. "That's just Marlow. Don't worry about him. He may be old, but that dog can take care of himself. He's kinda restless these days, that's all."

Relief hit Sara in a rush. She buttoned up her sweater and nodded. "Glad to hear it. Thanks again for the directions."

The bell chimed merrily as she walked out into the gusting wind and darkness.

For some reason it seemed as if she had left all warmth and safety behind her as she drove across the dark parking lot and headed out.

It took three tries, but Sara finally found the spare key that Hannah had said was shoved between two stones to the left of the front porch. In her car lights she saw a small cabin that was a quirky mix of river stone, adobe and hand-carved rustic wooden beams. Small but snug, Hannah had called the cabin she was currently renting. She hadn't mentioned that it was ten miles to the nearest town.

Behind her, Sara saw the lights of Sedona twinkling below the nearest mesa. But here on the rim the darkness was absolute. Something rustled in the bushes behind her.

Quickly she swung open the cabin door. She was immediately struck by a smell of dust and disuse. "Hannah," she called loudly, flipping on the light switch at the door.

There was no answer. The living room was filled with mismatched wooden furniture in brightly painted colors. At least one of the chairs looked as if Hannah had painted it herself. Several manila envelopes lay on the coffee table, and after a long hesitation Sara scanned each one, hoping to find a clue to her sister's whereabouts.

One envelope held what looked like some kind of spreadsheet listing dates and hours. The vertical line had a variety of abbreviations that made no sense to Sara. *Trans. Hand. Comp.* What was that supposed to mean?

But her head was aching from too much coffee and too much driving. Exhaustion from the past eleven hours on the road finally caught up with her. She yawned, checking out the rest of the cabin.

There was no sign of Hannah anywhere. Her suitcase was unpacked, and her clothes appeared to be distributed normally through the small closet, with no spaces. Her beading and jewelry supplies were still in a drawer in the kitchen. Since Hannah never went anywhere without her crafting tools, Sara decided her sister would be back eventually, after whatever restless urge that had struck her faded.

Probably this was one big wild-goose chase. She almost regretted giving up the shot at a job in New York photographing the Macy's parade. That could have led to more high-profile jobs, and heaven knew, Sara needed more referrals. She had been working hard for too long, hoping to break into the competitive commercial photography field. But after eight years of close-but-no-thanks calls, she had learned that great portfolios were a dime a dozen. More often than not it was *who* you knew, not how well you shot.

But Sara wasn't giving up the dream she had chased ever since she held her first camera. And this rugged corner of Arizona would be good for one thing. The high country around Sedona had stirring dawns and world-class sunsets, and she was determined to capture a few before heading back to Chicago.

After she made sure that Hannah was safe.

With sleep overtaking her, she had no more energy to ponder the mystery of her sister's latest whim. She opened her camera bag and placed her beloved Nikon on the coffee table. After locking her car, she brought in her single suitcase and the rest of her photographic supplies, then collapsed onto Hannah's neatly made bed.

She dreamed about skies that went on forever and a dog with melted-chocolate eyes.

CHAPTER
~TWO~

"So what did you think?" Charles Hamilton Vernon, ex-astronaut, ex-playboy and current pastry chef for the Red Rock Café and Grill, put down his nearly finished hand-knitted sock and leaned back in his chair. "Nice smile when she used it. Which wasn't often."

"No need for idle speculation, Charly. She's probably a journalism student or a friend of a friend going up to visit Liz Stone."

"Or going to see that young woman who was working for Liz." Emmett, the café owner, propped an elbow on the counter. "Hannah something."

"Winslow," Charly finished. "But it's a little odd to me. This Winslow girl shows up on Liz's doorstep, broke and looking for work. Then Liz takes her on as a paid assistant without a second thought. Stupid thing to do if you ask me."

"But nobody did ask you," Emmett said firmly. "You know how Liz is. She's used to being on her own and making her own decisions. She's got a good sense of people. If she trusted that young woman, it was with good reason."

The tinkle of the doorbell caught them by surprise. Charly's chair went out from under him, banging onto the oak floor.

"Somebody told me I could get a decent cup of coffee and a mediocre slice of pie in here. Probably it was a lie. Seems like everybody lies these days."

Coconino County deputy sheriff Jesse McCloud shoved back the well-worn brim of his hat and frowned at the silent group. "What's got all of you tongue-tied, like something a coyote just tossed up?"

Charly went to get some coffee and the pie for the deputy, piling on extra whipped cream just the way Jesse liked it. "It's the young woman who came in not ten minutes ago. She was wearing red cowboy boots."

"Not a crime last time I checked." Jesse's boots rang out as he crossed to a table. "Anything else suspicious I should know?"

"She was asking the way to Navajo Ridge," Charly answered flatly. "Only one person I know lives up there, and that's Liz Stone."

The tall deputy folded his long, lean body into a chair near the big picture window, scanning the parking lot as he did so. His eyes missed nothing despite his casual posture. "Maybe she was lost. Any of you think to get a license plate?"

Feet shuffled. There was a low ripple of muttered excuses.

"I thought not. I've been on since 4:00 a.m., Charly. If you'd allow me to eat this tolerable piece of pecan pie in peace—"

Charly slapped silverware on the table next to Jesse. "Tolerable? That recipe won a blue ribbon at the Sonoma Food and Wine Festival. But you're only as good as your last cookbook," he grumbled.

The lanky deputy sheriff of Coconino County hid a smile. Pulling Charly's chain was one of his special pleasures, and his friend knew that, too. The two had sparred amicably ever since Charly moved to Sedona five years before. Jesse knew everyone in the room, knew most of their grandmothers and all of their grandchildren.

These people watched out for each other, which made his job a little easier.

"Heavy on the molasses this time, Charly." Jesse made

a big deal of savoring his pie, staring into the air. "Excellent bouquet. Strong opening notes, but a weak finish," he mused.

"Blast it, Jesse." Charly snorted. "I had that recipe from my grandmother, and she baked it for three presidents."

Jesse knew that Charly had a deep fond spot for his recipes, and that his pecan pie was a prized family secret.

All the better to ruffle his feathers.

"Oh, shut up and sit down, Charly. The man's just toying with you, can't you see that? Your pie is the best thing west of the Mississippi. Everybody knows that." Rosa Harrington put down the chemo cap she was knitting, then stood up. Without ceremony she walked to the kitchen, found a fresh pot of coffee and topped up the deputy's cup.

Then she took a deep breath, bringing up the subject that no one wanted to face. They were all wondering why no one had seen Liz Stone or her new assistant. "We haven't see Liz for almost a week, Jesse. What do you think? Is that woman in the boots some kind of clue?"

"Could be." The lanky deputy stared at his coffee. "You sure she wanted Navajo Ridge?"

"No mistake about it. Darned attractive, too," Charly muttered. "Nice eyes and a thoughtful way about her. She probably got those boots in New York or maybe on

Rodeo Drive." Charly shot a glance at Rosa, whom he'd been trying to sweet-talk for the past few years. "Not that I noticed."

"And I'm the pope's daughter," the stunning white-haired woman muttered. "But what about Liz?" She glanced anxiously at Jesse, who was finishing his last bite of pie.

Jesse realized they were seriously worried, though Liz Stone was a strong woman who hated cities and liked living alone on her land up on the mesa. She could take care of herself, she always said.

He had no reason to suspect anything had happened to her. She often spread out her visits to town. But if these people were worried, he couldn't brush off their concern lightly.

He drummed his fingers on the table. "I'll drive up there and have a look tomorrow. How about that?"

"I think you should," Rosa said quickly.

"So do I." Charly stared from one person in the room to the next, giving voice to what all of them were thinking in their worries about the wealthy landowner. "I mean, where is she and why isn't she answering her phone? Why is her car still parked in her drive up there on Navajo Ridge Road?"

"You think something has happened to her, Jesse?

Remember there was a string of burglaries over in Cottonwood last month."

Jesse stood up, frowning. He'd helped catch the burglars in question, though he didn't mention that. There were more recent criminal activities than Rosa knew about, too. "I'll check it out. You have my word." The deputy started to put bills on the counter, but the owner shoved them firmly back toward him.

The way he'd done for the past eight years.

Jesse sighed. They were a tough bunch here. Stubborn, self-reliant and nosy, the lot of them.

He couldn't think of a better set of friends.

"Meanwhile, if that woman comes back at least get her name and her license plate." Jesse knew that Liz Stone's son lived in Denver. He would call him tomorrow to see if he had any news about his mother.

He crossed the parking lot in the darkness, favoring his right leg. The three-inch scar above his knee was bothering him again, a bitter memento of his last tour of duty. Sometimes the pain snuck up on him, jolting him back into memories of swirling dust and sniper fire. He'd lost two good friends during that last tour.

He'd lost his sister about then, too.

Jesse made an angry sound. His hand opened, massaging the knot of muscles above his knee. Pain filled him, as bitter as it had been the day he'd received the official notice of Katie's death.

He stood outside his police cruiser, the throb in his leg blurring into memories of his sister laughing at him as she hung upside down from a cottonwood tree with the summer wind ruffling her hair.

She'd never climb a tree or laugh again, Jesse thought grimly.

And he was partly to blame, because he hadn't persuaded her not to go.

He slid into the seat, wincing as he tucked his long legs inside and closed the door. You couldn't go back. Things didn't always work out, not like in the movies. Sometimes all you could hope to do was stay one step ahead of your demons.

So far his demanding job in the second largest county in the U.S. hadn't left him much time to brood, and he was glad of that. Free time was dangerous time when memories were bad. Just the same, he couldn't remember when he'd last been out on a date or taken a woman dancing, with her warm skin touching his.

Jesse frowned. What had Charly said?

Nice eyes and a thoughtful way about her. But did she have something to do with Liz Stone and her assistant?

As he drove out into the darkness, Jesse couldn't seem

to get a pair of red cowboy boots out of his mind. A possible clue, he reminded himself, to a troubling disappearance.

Something was howling outside her window.

Sara sat up in a rush. The howling was actually an owl, calling to its mate. She ran a hand through her hair and grimaced down at her rumpled clothes. She had fallen asleep fully dressed.

She made a cup of coffee, then prowled through Hannah's cabin for a closer look. She found more unopened mail and an answering machine with twenty-two phone messages. Everything was neat, neater than she remembered Hannah usually being. There was absolutely no sign that her sister had been planning a long trip. It didn't make sense.

Sara found dry lettuce, some leftovers and a full quart of milk in the refrigerator. More signs that Hannah had meant to stay home.

After her search, all the old worry returned. She remembered seeing a small detached garage on the side of the driveway and she decided to take a closer look. When she opened the front door, pink light was just touching the trees to the east.

The view left Sara speechless.

Coral cliffs twisted into tight spirals, climbing to a

purple sky now streaked with the fuchsia edge of dawn. More cliffs marched away to the north, and a shadowy mesa cut a straight path about half a mile to the east. Her sister had called this area picturesque. Sara called it nearly the most beautiful thing she had ever seen.

She ran back inside for her camera to capture the blazing colors. Outside, as she lifted her Nikon, a hawk cut through the sunlight.

It was a powerful shot. It might even be an award-winning shot, she thought, working feverishly at her settings. When the hawk circled over her head, she moved back, trying to catch the flare of the powerful wings in her viewfinder. She barely noticed the rustling behind her, intent on catching the bird in flight.

The rustling grew louder. Sara knew the sound meant something, but she didn't know what. As the hawk sailed over her head, she clicked half a dozen shots.

Suddenly she heard the soft crunch of gravel.

"Nice camera," a husky male voice said. "Why don't you turn around slowly and let me have a look at it? Just don't make any sudden movements."

CHAPTER
∽ THREE ∽

S ara gripped her camera against her chest. How had the man managed to sneak up on her like that? And what was he doing up here near Hannah's cabin?

She started to spin around, but the low, cool voice cut her off. "No swift movements, ma'am. Take one slow step to your left while you tell me about that lens you're using. It looks like a 70 to 200 millimeter."

"It's a Zeiss 2/28 actually, but why?" Sara looked over her shoulder and saw a tall man with cool eyes measuring her. He was wearing a uniform, but she couldn't read the insignia.

"That's good. Now, one more step to the left. Take it slow."

He was watching something near her right boot. Something was hidden in the bushes, and he was trying to protect her from whatever it was.

Sara's heart began to pound. "What are you looking at?" she whispered.

"Nothing important, ma'am. Take another slow step. You're going to be fine."

She gripped her camera, did just as he asked. Her palms felt sweaty against the rim of her Nikon, and she had to force herself not to run.

"This is a good sunrise," he said quietly. "But there will be better ones. Some of them will pull the breath right out of your throat."

"This one just did."

Sara took another slow step to her left, and he circled around to her side. In one smooth movement he shoved her behind a rock and stared at the spot where she had been standing.

The rustling in the grass became a hollow rattle.

He moved closer, standing between her and the danger as a big, dusty gray shape rose, tongue outstretched, from the bushes near where Sara had stood only moments before. The sheriff stayed right where he was, immobile, his hands loose at his side. "Rattler. Looks like a diamondback," he said quietly. "Why don't you go on inside while I move this big fellow down to the far side of the cliff, so he won't do anyone any harm."

"Fine with me," Sara muttered. She was already backing up the path to the cabin.

Her hands were clammy. *A rattlesnake had been barely a foot away from her.* It could have struck at any moment.

Sara shut the cabin door and ran trembling hands over her face. If she'd been bitten out here with no one to help her, she would have died. Just like that.

And that meant the man in the uniform had saved her life. He'd been smart to talk to her the way he had. Anything else would have sent her running, and that would have provoked the snake to attack.

Smart.

His voice still played through her mind—low and smoky, absolutely calm. She hadn't gotten a good look at his face. All she knew for sure was that he had an intense way about him, looking at you as if everything else had dropped away and you were the only important thing in the world.

The memory made Sara flush. She ran a hand through her tangled hair as she heard footsteps crunch outside. Quickly she pulled off her torn gray sweatshirt and exchanged it for a tidy cardigan. She took a deep breath, composing herself as she heard a knock.

She swung the front door open.

And went completely still.

He was taller than she'd expected—maybe six-five. His eyes reminded her of a mountain pool she'd seen once up near the Canadian border, deep and smoky blue in spring right after the ice began to melt. But his cheeks were gaunt, as if he had been sick. With the keen eye of a photographer, Sara noticed that he favored his right leg.

An accident? Some kind of service wound?

None of your business, Winslow.

She held out a hand. "I'm Sara Winslow. My sister, Hannah, lives here. I don't know how to thank you. I didn't have a clue that snake was there."

He stood in the doorway, looking thoughtful. "Jesse McCloud. Snakes have a way of doing that. Up here you have to watch every step. Never put a hand or foot in a crevice or blind spot. Look first. Keep your distance and they're fine. They were here first, after all."

Sara continued to stare at him, taking in the sharp angles of his face and the line of shadows cast by the sun rising over the trees. He had the look of someone comfortable with himself and the world. With bones like that, he would probably always look thirty years younger than his real age.

Wasn't it just unfair to waste a gift like that on a man who would never care how old he looked?

"What's unfair?"

Sara frowned and realized he was still standing in the doorway, staring at her. "I guess I'm a little shaken up. Come in, Mr.——McCloud. Or maybe I should say Sheriff McCloud." She had finally deciphered the words on his uniform patch.

"Deputy Sheriff. Most people here just call me Jesse." He moved inside with a spare grace that made Sara wonder if he had been an athlete at one time.

And there it was again, her curiosity getting her into trouble. Who he had been or who he was now was none of her business.

But maybe he could tell her the whereabouts of her sister. "How about some coffee? Then you can tell me why you came up here."

"Coffee sounds good." He moved around the living room, the casual sweep of his gaze missing nothing. When he followed her into the small kitchen, Sara felt oddly self-conscious.

"I like French press. But maybe you like something stronger, with a little more spice." She opened a ceramic canister of sugar and fumbled with the electric coffee-maker. When he didn't answer, she shot him a glance.

He was staring at her. Just staring. Looking surprised, as if he was trying to work out something that was important. Sara had a sudden urge to touch the tiny notch in the corner of his cheek and see if it made him smile. Something told her this man smiled far too little.

She forced down the temptation to move closer, calling herself twenty kinds of names. Men in uniform ought to be outlawed, she thought irritably. They had an unfair way of digging under all your well-intentioned defenses.

Sara shoved the coffeepot back into place and frowned at him. "Is something wrong? Do I have dirt on my face?"

"No, ma'am. Nothing wrong. It's your mouth." He rubbed his neck. "What I mean is, it's about the nicest mouth I've seen in my life."

Sara stared back at him. He wasn't smiling, and he looked absolutely serious. Something told her Jesse McCloud was serious about most things in his life. "Oh." What were you supposed to say to a thing like that? "Do you like it sweet?"

One dark eyebrow rose. "I beg your pardon?"

"Ah—your coffee. Sugar, raw sugar, agave or honey? My sister is a health food nut, so you've got your choice."

"No sugar. I take it straight."

"Why doesn't that surprise me?" Sara murmured. As she reached around him for a saucer to go with the brightly painted cup, their bodies seemed way too close in the small kitchen.

For some reason she couldn't explain, her hand wavered. Maybe it was the smell of his skin, full of the outdoors with just a hint of leather and citrus. Bottle that smell and you could walk away a millionaire, she thought wildly.

Annoyed by the way he was affecting her, Sara moved around him. Jesse moved at the same time. Their legs bumped together, and the empty cup tumbled from her fingers.

He caught it in midair. "Let me do that." Reaching behind her, he took down a second mug and filled them both from the steaming pot. He glanced at her with the hint of a smile. "I take you for no sugar and just a splash of milk. Am I right?"

It galled her, but he'd nailed her perfectly. "Nice guess."

"I wouldn't call it a guess. Doing what I do, meeting all kinds of people in all kinds of circumstances, you get to know something about them. Call it instinct or luck or experience. Somehow I almost feel as if I know you." There was a husky edge in his voice that made Sara's toes curl.

She ignored it ruthlessly. "So, Deputy McCloud, what brings you all the way up to Navajo Ridge at dawn? And don't tell me it's for the coffee, because my coffee isn't very good."

He leaned back against the kitchen counter, looking

comfortable yet completely alert. Sara decided that the mix of calm blended with alertness suited him.

"The folks down at the café told me you came in last night asking for directions. Can I speak with your sister?"

"She's—not here now."

"I thought I'd better see if everything was okay up here. This area is pretty isolated, in case you haven't noticed."

"Oh, I noticed. Last night I didn't hear a single car horn, and the only bright light came from a shooting star. It couldn't be more different from where I live."

He looked at her over the rim of his coffee cup. "And where would that be, Sara?"

"Chicago. Not the nice part, either. But there's a vitality to the bustle and noise, and somehow they grow on you." She swirled her coffee, frowning. "Last week I was walking along Lake Michigan and I took a shot of a dog—"

Sara stopped. Why was she telling him these things? What in the world made the man so easy to talk to?

She blew out a little breath. "How about more coffee?"

"I'm good. You took a shot of a dog," he prompted. "You're a photographer?"

Sara nodded, but she wasn't giving him anything more. She didn't know a thing about the man. On the other hand, a deputy sheriff had resources that she didn't.

She rubbed her neck, torn between reticence and the need to ask for help. Not yet, she decided. Not until she was certain that Hannah hadn't simply taken a road trip on the spur of the moment in her usual unpredictable way.

"I've done a few things," she went on coolly. "What about you, Deputy McCloud? What do you do when you're not riding around in that cruiser, working hard to serve and protect?"

Later Sara would wonder if she had imagined his little reflex and the way his hand had opened over the side of his leg. The long fingers had massaged lightly, as if he was caught by old memories. "We're a big, sprawling county, Sara. I don't have a lot of free time."

"But when you do?"

"Persistent, aren't you?"

"So I'm told."

He set his empty cup on the counter, shaking his head when she offered a refill. "Well, let's see. Before I shipped out, I used to like rock climbing and—don't laugh—I considered myself a bit of an amateur archaeologist. There are quite a few ruins around here. Climbing is the best way to see them."

But Sara latched onto the one point he had glossed over. "Shipped out? You were in the military?"

He nodded. "Seems like a long time ago."

"Where? Afghanistan or Iraq?"

He shrugged. "It doesn't matter. There's nothing worse than old news." Clearly he didn't choose to talk about it.

But Sara couldn't let it go. "You favor your right leg. And you massage your knee occasionally. Were you wounded over there?"

His face changed, his expression turning distant. "I don't know what you mean."

"Hurt, Deputy McCloud. A four-letter word that means suffering injury or harm. I assume you're in pain, probably from a mortar round, small arms fire or a land mine."

He just looked at her. There was an intensity to his gaze that hadn't been there before. Now the kitchen fairly shimmered with an awareness between them so sharp that Sara felt the little hairs stand up along her neck.

Something was happening here. For the life of her she couldn't decide if that was good or bad.

"You saw all that in a matter of fifteen minutes?" There was a hard edge of disbelief in his voice.

"I'm a photographer. I see things. I watch what other people don't watch. I'd be no good at my work if I didn't."

After a long time he nodded. "You're right about the

leg and the wound, Sara Winslow with the pesky knack for detail." He looked away. "Our convoy was ambushed north of Kabul." He didn't say anything more.

But Sara imagined the rest.

Shouting and noise, blown sand and the sudden orange fury of flames. Even then she couldn't leave it alone. "Was anyone else hurt?" she asked quietly.

He was staring out the window, watching the hawk cut lazy curves in the dawn sky. "Four of my best men. No way we could have foreseen it. There hadn't been any trouble on that road for six months, but we were in the wrong place at the wrong time."

There was more, but Sara was sure he wouldn't tell her. Probably he hadn't told anyone.

"So you haven't done much rock climbing since you got back. Maybe we can try it sometime. I've always wanted to learn how." The moment she said the words, Sara felt her face flush. He was a complete stranger, and he might even be married. What was she doing asking him out on what sounded dangerously like a date?

"I'd like that. I'm a little rusty, though. I won't be doing any quick footwork, but I still have my equipment. I could take you up north and get you started. There's a quiet ridge I know with great views. Thank heavens the weekend warriors from Phoenix and points south haven't discovered it yet. If you brought your camera, you could get some amazing shots of the Mogollon Rim. Maybe Humphrey Peak's snow line on a good day."

He watched her consider the offer. His hand opened, caressing the coffee cup slowly. Something about that gesture made Sara's breath catch.

Dangerous ground, Winslow. Watch that next step. If you fall here, it could be a long one.

Still, she could hardly say no, given that she had been the one who had done the asking. "Sounds like a good plan, but I can't do anything until Hannah and I figure out our plans."

He studied her lazily. "So how's your sister doing?"

Sara summoned a smile. Lying had never been easy for her. "Oh, Hannah is fine. She went to Flagstaff for some supplies. She should be back tomorrow. Late," she added casually.

"I'm glad to hear it. It gets lonely up here. Sometimes you have to leave for a change of pace."

He sounded genuine and completely sincere.

Uncomfortable about her lie, Sara put her empty coffee cup in the sink. She needed to change the subject and reestablish some distance between them.

When he pushed away from the counter, she could feel the unwavering force of his gaze on her face. "Well, I should go. I've got two stops to make." He rested his cup in the sink next to hers.

Their fingers touched for the barest space of a second.

It was enough. Even that brief moment of contact made Sara feel oddly restless. "I certainly don't want to keep you. Clearly, you're a very busy man." She moved awkwardly to the door and held it open. "Have a good day, Deputy McCloud."

"Call me Jesse," he said quietly. He pressed something into her hand. "Here's the dispatcher's number in town. They can reach me anytime."

Sara shoved the number into her pocket without looking and gave a jaunty smile. "Thanks for the offer, but I'll be just fine."

And she meant it. He seemed nice enough and heaven knew he was easy on the eyes. But having a man in her life? No, she wasn't interested. Not even slightly. She was going to pack up her camera and go for a walk. She hadn't had time to see any of the country near the cabin, and Sara was convinced if she looked hard enough she could find a clue to her sister's disappearance.

After all, seeing things was her business.

She found her first clue under a young cottonwood tree up the slope from the driveway. Sara wasn't sure what it meant, but it appeared that someone had stood beneath the tree, smoking. There were a dozen or so cigarette butts on the ground, but she wouldn't have no-

ticed if she hadn't been looking. Hannah didn't smoke—
at least she never had before.

No indication of a boyfriend or roommate.

Dropping a cigarette butt in dry country like this was
dangerously irresponsible, but this went beyond being
irresponsible. Someone had been watching the cabin.
Someone standing motionless and silent.

Planning.

Sara felt a cold touch of fear. She gave herself one
more day, and after that she was going to call the deputy
sheriff. She was also going to hire a detective, though it
would strain her meager savings. She couldn't dismiss
her fears any longer.

Worry left her oblivious to the beauty of the red cliffs
and the blindingly blue sky. She continued to search for
any sign of something that Hannah might have dropped,
but she came up empty. Even Hannah's car was gone.

The missing car could mean that her sister had simply gotten restless, nothing more. Except Hannah would
have let her know via e-mail or a terse phone call. She
knew that Sara was a champion worrier.

At the edge of the rocky wash that snaked across the
road below the cabin, Sara found her second clue. It had
rained not long before, and the ground was still damp
beside a mound of low, spiky grass. Nearly hidden by the
dense greenery was a trailing outline of feet captured

in the drying mud. The feet wore athletic shoes, cheap sneakers, heavy work boots. Some feet wore rough shoes with tire-tread soles.

She stared down at the footprints. Why would a dozen people walk through this isolated wash? Hikers or weekend visitors maybe?

She continued to stand motionless, staring at the marks in the wash. She didn't dare go any farther into the vegetation, not after her rattlesnake encounter. The wind seemed to snap through the grass as she studied the ground, trying to understand the meaning of those chaotic footprints left in the mud.

What had her sister gotten involved in?

By noon Sara had been through most of the cabin, all of the yard, the garage and the tiny shed at the far side of the gravel driveway. Her house key opened all the locks, and she had looked in every corner, shifting aside boxes and old papers feverishly. Nowhere was there anything to explain her sister's disappearance. She did find several surprising things during her search—a course syllabus from Northern Arizona University, bank statements that showed a slow but steady stream of work deposits, and a neat notebook filled with handwritten reports about her duties for Liz Stone. Clearly Hannah was taking her job seriously. Not only did she oversee repairs to the roof of the main house, but she maintained the irrigation system and had begun to research how to restore the ranch's peach orchards to their former glory. Any one of those jobs would have made Sara blink in surprise. When all three were added together, they painted a picture of a very changed person. Yet if her sister was making meticulous notes and shouldering more responsibilities, why had she left with no warning or explanation?

That was the question that Sara kept coming back to. And she still had no answers.

By one o'clock her head was aching. The third time her stomach growled she rummaged through her sister's refrigerator, pulled out two dry pieces of bread and a can of tuna. She ate her sandwich on the front porch, taking in the drama of a distant thunderstorm boiling over the cliffs to the west. She had to admit that this was one of the most beautiful landscapes she had ever seen, and she stopped eating several times to capture a photo.

But the uneasiness that had begun when Sara had found the pile of discarded cigarette butts continued to grow. She found herself watching the shadows behind the house and searching the curves of the wash, wondering if she was being watched. As the sun touched the sharp peaks to the west, the uneasiness changed to a sense of menace. She had finished looking through her sister's papers, letters and bank statements. After that she had scanned Hannah's phone messages. Most were calls from workers relating to duties at the ranch, and others involved requests for transportation for several of her employer's elderly friends. One whole page of Hannah's notebook had been devoted to the names and phone numbers of neighbors that her sister visited on a weekly basis, doing light errands and handyman work, picking up medicine and helping with occasional rides to town.

Yes, her sister had definitely been busy here in Sedona. She seemed to be part of the community, Sara realized. There was still no indication that she was seeing a man or involved in a distant relationship.

That left Sara right back where she had started, with no answers.

The sky was a glorious explosion of red when she noticed something behind a rock at the edge of the wash. As the angle of the sun had changed, she could see a line of color that had not been visible before. Picking up her camera, Sara triggered the powerful zoom lens and focused on a wedge of reds and blues.

A piece of fabric appeared to be jammed beneath a boulder. One end looked as if it was streaked with mud, but Sara couldn't make out any other details.

Carefully she picked her way over the uneven ground until she came to a spot above the wash. From her vantage point the fabric resembled a small, ornately woven blanket. As she leaned down, Sara saw more footprints captured in the soil at the bottom of the wash. Using a stick, she carefully pulled the cloth out from beneath the rock.

One corner was torn. The other corners were streaked with mud, but the fabric was beautiful, an intricate pattern of stylized birds and mountains. Sara held the old piece in her hands, feeling the last rays of sun on her back, struck by the sense that this was a valuable piece of family history. No one would have dropped it casually.

And she realized now why it was so small.

It was a baby blanket.

The drive down to Sedona in the dusk should have been awe inspiring, but Sara's mind kept racing through dangerous possibilities.

The police department was quiet, and the desk sergeant shook his head when she asked for Deputy Jesse McCloud.

"Not here, ma'am. County sheriff's office is up in Flagstaff. He's on duty until seven tonight."

Sara smothered a wave of disappointment. "He left me a number, but I lost the card. Would you tell him that I came by? I'll leave you my cell phone number. I—I'd really like to speak with him. Tonight, if possible."

When she walked outside, she saw the bright lights

of the Red Rock Café at the top of the hill. Her stomach growled. Sara realized she hadn't eaten anything since her hurried tuna sandwich at lunch.

Maybe a slice of pecan pie would make her feel better.

And maybe someone inside would have more answers.

The same cars were parked in the café's parking lot. The same faces were ranged along the long oak table. Knitters sat on one side, and poker players sat nearby. All of them chatted across the tables.

Sara had barely sat down before she had silverware, iced tea and a menu in her hands. The rich, smoky smell of chili hit her, making her mouth water. "I don't need to look at the menu," she said with a smile at the owner. "Whatever that delicious smell is, I'll take your biggest bowl. And another slice of that amazing pie."

One of the men stood up, and Sara saw it was the ex-astronaut. A smile creased his tanned face. "Coming right up, ma'am. Nice to see *someone* who recognizes the finer points of high cuisine."

Behind him, somebody muttered at the long table. The astronaut—Charly—ignored him. He was too busy cutting a slab of pie and mounding on freshly whipped cream.

Sara's mouth watered. In two minutes she had more food in front of her than she could eat in one evening.

Someone was always filling up her coffee cup and bringing more slices of freshly baked bread. The chili was a delight to her tongue—smoky and sweet at the same time, rich with chipotle chilis and what might have been a deeper hint of coffee. Finally Sara pushed away her plate, absolutely sated.

Even then the café owner—Emmett—tried to refill her bowl, but she put her hand over the rim. "I couldn't possibly. It was wonderful. Would you consider giving me the recipe?"

"Done. Anything else I can do for you, ma'am?"

"Call me Sara, please. Have you seen Deputy Mc-Cloud this afternoon?"

"He was in just before lunch. He was heading north to Flagstaff. Is something wrong?"

Sara hesitated. She wanted to trust these people, but right now trusting the wrong person might be dangerous. There were still too many questions. "Not really. I just want to ask him a question. He came up to the cabin this morning…."

Behind her all movement stopped. She heard someone clear his throat.

"He drove up to Navajo Ridge this morning, did he?" The astronaut frowned at her. "Nothing's wrong, I hope."

"Just a routine visit, from what he said." Sara decided it was time to change the subject. "That is definitely the best piece of pie I've ever had." She frowned a little. "Actually, my grandmother would tie you for first place, but she doesn't count. When she was young she was a professional pastry chef in Paris for five years." It hurt to remember her grandmother's expert hands and featherlight pastry. It hurt to remember the reason Sara and Hannah had gone to live with their grandparents after the freak accident that had resulted in their parents' deaths one snowy night in December.

She glanced up, surprised to see that the big wall clock now read 8:45. Probably Deputy McCloud had gotten caught up in official business. It might be hours before she heard back from him.

Sara lifted her purse and took out her wallet, turning over the check.

Five dollars? It had to be a mistake. "I think you forgot to add in the cost of my dinner. This is only the cost of the pie."

"No mistake." Emmett beamed at her as he stacked clean glasses on the counter. "You're Hannah Winslow's sister, aren't you?" Emmett took Sara's hesitation in answering as a yes. "She's a friend of Liz Stone. And any friend of Liz Stone's gets the local rate in this café. Liz loaned me my first hundred dollars when I opened this place twenty years ago."

"But—"

"No buts. Friends stick together. That's the way it is."

He hesitated and then scrubbed a corner of the spotless counter with a towel. "We haven't seen Liz in town for a while. Your sister hasn't been in, either. Frankly, it's got us all a little worried."

Sara decided there was no more point in lying. She had to trust *someone*. "I'm worried, too. I haven't heard from Hannah and she didn't mention any trouble when we last spoke. Have you heard about any...problems... here?"

"Only the usual stranded hikers. High school kids getting drunk and blowing off steam. An occasional DUI and a stolen car. That's the extent of it."

None of those things would explain her sister's absence. Nor would they explain the footprints in the wash and the pile of cigarette butts near the cabin's driveway.

"Sorry I can't help you, Ms. Winslow. But I think you're in luck. This is the man you should be talking to. Why don't you ask him?"

The little doorbell chimed.

Sara caught the scent of sage mixed with the damp green smell of rain blowing in. She heard boots cross the room. A chair slid out next to hers.

Spirals of heat worked across her face as Jesse McCloud sat down. The midnight-blue eyes were startling against the deep tan of his face, and he smelled like leather and a spring night.

He was more handsome than a man had any right to be. When he leaned forward, their knees bumped under the table, and Sara felt the contact zip through her like an electric shock.

She didn't want to feel any sparks. She didn't want to be distracted from finding Hannah.

Her hand lurched. She dropped her bill and her napkin.

Jesse picked up both and held them out to her, watching her face. "Ask me about what, Sara?"

CHAPTER
⤙FOUR⤚

Sara cleared her throat. Something funny was happening in her chest. It wasn't a heart arrhythmia, nothing that you'd find in a medical textbook, but it felt nearly as disorienting.

She rubbed one hand over the spot that shouldn't have been hurting. Emotions shimmered, strong and clear in ways that felt totally new.

She didn't let emotion clutter up her life. To her way of thinking, attachments were something you added to an e-mail message. Her life was her work—chasing the next new technique for a great photograph or the chance to learn from an expert. Since the death of her grandparents, Hannah had been the lodestone and only personal connection in her life.

Yet a sharp sensation continued to tug at the center of her chest. Those blue eyes measured her, calm and intense, and Sara realized her cautious position on emotions and attachments was about to change.

She forced her thoughts back to the reason she had been looking for the deputy and lowered her voice, aware of the silence that had followed Jesse's question. "I'd like to apologize for not being exactly forthcoming before—it's hard to know who to trust. My sister didn't go to Flagstaff, and I don't think she's fine. I found some things that could be important." She ran a hand through her hair, the worry and the sleepless nights beginning to catch up with her. Now her nerves felt raw. She couldn't stop thinking about her sister, and what kind of dangerous situation she might be caught up in. She looked down at the table and saw that her fingers were trembling.

The deputy leaned over. His big, solid hand settled over hers and squeezed lightly. "It will be okay, Sara. We'll get this untangled. Trust me."

It didn't make sense, but she did trust him. His husky voice was cool against her ragged nerves. This was a man you could rely on, she thought. This was a man who would watch your back and guard your steps. Not because you'd asked him to, but because it was the right thing to do.

Friends stick together.

That's the way things are.

Sara remembered Emmett's words. These weren't simple platitudes. These people meant what they said.

Suddenly her life seemed a little safer.

She reached into her purse and took out a plastic bag containing the cigarette butts she had collected. They were all the same variety, and Sara hoped they could be useful. "I found these outside the cabin. There were a dozen of them under a tree. I think—" Her voice trembled, and she forced down her worry. "I think someone was watching the cabin. I think that person was there for a long time. As you can see, the cigarettes all look like the same type. That's why I think it was one person, not different ones." Jesse took the bag. There was no expression on his face as he turned the cigarette butts over slowly, studying them through the plastic. He was wearing a cop's face now, Sara realized. Giving away nothing.

"By the driveway, you said?"

"Under a cottonwood tree. You could see anyone in the cabin, but they couldn't see you."

"What else, Sara?"

"I was taking a walk. At the bottom of the wash, just

below the cabin, the ground was damp. You must have had a rain recently."

"About a week ago."

Sara nodded. "There were footprints at the edge of some wild grass. When I walked, I saw more. I counted at least twelve people, judging by the shoes. But there were all different kinds of shoes—sneakers and jogging shoes, plus one set of prints from an expensive boot."

"How would you recognize all those?"

When he frowned, Sara explained. "Last year I did a photo layout on shoe prints, and I recognized the expensive one in particular. That design is used only on an imported Italian shoe. Bottega Veneta is the brand." She shook her head. "Why would someone with that kind of expensive shoes be walking up an isolated wash at Navajo Ridge?"

Why indeed? Jesse McCloud wondered grimly.

The answer was money. Smugglers of illegal immigrants used the isolated washes and mesa country to hide their human cargo while waiting to arrange a pickup in drop points from Kingman and Flagstaff to Albuquerque and every direction from there. Jesse had seen federal law enforcement reports about an upswing in activity in this area for almost a year now.

It was an old problem, and there was no sign of any

decrease. Now they were moving into this isolated area, it seemed.

Jesse studied the bag of cigarette butts, mulling over what Sara had told him. She had been the first to find this clue. It would be very helpful. He sat back, studying her. "Anytime you want a job in law enforcement, I think I could swing you a spot."

She smiled, the first smile he had seen since he came in. "Crime scene photographer? I doubt I have the stomach for it. Thanks anyway."

China rattled behind them. Charly put fresh bread in front of Jesse. The café owner brought a steaming bowl of chili topped with caramelized onions, fire-roasted chipotles and shaved cheese.

"Best chili I ever ate," Jesse said.

"After all this time, I guess I ought to know what you like," Emmett said.

After they walked away, Jesse began to eat, quietly and thoroughly, the same way he did everything.

"I have something else to show you." Sara held out a larger bag with the muddy textile. "I found this in the wash not far from the footprints. It was shoved beneath a boulder. It looks expensive, with a lot of handmade detail. I doubt anyone would leave this on purpose."

As she unrolled the small blanket on the table, the bright lights of the café touched the woven mountains and stylized birds. They seemed to shine, full of hope for a bright future.

Jesse doubted there would be a bright future for the people in that wash. If smugglers, known in the Southwest as coyotes, were truly working near the isolated cabin on Liz Stone's land, the consequences could be very dangerous. The two women could have run afoul of people with a reputation for leaving no witnesses behind.

Jesse finished his chili. Like magic, a to-go cup of coffee and a piece of pecan pie appeared in a bag in front of him.

Just the way they always did. His effort to pay was waved off in short order.

"They wouldn't let me pay, either," Sara said quietly. "It doesn't feel right. How can five dollars be enough for a whole dinner?"

"You'll have to get used to it. Things get done differently here." He picked up his food, the blanket and the plastic bag. "I'd better drive up to Navajo Ridge with you and take a look around. I won't be able to see much in the dark, but Marlow isn't bothered by that."

"Marlow?"

"The brown Lab out in my cruiser. He's not doing too well right now. Freshly retired from K-9 service and he's taking it hard. A lot like a human, I guess. He was in a search-and-detection unit, and I'm fostering him for the moment, but I don't know how long he can tag along with me. Rules are rules. Besides, he needs a place of his own."

"I'll take him. At least, as long as he needs a place." Sara heard the words spill out of her mouth and realized just how much she wanted Marlow. If this was the same dog she had seen sitting by the road, she was already hooked. Something about those melting brown eyes had drilled through her defenses from the first moment she'd seen him, looking lost and unhappy.

"You mean it?"

Sara nodded. "You'll have to give me some instructions. I've never had a pet before."

"Marlow's easy. Well behaved and good-tempered." Jesse held the door open for her. "All you have to do is feed him and love him. I'll get you a kennel for the evenings, along with his special leash and toys. Mainly he needs to have exercise and feel like he's working again. Keep in mind that Labradors love to play. The best work is play for them." Sara walked out as he held the door. When Jesse looked back, Charly was trying to hide a smile. Marie, the town vet, gave him a covert thumbs-up signal.

No secrets in this town, Jesse thought. By morning the news would be all over the county that he had driven up to Navajo Ridge with Sara Winslow. The story would probably be blown up to feverish proportions.

He slid into the cruiser and flipped his lights at Sara, motioning her to go in front of him. Marlow was curled up on the passenger seat, tail wagging. He looked out the window at Sara, sat up and barked noisily.

"I know just how you feel, boy."

Jesse walked Sara to the door of the cabin and made sure she was safely inside. Then he checked the locks on all the windows and doors to be sure they hadn't been tampered with. Once he was satisfied, he pulled out his heavy flashlight and clipped Marlow onto his service leash. Immediately the dog tensed with excitement. His leash meant that he was doing something important, following the careful tracking and detection rules he had been taught as a police dog.

Jesse pulled out the blanket that Sara had given him and put it on the ground in front of Marlow. He let the dog take his time, smelling the textile thoroughly. Then Jesse gave the order to search.

Almost immediately the big dog strained forward, heading toward the wash. Jesse's flashlight beam cut back and forth over tall grass and boulders as Marlow led him straight to the spot that Sara had described, a rugged boulder in the curve of the wash downhill from the cabin. Marlow's body quivered with excitement when he sniffed the base of the rock. Then he headed for the brush at the opposite slope.

Jesse wouldn't take him any farther in the dark. But they'd be back here at dawn to pick up the trail.

"Heel, Marlow."

Instantly the beautifully trained veteran sat down, looking intently at Jesse, who offered lavish praise along with two dog treats he kept in his pocket.

Then the two headed back to the cabin. Twice Marlow turned, staring into the darkness. Jesse felt his muscles lock. He ran his hand along the dog's back, murmuring softly.

Sara threw open the door at his first knock, her face pale. "Did you find anything?"

"We can talk inside," Jesse said quietly.

"But—"

"Inside." The word was gentle, but an order just the same.

As Marlow lay curled up near her feet, Sara blurted out the whole story of her sister's disappearance. When Sara hadn't heard from her sister for five days, she had decided to push up her vacation and head out to Arizona earlier than planned. Hannah was known to take spontaneous road trips, but not without letting Sara know.

This was different. Sara was certain her sister was in some kind of trouble.

Jesse had checked and knew that neither woman had any criminal record, and he was inclined to rule them out as suspects. But for the moment he was drawing no conclusions. He had already put in a request for Liz Stone's cell phone and recent credit card usage. The information was being processed, and the delay was frustrating. He made a decision to pack some supplies and take Marlow into the rugged backcountry first thing in the morning, following whatever trail the dog could pick up.

When Jesse looked down, he saw Marlow was draped across Sara's feet, wagging his tail as she scratched a spot behind his ear. Jesse knelt beside the dog and laughed when Marlow licked his hands. "You be good to Ms. Winslow tonight, Marlow. Don't cause her any trouble."

The big dog barked once, his tail thumping on the floor.

"I'll take that as a yes." Jesse stood up. "I feel a lot better with Marlow here. For safety I think you should move into town tomorrow, until we get things sorted out."

Sara looked undecided. Then her mouth set in a firm line. "No. I don't need—"

"I don't know what's going on up here, Sara. Until I do, you need to be someplace safe. Rosa has an apartment in town for short-term rentals. I happen to know that it's free right now. Since you're about to become a material witness in a criminal investigation, there would be no fee for you to stay there."

"Material witness." Sara repeated the phrase slowly. Then she squared her shoulders. "Whatever you need me to do, I'm available." She didn't give way to panic or nervous questions, and that was one of the things Jesse liked about her. Her mouth was another.

It was getting harder to curb his impulse to see how her soft mouth would taste.

But instead of doing what he wanted, he walked to the door.

A hand touched his shoulder. He turned and his breath caught as Sara stood on her toes. Her hands slid around his shoulders. She brushed a kiss lightly across his mouth.

Once.

Twice.

Jesse felt a little dizzy when she finished. He cleared his throat. "Should I ask what that was for?"

"No," she said softly. "Not yet."

Jesse nodded. He had always liked a good mystery. But now he had to concentrate on finding her sister and Liz Stone. As a seasoned officer, he knew the first twenty-four hours were key to locating a missing person. With every hour that passed, the chance for a safe recovery faded.

He would have many things to do before morning, and he would have to be very fast. Meanwhile, he did not want to leave Sara alone here in this cabin.

He needed to pack a few things and come back. Tonight he would sleep in his cruiser parked down the road, out of sight behind a big mesquite tree.

Sara stood in the darkened living room after Jesse left.

For a long time she listened to the sounds of the night. An owl *hoooed* somewhere nearby and distant thunder rumbled out over the mesa. Every hiss of the wind and stirring in the long grass made her conjure images of shadowy figures waiting in the darkness.

Marlow's head rose. He stared at the front door, suddenly tense, his head cocked. His nose worked, pulling scent from the air as he focused intently on something outside.

Sara held her breath, listening but hearing nothing.

Only the wind, swaying the trees near the driveway.

Marlow huffed out a little breath, then turned in a circle and settled at Sara's feet.

Whatever had been bothering him was gone. Some of Sara's uneasiness faded as she ran her fingers over Marlow's soft fur, remembering Hannah and her spunky laugh. The little games they had played as lonely girls growing up.

Her fingers tightened. Marlow looked up, licking her hand.

Sara felt a tug of sad memories. "I have to find her, Marlow. She needs me, just like when we were kids." Something continued to bother her. She couldn't put her finger on it, but it had to do with the woven baby blanket shoved under the rock in the wash. There had been something else....

The image of the blanket continued to gnaw at Sara all the way to dawn.

CHAPTER
❧ FIVE ❧

After a restless night, Sara pulled out her sister's notebook and began working through every page, looking for any detail that might be useful. A number of times she came across references to a volunteer organization in Maryland called Partners In Care. The group offered unique resources to help the elderly who were alone or isolated. Volunteers gave arm-in-arm service, escorting members to medical appointments, picking up medications, helping with handyman jobs or buying groceries. Sara was intrigued at the way all the volunteer services were banked via a service exchange. Volunteers could draw on their service hours as needed or donate them to the organization. With

2,600 members, Partners In Care had become a life-saving support network for overwhelmed seniors and overtaxed families.

Sara found a brochure for the organization tucked into the back of her sister's notebook, and the more she read, the more she could understand how crucial a volunteer organization like this would be. She had seen her grandparents' friends struggle with ill health and arthritis, challenged by the smallest daily tasks. An organization like this would have gone far toward improving their quality of life.

It appeared that Hannah was deeply involved in planning how to bring similar services to elderly residents of the area. She had made notes of conversations with those who would be willing to contribute their services. Hannah also listed a Web site for the Partners In Care network in Maryland. As she scanned the warm-house and ride-partners programs on her sister's computer, Sara understood why her sister had been so excited, and how many lives would be touched by a caring local network like this.

The phone rang.

Emmett from the Red Rock Café was calling to see if she needed any groceries delivered. Sara assured him it wasn't necessary because she would definitely be back for dinner. Then Charly called, alerting her that he was on his way up to her cabin to check on her. When Sara tried to argue that it was too much trouble, he simply laughed and hung up. She was bewildered at the kindness shown to her by near strangers. It had to be because of her sister, but Hannah had never been known for her long-term sense of responsibility or community attachments. She had a good heart, but acted on whim and the moment, never tied down. Clearly she had changed since arriving in Sedona.

Sara opened a drawer on her sister's desk and pulled out a thick file filled with records. Flipping through the papers, she began to understand Hannah's abbreviations. *Comp* indicated computer work. *Trans* indicated transportation. *Hand* meant handyman work. All of those services were recorded in Hannah's neat and careful notations on a homemade ledger page. The entries dated back three months, and Sara was stunned to see that almost a hundred people were listed with address, date of birth and phone number. When she scanned the birth dates, Sara saw that all the recipients were older than sixty-five, with several in their nineties.

After years of restlessness, Hannah had finally found a worthy goal.

Sara closed her eyes, feeling another stab of worry.

The sharp rapping at the front door, coupled with

Marlow's excited barking, made her stiffen. Then Charly called out from the front porch.

"Bread delivery. Hope I'm not too early."

Sara caught a breath, staring down at her rumpled pink flannel pajamas.

As she turned to change, the banging at the door came again. "Hello? Sara, are you okay in there?" This time Charly sounded worried.

She tugged on her robe, crossed to open the door and was immediately assaulted by mouthwatering smells of fresh bread, sun-dried tomatoes and smoked chilis. Charly was carrying a paper bag under one arm. "Everything okay here?"

"Just fine."

Charly glanced around the room and nodded. "Good. I thought I'd bring you a few things, since I was coming up." His mouth curved. "I put in what Jesse likes."

Sara flushed a little, looking away. "You shouldn't have. But this is one of the nicest things anyone's ever done for me."

After he put the packages on the table, Charly frowned at her. "I'm sorry to hear that, Sara. People are meant to take care of each other. Liz Stone sets a high example in this county. We all owe her a lot for the ways she has helped us."

"She sounds very special." Sara poured him a cup of coffee. "No wonder my sister likes her work here."

Charly eyed her over the rim, then grinned. "Nice pajamas. Hello Kitty, aren't they? My granddaughter's favorite."

Sara frowned. She wasn't used to worrying about what she wore to sleep in. It had been a long time since she had been involved with a man.

But that thought brought a picture of the steady, cool deputy sheriff with the smoky-blue eyes. Suddenly getting involved seemed like a wonderful possibility.

Sara shoved away the thought. "They're comfortable. That's all that matters."

Another car pulled up, and boots crossed gravel. "Sara, are you up? Jesse asked me to drop by and see how things were going."

When she opened the door. Sara found Rosa Harrington carrying a dog bed, grooming tools and a big bag of dog food. "For Marlow," she explained, patting the excited dog pressed against her knee. "I remembered the kind of food he likes. When Jesse said he was bringing Marlow to you, I figured you could take the bag and the bed along when you come down to town." She set down the dog bed and raised an eyebrow as she looked at Sara. "Nice pajamas."

Charly coughed in what might have been a stifled laugh.

Sara ignored him. "It gets cold up here. The flannel was the only thing that helped last night." She didn't add that uneasiness had made the temperature seem worse. Or that she had slept sitting up in the rocker near the door, yanked awake by every suspicious noise outside. There had been too many for her to sleep well.

"What you need is a fire in that fireplace. Charly, don't just stand there. Show the young woman where the logs are and put out some kindling for her. I'll show her how to set everything up."

"Yes, ma'am."

Charly bustled off, and Sara poured Rosa a cup of coffee. "You sure that everything's okay?" The older woman sent a casual but thorough glance around the kitchen and neighboring room. "Jesse said he was going to keep an eye on things. Slept outside in his cruiser all night, just down the hill."

Sara felt tendrils of heat curl up to her face. He had been outside all night, and he hadn't said a word to her? The gesture was all the more touching because he had done it without fuss or comment.

"He didn't need to do that. I was fine."

"Good to know. But his being parked in that cruiser all night might be the reason you were fine. He told me that you were coming down to stay in town until he finds out what happened to Liz and your sister." Rosa peeked into the bag Charly had brought and nodded. "Good choice. You can have breakfast before you leave—burritos with fried new potatoes, Hatch green chilis and applewood-smoked pork. I have to say that boy can cook."

Boy? Charly had to be at least sixty-five, but probably closer to seventy.

Of course, like everything else age was relative. These people acted as if they were barely forty, Sara thought. Maybe it was something in the water. Or maybe it was clean air, clear skies and basic human kindness.

She took down a plate, loaded two burritos and slid them into the microwave while Rosa studied her pajamas.

The older woman nodded. "Jesse likes pink," she murmured. "He told me that last Christmas."

Sara definitely didn't need any matchmaking activity. "He's nice, Rosa. I've been worried about my sister, and Jesse is helping me find her. But that's all. It's nothing...personal."

"Isn't it?" Rosa smiled and shrugged in a way that meant she wasn't buying this casual story, not for a second.

Another car pulled up outside. Boots tapped across

the porch. This time it was Jesse who put his head in-side. "Sara, is everything okay?"

"Just fine. I'm making coffee and breakfast burritos, courtesy of Charly. Come in." She crossed the room, frowning at him, and lowered her voice. "Did you sleep outside in your cruiser all night?"

"I did." His eyes narrowed on her face. "I was wor-ried about you."

"You should have told me."

"Why? It was the right thing to do. No need to ex-plain."

He was a hard man to argue with. The intense way he studied her face was impossible to ignore. Sara felt as if the ground shifted a little. They didn't feel like strangers now.

There was more than trust growing between them. She saw that he had a scratch on his jaw, and she raised her fingers, touching it gently. "You cut yourself."

The muscles at his jaw locked. Emotion swirled through his eyes for a moment. "Shaving. Not the easi-est thing to do in the dark."

Sara didn't take her hand away, savoring the warmth of his skin and the ripple of muscles at his jaw. She shook her head. "Idiot," she said softly.

He nodded. "You may be right."

Rosa and Charly were talking next door in the living room. Sara realized she was standing very close to Jesse, and that he was staring at her mouth.

He had said that he liked her mouth. Sara wondered what he would do if she—

Outside, another car pulled up. A door slammed, and more boots crunched across the gravel drive.

"Jesse?"

Jesse opened the door to a man in a deputy's uniform. "Right here, Miguel."

"We need you in town. That paperwork you ordered just came in from Mexico. And there's something from the NCIC."

"I'll be right there." Jesse looked down at Sara and slid a curve of hair off her cheek. "Afraid I'm going to miss that burrito and coffee. I have to go. You can follow me into town." His gaze slid over her from head to toe, and his eyes glinted as if he liked what he saw. "Nice pajamas," he murmured. "I like pink. I especially like it on you."

Then he took a step back.

Almost instantly his face became unreadable. He looked at the road and called to the two people in the living room, "Why don't you two take Sara over to Liz Stone's house before you go? You know where she leaves her key. Show Sara inside and let her look around. I've already searched the house, but maybe she'll see something in there that I overlooked." He studied Sara and a muscle moved at his jaw. "If you find anything, call me via the dispatcher. After that, you need to pack. Charly will get you settled. I don't want you up here alone any longer."

Jesse frowned at the papers spread over his desk.

The statements had come through from Liz Stone's credit cards and cell phone.

There was nothing. Stone-cold zero. She hadn't used her cards in the past six days. No one had stolen them and tried to use them in her place. Her cell phone activity had stopped eight days earlier.

Jesse scanned the other documents on his desk, including current data on illegal smuggling in the state. Ten days earlier a farm truck had collided with a drunk driver on a rural road outside Tucson. The drunk had been untouched, his car totaled. The only witness said that there had been a little drizzle when the farm truck had overturned, and people were crowded into the truck bed. Footprints at the scene confirmed that there had been almost two dozen people riding on the truck. All of them were gone by the time the police arrived.

Like water spilled in the darkness, lost in the quiet Arizona night.

Jesse stared down at the photographs from the accident site. Shoe prints were stamped in the damp ground. Boots, athletic shoes.

He saw another print. An ornate *B* above a capital *V*.

Sara had told him about a similar logo on the footprints she'd seen in the wash. Was this simple coincidence, or were they putting together another solid clue?

Miguel Rodriguez, the young deputy, cleared his throat. "There's something else, Jesse. I sent the photographs of that blanket via e-mail to my cousin in Mexico City, just the way you asked. His specialty is textile art, and he said there's no question about it. The blanket is Oaxacan. He can tell us the village and even the family specializing in that pattern." The deputy rubbed his neck. "He asked a friend to check in the area. Only three families weave that kind of bird and mountain designs, and one of the granddaughters disappeared about two weeks ago. She's only seventeen, Jesse. She had a three-month-old baby with her. They say she had a baby blanket with a pattern that sounds a lot like the one you showed me."

Jesse felt a little wave of excitement as he finally made traction on the case. "Nice job, Miguel. Let's get everything you can on this young woman. Where was she last seen? What do the police assume to be the cause of her disappearance? Any known relatives in Arizona? You know the drill."

"Already working on it." The young, handsome detective frowned. "Something else you should know." He cleared his throat. "I saw Hannah Winslow up in Flagstaff a few times. She was doing research at the university library. We had coffee, talked. She's—nice. Just thought I should tell you."

Jesse rocked back in his chair. "How did she strike you? Did she seem worried or bored?"

The deputy shook his head. "Not bored. She was all fired up about this idea of a service-exchange program to help the elderly in Coconino County. I don't need to tell you how hard it is for people who are isolated with no transportation. Hannah said she had been reading up on it, and she and Liz were trying to start something official. They hoped to visit Baltimore and meet the people who had set up a similar program there."

"Liz never said a word about it to me. Nor to anyone else, so far as I know."

Miguel shifted, looking a little uncomfortable. "Hannah asked me not to say anything yet. She said Liz didn't want to fall flat on her face before they had all the details worked out. You know how stubborn Liz can be."

"Tell me about it." Jesse looked up as the dispatcher waved from the front of the office.

"Got something for you, Jesse. There's a Navajo elder by the name of Albert Begay, lives up near Chinle. He says he needs to talk to you right away. Something about Liz Stone."

"You can put the call through here to my desk, Maryanne."

"Not a call, Jesse. He's out in the waiting room with his daughter."

Jesse ushered the white-haired man and his daughter into a quiet room, then sat down across from them. "Mr. Begay, I understand that you came here about Liz Stone."

The elderly man nodded. "I do not like to bother anyone, but I am worried. Liz was to meet me in Flagstaff. She seemed anxious on the phone the day she called me. First she was excited. She told me she was working on a project to help older adults. I've never heard her so excited before," the man said quietly. "She told me not to say anything yet, not until she was ready to make these things public. Then she asked me if I could meet her about something else. She grew worried then, but she would not discuss it on the phone. She planned to come north last week and meet me in Flagstaff, but she missed the appointment. I have tried calling her many times, but never had an answer."

"What did she want to meet you about, Mr. Begay?"

"She asked me to bring my son, who is with the border patrol south of Tucson. I think she wanted to get advice from him." He stared at Jesse for a long time.

"She is a determined person, Deputy McCloud. When she did not contact me, I began to wonder. Now…I am worried. Maybe I should have come here sooner, but I kept hoping I would hear from her."

"Do you have any idea what kind of problem she had?"

The old man shook his head. "Only that she wanted my son to be present. She changed the date so that we would be certain he could come. From this I think her problem involves immigration. I can tell you no more than that." The older man stood up. "If I can be of help, please call me. My daughter has written down the number for you. Now I must go." But he did not move. His dark eyes were troubled. "Liz Stone has been a good friend to me. Her generosity has helped many people. Find her, Deputy McCloud. She has much good work to be done. I can feel this clearly. But you do not have much time. This also I can sense." The tall man looked at Jesse and then said another phrase. It was low and soft, ancient words in an ancient tongue.

After he left, Jesse turned to his daughter. "I appreciate you coming. We'll do everything possible to find Liz Stone. But what was the last thing your father said?"

"It is an old saying among the Dineh," the young woman explained. "'The Coyote is always waiting, and the Coyote is always very hungry.'"

As Jesse held the piece of paper with the old man's

number, he had a sudden image of the official telegram notifying him of his sister's death in Afghanistan, where she had been serving only a month as a humanitarian aid worker.

His hand tightened. He wasn't going to lose Liz Stone or Sara's sister. No matter if he had to walk every inch of that wash with Marlow, tracking them all the way to the next county, he would find them.

But every instinct told him that time was running out.

Clouds blocked the sun. Above the cliffs, a hawk cried shrilly.

Hannah Winslow's throat was raw and her wrists hurt. She was in a dark room with her hands bound. She would have given her bank account for a full glass of water.

But the men with the rifles guarding the little shack at the mouth of the canyon kept the water jugs for themselves, offering only limited amounts to their captives. Their scant daily meal of bread and dried fruit left her stomach growling, but the thirst was starting to drain Hannah. Her head ached constantly and her mouth felt raw.

She glanced over at the woman sleeping restlessly at the opposite wall of the shed. Liz Stone was tough, but their climb through the canyons had nearly done her in.

Despite Hannah's arguing with their captors, they refused to release the older woman or give her a bottle of water for her own use.

Hannah's argument had earned her a split lip and a bruised face. Now her mouth was covered by a gag. But even with her hands bound, she managed to turn and pull the torn blanket up to cover Liz. The sleeping woman reminded Hannah of her grandmother—tough, quiet and stubborn. Hannah was prepared to do anything to protect Liz from these vicious criminals who preyed on anyone in their path.

Someone in Sedona would discover they were gone and come looking for them, Hannah thought. And there was her sister. Sara would worry when she didn't hear from Hannah. Her sister was a worrier, and no one was more reliable.

Hannah took a deep breath, remembering the message she had left back in the wash. She'd had only minutes to act before their captors herded them up, driving them into the wash like sheep. Hannah had heard the men mention a place in English and then again in Spanish. Her high school Spanish was limited but adequate for the translation.

Cross of the Eagles.

They were being taken to a remote canyon there.

Hannah prayed that Sara would see her message in the wash and understand it.

Sara had to come.

Hannah closed her eyes as exhaustion hit her, more powerful even than fear. She needed to sleep while she could. Some of the men had left early that morning on an errand that seemed important. She hadn't been able to hear what they'd said, but they'd seemed edgy.

She prayed that her sister would hurry.

Jesse was on the phone with Liz Stone's son when Miguel sprinted down the narrow row of desks. "Jesse, the dispatcher has Charly on the phone. All hell's breaking loose up on Navajo Ridge. Deputy Harris has been shot, and Rosa is hurt." Miguel was already unlocking his desk drawer, digging for his rifle cartridges. "I couldn't get a clear story because Charly was yelling." The deputy pulled on his jacket. "But he said that Sara's gone."

CHAPTER
∾SIX∾

J esse drove north, forcing his mind to stay calm and logical, but it wasn't easy. These were his friends, people he'd known for years. Liz, Charly, Rosa, the deputy who had been shot.

And Sara...

No emotion. He couldn't afford any distraction.

The dispatcher's voice crackled over his car radio. "Jesse, I've got Charly on the phone again. He says that he's going after her. He says he can't wait—"

"Patch him through, Maryanne."

Charly was still distraught, but his panic had given way to anger. "Jesse, I'm going up into the canyon. If I hurry I can probably find her and—"

"You'll get yourself killed, Charly. I'm on my way. Stay there and keep an eye on Rosa."

"But—"

"Do *not* leave."

When Jesse pulled up the drive to the cabin, the first thing he saw was the wounded deputy sitting up against a tree. His right arm hung motionless at his side and his eyes were closed, but he was alive. Jesse stopped the car and knelt by the officer. In the distance he could hear the ambulance on its way. "How are you doing?"

"I've been better, Jesse. There were three of them. They must have been in a car parked nearby. Marlow heard them and set up a racket. Sara went after Marlow, and suddenly all hell broke loose. Someone started firing from beyond those cottonwoods over there. I returned fire, and then I was hit. I must have blacked out. I'm sorry, Jesse—they took her."

"And we'll get her back. Now you need to relax. There's the ambulance."

Jesse stood up and stepped back as two medics ran up the drive. Then he saw Charly stride around the side of the cabin, his face pale.

"They went north, Jesse. Up the wash."

"You saw them?"

"No, but that's where Marlow was, and I heard them in the grass. We need to—"

"I need you to stay here and help get things sorted out, Charly. I'm going on alone."

Charly followed Jesse back to the cruiser, his face hard with anger. "You can't do this alone. You're going to need backup."

Jesse was already changing into a camouflage jacket and tugging a big khaki bag over his shoulder. "I don't have time to argue, Charly. Every second we waste gives them more time to hide. I need to go talk to Officer Rodriguez and brief him before I—"

Charly blocked Jesse's path. "There's one more thing you should know. Right before we were to leave, Sara told me she'd found something in a photograph she took yesterday. It was bothering her, so she went out to have one last look before we left for town. I should have stopped her. If only I had left fifteen minutes earlier—"

"No point worrying about what might have been, Charly. Now, go on. What did she find?"

"She said it was some kind of code she and her sister made up as girls. They'd hide from each other in the woods and leave messages using rocks and sticks to spell out words. Sara saw one of those messages in the wash. It was a pile of rocks not too far from the place where she found that baby blanket, but it didn't make sense. The first part was three men and danger. Then it said something like bird and cross." Charlie scratched his head. "She was going north into the wash to see if she could find any more messages from her sister. I could hear Marlow somewhere up ahead of her in the bushes. Then Rosa shouted, and I heard a rifle. When I looked around, Sara was gone."

"I'll find her." Jesse shoved a pair of gloves and a compass into his pocket. Then he checked to be sure that his two canteens were secure. "Now I've got to go talk to Officer Rodriguez, Charly. You two can fill in the other officers when they get here."

"But what did it mean? Is bird and cross some kind of code?"

Jesse stopped walking. "Not bird. She could have meant eagle—as in Eagle Crossing."

Charly shaded his eyes and looked north where the red cliffs towered above the cabin. "There's a box canyon in Eagle Crossing. It would make a good spot to hide, and there's no way to get a truck in there, not even one with four-wheel drive. We'll have to get horses."

"Tell the officers exactly what you've told me, Charly."

"What are you going to do?"

Jesse opened a pocket in the canvas bag. He pulled out a coil of rope and slid it over his shoulder. "I'm going up the one way they won't expect me." His fingers smoothed the heavy coils as he turned toward the trees. "I'm heading up past the old Sinagua ruins, over the rock arch and then straight up the cliff."

They had taped Sara's hands behind her. She was blindfolded, stumbling over gravel and ruts in the sandy trail. Every time she swayed a man cursed and dug a gun into her ribs.

She was beyond exhaustion, almost beyond fear after what felt like endless hiking up rocky trails. From the way the sun hit her face, she knew they were headed northwest. She kept waiting to hear a shout, or to hear twigs snap and feel Jesse's quiet touch.

He was out there somewhere. She was certain of it. And when he appeared she would be ready.

Her foot struck a loose rock and she pitched forward to her knees. With her hands bound behind her it was hard to keep her balance on the rough trail. A man cursed at her in English, and his voice held no accent. She recorded this like the other facts.

They used code words for names. Ace, Duke and Primo.

Primo was the one who cursed at her as her shoulder hit the earth. She rolled slightly, gravel in her face.

A boot heel dug into the small of her back. "Get up

and walk. If you keep falling, I'll leave you here with two bullets."

Gritting her teeth, Sara stood up. At least they were taking her somewhere. She prayed Hannah and her friend would be waiting when they stopped.

And despite their threats they hadn't shot her, Sara thought grimly.

Yet.

Jesse watched them below on the trail, watched the tall man press his boot against Sara's back.

Anger blurred his vision as he saw her struggle to her feet. His hands clenched on the rope looped over his shoulder and he fought the urge to pick off her captors one by one.

But he had to let these men lead him to their hiding place. If he went in now, they would almost certainly shoot Sara. So he followed silently and prayed that Liz Stone and Sara's sister were alive somewhere up the trail.

With his climbing skills rusty, his last cliff ascent had strained the wound in his leg, but Jesse knew he could go on climbing for a week. He would not rest until Sara and the others were safe. Then he was going to take a great deal of pleasure in bagging and tagging the men walking beside Sara down on the trail.

* * *

Jesse followed in silence, a shadow unnoticed as the men wound up through the rugged terrain, heading northwest. Finally the group stopped. Crouched in the grass nearby, Jesse heard the leader giving orders to one of the others.

"We'll be at Eagle Crossing within the hour. Radio ahead and tell them to get everyone ready. There's no reason to stay. We got what we needed back at the house."

"We shouldn't have gone back," the shorter man said, shaking his head. "It's too dangerous. I don't care how much cash or how many credit cards the old lady had, we need to reach the pickup point in Kingman. We're wasting time."

"You call this wasting time?" Laughing harshly, the other man waved a handful of credit cards and a wad of money. "If you don't want your cut, that's fine with me. I'll keep all of it."

They stopped arguing as a third man gestured to them from the top of the trail.

The man with the stolen credit cards waved back. "Where are the others?" he called.

"I've got 'em locked up in the canyon."

In the distance, Jesse heard the low drone of a helicopter. He was almost certain that a chopper had been dispatched from Flagstaff. He needed to move before these men turned antsy and did something stupid.

"Let's go." The man with the cash and credit cards vanished around a bend in the trail. The other man turned, staring north. It was clear that he had heard the helicopter.

As the man studied the tree line, Jesse tackled him and took him down hard, one hand clamped over his mouth. They struggled in the dust, but Jesse was bigger and faster. He left the man bound and gagged, tied to a tree twenty yards off the trail. Then he circled up the slope.

Two more smugglers were walking nearby. One was directly up the hill, and one was on the trail to his left. How many others were there? And where were the captives being held?

Jesse continued up the slope, staying parallel to the trail. With luck he would come across more men. He would take them out one by one.

Something bumped his leg. He froze, snapping a look down into the underbrush, startled to see a brown shape half-hidden by deer grass.

Marlow?

The big dog was flat on the ground, looking up at him alertly. He must have followed Sara when she was taken up the trail. Then he had tracked Jesse here, in full service mode.

Jesse reached down and scratched the big dog behind his ears. He leaned closer, whispering, "Stay. *Stay*, Marlow."

The dog was well trained. He would obey a clear order from someone he trusted.

Jesse took a step and halted, surprised to feel Marlow's teeth close gently on his wrist. The dog stayed right where he was, holding Jesse in place. Then Marlow began backing up. The dog's behavior made no sense until Jesse saw a faint trail leading up the slope to the right. He hesitated and then allowed Marlow to pull him a few feet back. Once the dog was sure Jesse was behind him, he trotted off into the brush, obviously tracking something. Jesse stayed close, moving at a crouch as the trail grew wider, snaking back and forth between boulders and low overhangs.

Suddenly Marlow stopped.

He looked forward, his head cocked.

Without a sound he turned and launched his paws against Jesse's chest, forcing him down. A man emerged from behind a cliff at the top of the trail, speaking into a walkie-talkie and looking at his watch. Thanks to Marlow's warning, Jesse had time to pick his spot, waiting until the man was nearly below him, then dropping down to tackle him.

Within minutes another captive was tied and gagged, then pulled away off the trail.

When Jesse looked around, Marlow was gone.

They forced Sara up the trail into a cabin. She stumbled at the threshold and went down hard. She heard the man behind her laughing as she fell.

Then she heard something else. Off in the distance she was certain she caught the drone of a helicopter. She prayed it was headed their way, dispatched by Jesse or the deputy back at Hannah's cabin.

She gasped as she was shoved forward and the dirty blindfold was yanked away from her eyes. A man in a dark ski mask gestured to her.

She squinted, trying to see him clearly as her eyes adjusted to the light.

"You'll stay here and shut up." He pointed across the dusty floor of a small room. "If you make any trouble, you'll end up like her."

Sara stared into the gloom. The room had one window, but big planks of wood had been nailed randomly over the glass. She couldn't see anything except a shadowy shape, propped against the opposite wall. Her heart leaped into her throat.

It was Hannah.

The man banged outside, and Sara heard the loud snap of a padlock being shoved in place on the door. All she could think about was her sister as she scooted closer. Hannah turned, unable to see behind her blindfold. Even in the gloom, Sara saw three big bruises on her face and neck.

"It's me, Hannah. I'm here, honey. What have they done to you?"

Behind the gag her sister bit back a sob.

"Thank God you've come." Her words were muffled but Sara knew what she said. She couldn't do much with her hands bound behind her, but she leaned against her sister, speaking softly. Sara was overcome by a rush of love for her sister, and heartsick to see her helpless and immobilized. Hannah had so many good plans, and a new dream that would touch the lives of hundreds of people.

Somehow they had to find a way to escape.

Marlow lay silent at Jesse's feet.

Jesse calmed him with a hand on the head, then turned to study the rickety shed. The wooden door was peeling and there were big gaps between the rough plank walls. Jesse was surprised to see a dented bottle of water sitting on the single step outside.

Marlow kept watching Jesse.

As Jesse crept closer to the little shed, he felt Marlow right beside him. The dog's head rose as he sniffed the air. His tail banged against Jesse's leg. It was all the signal Jesse needed.

He pushed open the door silently, and his mouth flattened when he saw Liz Stone stretched out in the gloom. Her face was tight with pain, and a piece of splintered wood was wrapped around her lower leg, secured with three strips of cloth torn from her shirt.

"Liz? It's Jesse," he whispered.

Marlow ran past him, headed straight for the elderly woman on the floor. The big dog sank down and licked Liz's face while Jesse carefully removed the muddy piece of cloth from her eyes.

"You came for us. I knew you would, Jesse."

"You're just determined to make my job interesting, aren't you?" Jesse's voice was gruff as Liz gripped his arm with trembling fingers. He ran an experienced eye over her leg, glad to see there was no sign of blood.

She blinked up at him and her tanned face lost some of its strain. "I never meant to make it *this* interesting," she said hoarsely. "I was a fool, Jesse. I should have come to you as soon as I suspected those people were using my land. But I didn't want to look stupid in case I was wrong. I should have known better."

"You can tell me what happened as soon as I get you

out of here, Liz. I'm going to help you outside into the grass. You'll be safe there."

She was tired and obviously in a great deal of pain, but her smile was as bright as a Sedona sunrise. She licked her cracked lips and took his arm. "I'm ready when you are. I think my leg is broken. I made a splint, but you'll have to help me."

The woman had a spirit of iron, Jesse thought. He was impressed beyond words as he lifted her gently. Sliding an arm around her waist, he helped her hobble to the door.

"Once you're clear, I'm going for the others. Where is Hannah Winslow?"

Liz's voice wavered. "I heard them say they were taking her higher up in the canyon. It's not far, straight north if you have a compass. I made a mental note of whatever I heard them say."

Jesse scanned the brush. It was slow going on the uneven ground and he was afraid to hurry Liz. Her hand felt very frail on his arm, but the force of her clenched fist was unmistakable.

This woman could teach a lot of men he knew about courage, Jesse thought. "Why did they leave you alone down in this shed?"

"After I fell, they figured I couldn't move anywhere. They left me a little food, but they didn't bother to guard me, so I made a splint, and I found some rainwater in a broken cup near the shed door."

"They didn't give you anything to drink?" Jesse glanced at the water bottle.

"Only a glass once a day. They left the bottle there to torment me because they wanted my bank code and the location of my cash and credit cards in my house," the old woman said angrily. "I delayed as long as I could, acting confused and telling them only bits and pieces. All of them should be shot. And those poor people think they're going to be taken someplace safe and given work." She shook her head. "All they will do is lose their money. Maybe their lives. It breaks my heart," Liz whispered. "Especially that young woman with the baby. These people are simply cargo."

"Don't talk, Liz." Jesse helped her lie down behind a cottonwood tree completely hidden by a mound of tall feather grass. She started to speak, but Jesse shook his head. He held his canteen up and helped her drink, then set the canteen in the grass next to her.

The white-haired rancher gripped his arm. "You have to find Hannah. They hit her when she insisted that they give me more food and water. It was me she was worried about, not herself. I owe her, Jesse."

"We all owe her," the deputy sheriff said flatly.

* * *

Sara had managed to peel away most of the tape on Hannah's ankles with the help of a rusty tin can lid Hannah had hidden between the cracks in the floor. While Hannah finished wriggling free, Sara went to work on her sister's hands. When she was done, Hannah removed her blindfold and returned the favor.

"We have to go find Liz," Hannah whispered. "They left her somewhere down the hill. I'm very worried, Sara. I think her leg is broken. And they wouldn't leave her any extra water, just a glass every day until she told them where her cash and credit cards were hidden."

"We'll find her." Sara stood up and took her sister's arm.

She froze as the grass outside the door rustled. A shadow moved beyond the rough slats of the boarded-up window.

Without a word Hannah dropped to the floor and curled up in a ball, moaning. Sara slid behind the door and pressed against the wall, waiting.

The minute the man came in and bent over her sister, Sara used a heavy rock hidden near the door and smashed it down on his head. He swayed and then turned furiously, swinging at her face. She ducked and then her sister launched herself from the ground and grabbed his legs while Sara hit him again and again until he cursed and toppled sideways.

When he hit the floor, it was one of the nicest sounds Sara had ever heard. Hannah sat up and smiled. Her face was bruised and streaked with dust, but she was full of enthusiasm. "That will teach them to mess with the Winslows."

Between them, the two women dragged the man across to the far corner and then Sara closed the door of the cabin, replacing the lock. She helped her sister, who was still wobbly, as they followed a narrow trail toward the cliffs, winding through rugged boulders and patchy brush. So far there had been no shouts or signs that they had been seen. But they needed water. If they didn't get it soon, their survival chances were slim.

Something moved in the tall feather grass beyond the trail. Remembering her confrontation with the snake, Sara grabbed her sister's arm. The grass rustled again, then parted, and a big dark shape nosed closer. Something wet pressed against Sara's hand.

"Marlow." Sara looked up and caught her breath at the sight of a man farther up the narrow trail.

Jesse.

He pressed one finger to his mouth, beckoning her toward him. Sara helped Hannah the last ten feet and felt Jesse squeeze her shoulder hard.

Then he scanned the trail. "We have to go. Head to your right." He passed a canteen to Sara's sister. "Have a little of this while you walk, but take it slow."

Hannah sipped, then gave the canteen to Sara, who had to force herself not to gulp down the whole thing. When Jesse led them to a shady spot concealed from the trail by a cottonwood tree, Sara saw a wiry, white-haired woman propped against the trunk with a canteen cradled in her lap.

Hannah muffled a cry of relief. "You found her. Liz, are you all right?"

"I could do with a gallon or two of coffee and one of Charly's pecan pies, but I think I'll survive. Thanks to all of you," the elderly woman whispered, her voice breaking with emotion.

Once the three were comfortable, Jesse straightened the grass that had been flattened when they'd walked in. He left a canvas bag next to Sara. "There's more water in there, along with some chocolate and protein bars, which I imagine are more appealing than the food they gave you here. I'll be back for you as soon as I can." He looked at the three and shook his head, his mouth curving in a grin. "You three ladies are something, you know that?"

Then he vanished like a shadow into the tall grass.

When the government helicopter set down on the cliffs above the canyon, the officers saw a curious sight.

Three men were standing in a clearing, their hands and feet roped together. Deputy Sheriff McCloud waved a shirt like a flag, directing the team to the only trail that would lead them from the rim down into the canyon so that they could take custody of the assailants.

As the smugglers were rounded into custody, Jesse pointed to a second helicopter banking in from the south. His arm slid around Sara's shoulders. "That ride will be ours, honey. I'm cooking dinner tonight. It might be a long night."

"Is that a promise?" Sara whispered.

Their fingers linked.

Emotion shimmered in her eyes as Sara watched Jesse's fellow officer Miguel Rodriguez bend protectively over Hannah. It was clear that theirs was more than a casual friendship.

"Looks like your sister has a beau." Jesse slanted a searching glance at Sara. "Looks like you both do. Is that a problem?"

She cocked her head and ran a hand over his shoulder. "Not with me. By the way, that was nice climbing. You're not as rusty as you thought."

"All it took was the right motivation. But it was a fight not to drop down on the trail when they shoved you, Sara."

"You did what you had to do."

"So did you."

"What about the people traveling in that group, Jesse?"

"The people are fine. They'll be treated and given whatever medical aid they need. It's already being arranged." Jesse cleared his throat. "By the way, I think I'm going to be seeing a lot of your sister. I want to help with this new elder care project she's working on. We're way past due for this kind of program in the county. I'm ashamed it took an outsider to show us that."

Sara moved her fingers against his, feeling the calluses and the strength there.

A man she could trust. Her first instincts about him had been right.

She was about to tell Jesse that, when Marlow came bounding up the trail. He lunged, and his dusty paws slammed against Jesse's chest. The three of them sprawled back into the feather grass, dirty, exhausted, but happy. Their laughter was as bright as the clear Arizona sky.

∽—EPILOGUE—∽

Sedona

One year later

"Charly, I need two more pecan pies over here. One's for the Garcia family and one's for Molly over in Cottonwood." Little tendrils of hair tumbled around Sara's tanned face as she surveyed the controlled chaos of Liz Stone's big kitchen. Boxes were organized in neat piles, all of them stamped with a bright red "Home and Heart" logo. Tools were set out for the handyman, who was due to arrive in twenty minutes.

Two reams of paper and a printer were prepared for

the computer team, who would be going out on their rounds an hour later.

Sara was working hard, throwing her energies behind this dream that Liz Stone and her sister had brought to reality. Even a small ride, errand or home visit touched the lives of those in the program, and she had never enjoyed anything more in her life.

Sara's fingers opened, smoothing the gentle curve of her stomach where Deputy Sheriff Jesse McCloud's baby was now in its sixth month. This was her home now.

Someone kissed the top of her head. She smiled, closing her eyes. "Charly, I told you not to kiss me like that. Jesse will—"

She heard a muffled laugh. Jesse drew her around to face him, carefully sliding his arms around her waist. "Am I going to have to get medieval on you and Charly, Mrs. McCloud?"

"I think he'd be very excited by the thought of sparring for a few rounds with you, my love, but Rosa wouldn't like it, so let's just keep this secret affair between us."

Jesse smiled and kissed her as if it was the first time. As if they had all the time in the world.

Which they did.

But when he looked at the boxes stacked around her,

the tall officer frowned. "You're working too hard, Sara. You should be resting."

Hannah bustled up behind them with a grinning Deputy Rodriguez in tow. "That's what I've been telling her all week, Jesse. You're her husband. Can't you talk some sense into my sister?"

Jesse smiled faintly. "I may be able to." He took the boxes of printer paper and gave them to Miguel. "You two can finish prepping for the rounds today. We'll be back in three hours to help you plan next week's visits. Right now, I want to spend some quiet time with my wife. And daughter."

"Son or daughter," Sara corrected him. They didn't know the baby's gender, preferring to keep a little magic in their child's upcoming birth.

"Daughter," Jesse murmured. He turned, his brow rising at the sound of wild barking from the back of his pickup truck. Marlow was braced against one side of the truck bed, paws up and tail wagging. Clearly, he was ready to work, too.

"What's on Marlow's schedule for today?" Jesse asked.

Hannah checked her clipboard. "He's going to visit two homes outside Sedona. Then a tracking demonstration at an elementary school." Hannah smiled proudly. "After that he's being interviewed by a reporter from New York. It seems he heard about Marlow's work here and his bravery in the rescue last year up at Eagle Crossing. The reporter also wants to take some pictures of the people who donate services to Home and Heart."

Liz peered out from her office, beaming. "Are you sitting down, everyone? We just received a contribution from an anonymous donor in California. He saw the feature story about Marlow and the agency last week, and he's sent us a six-figure check."

"Way to go, Marlow." Jesse went outside, bent next to the truck and gave a high five to the excited dog.

When Sara moved in beside him, Marlow gave her a high five, too.

Strange how comfortable a place could seem after just one year, she thought, studying Jesse's rugged profile. But she'd never felt more energetic or alive. She had taken some of her best photographs in the past two months, and one had received an international award. That black-and-white shot of snow dusting Eagle Crossing Canyon was going on exhibit in Paris the following summer.

Paris.

A car horn rang out. Two more volunteers were arriving. There was work to be done.

Jesse pointed to the picnic lunch he'd packed and the blanket spread out at the edge of the mesa. "You can see for fifty miles from here," he said. "I thought you needed to stop and eat." His mouth curved. "And plan your next set of photographs. The way I see it, you'll be showing in China next, and I've always wanted to climb the Great Wall."

He had encouraged and nagged and supported her every step of the way. He was almost more proud of the award than she was, Sara thought.

As Marlow settled down beside them and the wind ruffled the tall grass at the edge of the mesa, she knew exactly what it felt like to be home.

* * * * *

Dear Reader,

A first view of Sedona is something you never forget. Walking the high canyons in crisp, cool air is exhilarating, even close to magical. Those who have visited this beautiful corner of the rugged Southwest seldom forget it. What better place than a town with red-rock vistas and stubborn, supportive residents for setting a story of discovery, hope and service?

As I researched this novella, the work of Barbara Huston and her dedicated team at Partners In Care touched me on many levels. For years, my mother and father both did private work with older adults in our county. Growing up, I had clear memories of my mother receiving a phone call, speaking quietly, then moving to her desk and pulling out one of a dozen files organized with her ever-changing list of government agencies, private donors or faith-based support centers. In her quiet way she touched many lives through those calls.

Now, years later, I am delighted to write about Barbara's work with service exchange, a tool that empowers older adults to remain independent with community support in the home of their choice. Barbara's skill is to take this innovative concept and build an ever-widening network of support.

Successful? You decide.

In the first half of 2009, Partners In Care's 2,600 volunteer members exchanged over 25,000 hours in services. They installed 103 pieces of home safety equipment and provided 6,457 rides to doctors and grocery stores. They've repaired homes, organized neighborhood social events and provided medical advocacy.

Barbara has a special gift for positive action. She is a firm believer that everyone has something to contribute and is valued for those contributions. With drive and resourcefulness she has created a way for older adults to live safely and independently with the support of a growing network of members. I am in awe of her dedication and enthusiasm.

To learn more about Partners In Care, visit their website at www.partnersincare.org. I'm sure the enthusiastic faces and the stories of the members will touch you just the way they touched me. Please consider becoming involved with donations or a contribution. With your support the network can keep on growing with all the warmth and beauty of a Sedona sunset.

With warmest wishes,
Christina Skye

KAREN THOMSON
⌁ Literature for All of Us ⌁

When Karen Thomson opens a book, she is certain of one thing: by turning a page, she is opening herself up to laughter, tragedy, beauty and a profound and deep understanding of how other people think, feel and exist.

She is opening herself up to the world and all its potential.

Karen is the founder and executive director of Literature for All of Us, a charitable organization that reaches out to more than 500 disadvantaged teens in the Chicago area each year with thought-provoking book groups. Most groups are made up of teen girls struggling with everything, including domestic violence, poverty, teen pregnancy and faltering grades.

Karen is convinced that by giving teens a safe place to explore the world and speak their mind about a book they've read, they will gain confidence—and with confidence comes change.

"I can't tell you what it feels like to look in on a group and see everybody's head buried in a book, because I know what the alternative is," she says, sounding perpetually energized and excited. "So this is really good."

Falling in love with her girls

Karen's own path to the present has been paved with fabulous books, thoughtful discussions and two epiphanies.

The first happened while having dinner with friends back in 1979 and musing over whether she would go back to work after staying home with the kids for eight years. Finally one friend turned to her and asked point-blank what Karen really wanted. She thought for a moment, then answered, "If I could do anything, I want to be a book group leader for women. And you know what? I'm going to do it."

For the next sixteen years Karen, who has a B.A. in English literature from Wheaton College and a master of arts in teaching English from Northwestern University, introduced hundreds of female readers to Virginia Woolf, Kate Chopin and Judy Chicago as her book-group business grew by word of mouth. She hosted groups in colleges, retirement homes and in Barnes & Noble bookstores. She ran women's retreats ("We talked intensely about our mothers in the woods," she says) and would have kept chugging along if it hadn't been for a friend who suggested she branch out to disadvantaged teens. Karen wasn't so sure. She had taught school for a short while before having her own kids and wondered if it would be the right fit.

It was.

Karen volunteered to lead a book group for teen mothers at the Illinois Department of Human Services. That first week she walked into the room with some trepidation and a stack of Maya Angelou poetry under her arm. Only one problem: the fifteen girls whizzed through the three poems she'd prepared—and she still had over an hour of time to fill. The solution? Have the teens write their own poetry.

"I noticed when they read their poems, their body language changed significantly," Karen says now. "They were proud of themselves."

Word got out about the transforming and fun book group, and by the next week attendance doubled.

"I fell in love with these girls by the second week," she says. "I just realized that they enjoyed the group so much and it was exactly what they needed. They were reading and writing. They were creating. It was about them."

For ten weeks the young women read two books and

opened up about their lives. They read parts of the books aloud to keep everyone on the same page and also to increase their reading skills. The teens wrote short pieces about their children's hair and other personal topics and kept a strict "no put-down" policy about each other's reading or writing. As their confidence grew, their disciplinary referrals dropped at school.

That's when epiphany number two hit.

"I thought, Oh my God. This is the rest of my life," says Karen. "I saw it unroll before me."

In 1997 she launched Literature for All of Us with a mandate to grow a community of readers, poets and critical thinkers.

More to be done

Today, Literature for All of Us has facilitated more than 240 book groups, reaching more than 6,900 young people. It employs five book-group leaders, a collection of fabulous young women who see the world as Karen does and keep her mission alive. While Karen fund-raises and designs the programs, they head out to Chicago schools to run groups for teen girls and boys. Twenty-five percent of all book-group members are boys now, a program that started after many girls said they wanted their partners and boyfriends to start reading, too.

Members keep the books they read so they can build their own libraries, but just as often they pass them around to friends and family. The organization is also committed to teaching the magic of the written word to young children. Its Children's Literature for Parenting program introduces parents to relevant and award-winning kids' books they can read at home.

Karen remembers one young mother she invited to a fund-raising event who agreed to talk about the charity.

"I have a son and I never read to him," the sixteen-year-old told the silent audience. Then she turned to Karen. "But I did what you said and I put him on my lap, with my arms around him, and I read him this book. And guess what? He was good and quiet. I fell in love with him. And I read to him all the time now."

Years later, that story still reminds Karen that books have power far greater than any one sentence on a page. They transform the soul and encourage readers to embrace the world so they can make a difference, too.

And while she admits that fund-raising is always tough, finding the time to take the organization to the next level and tend to her personal life is even more of a challenge some days.

"I'm a reader, so I need lots of time to read and write," she says with a laugh. "But I don't feel that we've fulfilled our whole mission yet. There's more to be done."

PAMELA MORSI

Daffodils in Spring

~PAMELA MORSI~

Pamela Morsi is a bestselling, award-winning novelist who finds humor in everyday life and honor in ordinary people. She lives in San Antonio, Texas, with her husband and daughter.

To readers: young, old and everything in between.
May there always be a good story in your future.

CHAPTER
ONE

Calla stepped off the bus on Canasta Street and made a quick stop at the Korean grocery before walking the three blocks to her home. Typically this time of year she made the walk all bundled up and with her head down against the wind. But this fall was gorgeous in Chicago and the city was, for a brief time at least, a place of bright sunshine and vivid autumn colors. Only the slightest nip in the air foretold of the cold winter to come.

She'd lived on Canasta Street for sixteen years. She and her husband, Mark, had moved into their house when their son was still just a toddler. Now, Nathan was in his last year of high school and had just completed his early action application to attend Northwestern, his first choice for college, next year. Calla smiled to herself. She couldn't help but be proud. She just wished that Mark had lived to see it.

As she approached her block, all the tiredness of the long workday seemed to lift. There was something about a home surrounded by neighbors and friends that just buoyed a person. Every step she took along the well-worn sidewalk was as familiar to her as the back of her hand.

From his porch, old Mr. Whitten waved to her. Next door to him, the Carnaby children, along with their cousins, friends and assorted other stragglers, were noisy and exuberant as they played in their front yard. Two houses past them, Mrs. Gamble sat on her steps, her daughter Eunice at her side.

"You're home early," the older woman called out.

Calla just smiled. She was home at exactly the same time she was home every day.

"Did you buy something at the store?" Mrs. Gamble asked.

"Just milk," Calla answered. "And a half dozen apples. You know Mr. Ohng's produce is hard to resist."

"Come and sit a spell with us," the older woman said. "We haven't had a good visit with you in ages."

"Oh, I'd better get home and see what Nathan is up to."

"He's sure up to nothing at home," Eunice said with just a hint of superiority in her voice. "He's across the street in 2B with Gerty's wild grandniece."

Calla kept her expression deliberately blank. Eunice undoubtedly wanted to get a rise from her, but she wasn't about to give the woman the satisfaction.

"Oh, come up and sit," Mrs. Gamble pleaded. "That way you can see him when he leaves."

Calla wouldn't have walked across the street to talk with Eunice. But Mrs. Gamble was a genuinely sweet older lady who was trapped all day with the bitter unhappiness of her daughter.

So she opened the gate on the Gambles' chain-link fence and made her way to the porch. Setting her little bag of groceries beside her, Calla tucked the hem of her skirt behind her knees and seated herself on the fourth step, just slightly below Mrs. Gamble and directly across from Eunice.

"How was your job today?" Mrs. Gamble asked.

Calla shrugged. "Fine," she answered. She knew the woman was eager for details. Calla had been a nurse in Dr. Walker's ear, nose and throat practice for over a decade. Mrs. Gamble loved stories about diseases. Especially ones where the patient had to overcome great odds to recover.

There'd been no such dramatic cases today. With the

coming of fall, the office had been full of allergy sufferers fighting off sinus infections. Calla was not sure how entertaining the stories would be when all the characters were blowing into tissues.

"It's been pretty routine at the office the last few days," Calla told her.

"Well, there's nothing routine about the goings-on around here," Eunice piped in. "That girl has got her hooks in Nathan and no good is going to come of it."

Calla couldn't stop herself from casting a nervous glance in the direction of the apartment building across the street. Gerty Cleveland had lived there for twenty years at least. She was about Mrs. Gamble's age and had a large family scattered across the city. Less than a month ago, Jazleen—or Jazzy, as Nathan called her—had come to live with her. Calla didn't know the whole story, but there were plenty of rumors swirling about.

The girl's mother was on drugs. Or maybe she was in jail. Jazleen herself had been in trouble. Or maybe she just was trouble. Gerty was Jazleen's last chance. Or maybe she was the only chance the teenager had ever had.

Calla had heard what everyone was saying. But what resounded with her louder than all the neighborhood whispering were the words of her son, Nathan.

"She's okay, Mom," he assured her. "She's a good person."

Calla trusted her son, but she worried, too. Young men could often be blinded by a pretty face or a good figure. Jazleen was no great beauty, but she had sweet features and the requisite number of teenage curves.

"Once you get to know her," Nathan said, "you'll like her."

That was slow going so far. Jazleen had been in their house many times. She was mostly silent and slightly sullen. Those were hardly traits to win the heart.

"I don't think we should jump to conclusions about the girl," Calla told Eunice. "Nathan says she's nice."

Eunice sucked her teeth. "Yes, well, I'm sure that's what the boy would tell his mother."

Calla was very tempted to remind Eunice that since she obviously didn't know one thing about mothers and sons, it might be best if she just kept her opinions to herself.

She was saved from making any comment by the now familiar tap of shiny shoes coming down the sidewalk.

"It's him!" Eunice breathed, barely above a whisper.

Calla didn't need to ask who she meant. Every woman on Canasta Street, single, divorced, married or widowed, like Calla herself, knew the only man who would attract such attention.

Deliberately Calla kept her gaze on Mrs. Gamble. She flatly refused to turn and look, though she could see the man perfectly in her imagination. Landry Sinclair had moved into the house next door to her just weeks ago. He was polite and friendly, but so far no one had really gotten to know him.

What Calla and the other women did know was that he was tall and trim, with a strong jaw, a handsome smile and thick, arched brows. He went to work every morning and returned every evening dressed in impeccably tailored suits. And, so far, there had been no visitors at his place. No wife or girlfriend, not even a one-night-stand. He seemed unattached, which provoked much speculation.

"That is the finest looking man I've ever seen in my life," Eunice stated in a hushed whisper. "And I think he's just about my age. Don't you think he's probably my age?"

Calla nodded. "More or less," she agreed. Though she thought the years certainly held up better on him than on Eunice.

"Have you noticed his accent?" Eunice asked.

Of course Calla had noticed. She noticed everything about him.

"I think he's from the South," Eunice said.

"No, he's not from the South," Calla replied, shaking her head. "I have relatives from South Carolina and Georgia. He doesn't talk like the South at all."

"Well, he's not from here," Eunice insisted.

Calla shrugged agreement. The man clearly was not a local. But he was almost as mysterious as he was good-looking. He wasn't secretive. He answered any question he was asked. But the men on the street seemed satisfied to exchange pleasantries and opinions on sports teams. The women were all too curious but didn't trust themselves to stick to casual questions. So the basic information of where he was from and where he worked remained unknown, as well as the most critical fact to some—whether there was a woman someplace waiting for him.

"Good afternoon, Mr. Sinclair!" Mrs. Gamble called out as he passed by the gate.

Calla turned to look at him then, as if she'd been unaware of his approach. The man was dressed attractively in a single-breasted brown suit with narrow beige pinstripes. He looked businesslike, successful. She smiled in a way she hoped would appear to be polite disinterest.

"Good afternoon, Mrs. Gamble, ladies." He doffed his fedora, revealing dark hair that was just beginning to thin on the top. "It's a beautiful afternoon to sit out and enjoy the weather."

"It surely is," Mrs. Gamble agreed. "Why don't you come and join us?"

Calla heard Eunice draw a sharp, shocked breath. She couldn't tell if Landry Sinclair had heard it or not.

"I wish that I could," he answered, smiling broadly. "I sure wish I could."

He did not give a reason why he couldn't, but for an instant Calla's glance met his. His eyes were deep brown with a sparkle that was as much intelligence as humor. Calla found him completely irresistible.

Which was precisely the reason she had never spoken to him.

That was the last thing in the world she needed, to get all goofy and lovestruck over some man. She'd had her man. They'd had a good marriage and raised a wonderful son. Romantic for her was over and done now. She was a grown-up, sensible woman, not some silly teenager.

It was after six when Nathan got home.

"It's about time you showed up," Calla said. "Dinner's almost ready."

"Yeah, I smelled your cooking all the way across the street and came running," her son teased.

He hurried to the bathroom to wash up as she set the table. Two plates, two forks, two knives, two spoons. It had been just the two of them now for almost five years. But two was an excellent number. She and Nathan were a team and they shared the same goal. Getting him through high school and into a good college. That goal had often seemed so far off that Calla had thought it would never happen. Now their dream was nearing realization. And it was as if all those years of reaching for it had gone by in a flash.

Nathan hurried to the table and took a seat. "Give me a pork chop before I bite into the table leg," he threatened.

Calla chuckled lightly as she seated herself and passed him the platter of meat. Everyone said that Nathan was just like her. But when she looked at him, she saw so much of her late husband. Nathan was lean and lanky. He had a bubbly humor that charmed everyone he met. But he also had a streak of kindheartedness that was as wide as Lake Michigan. Calla was absolutely certain he hadn't gotten *that* from her. And she worried where it might lead him.

"I guess you've been over at Mrs. Cleveland's place," Calla said with deliberate casualness. "Visiting her niece. That's very nice, of course, but you mustn't neglect your other friends."

Nathan eyed his mother with open amusement. "My other *friends* understand completely why I want to spend time with Jazleen."

Her son was grinning. Calla didn't like that much.

"She's pretty lonely," he continued. "It's bad enough to be going through a lot of stuff, but then to spend all your time alone—that just makes it worse."

"Isn't she making friends at school?"

Nathan hesitated slightly. "She's sort of blown school off."

"What do you mean by that?"

"She pretty much ignored it the last couple of years, and when she showed up this year to enroll, they transferred her to the alternative high school. That ticked her off. She said if she couldn't take classes with me, then there was no point going."

Calla raised an eyebrow. "That doesn't make any sense at all."

Nathan shrugged. "She was so far behind, she wasn't going to be able to keep up in my classes anyway," he said. "But it is kind of worthless to sit around all day watching TV, just waiting for me to get home."

Calla agreed with that. She was not happy, however, that the girl was planning her life, living her life around Nathan.

"What does Mrs. Cleveland say about her dropping out of school?"

"I don't think she knows, Mom."

"What do you mean? She must know."

Nathan shook his head. "Her job is way across town. She leaves to catch her train before seven in the morning and she doesn't get home until after five. She and Jazzy hardly say two words to each other. I seriously doubt they've talked this out together."

Calla's dinner was suddenly tasteless. "You know I'll have to tell her."

Her son nodded. "Yeah, I know. Jazzy really needs… she really needs something, someone…I don't know. Mom, she's clever and smart and doesn't have a lazy bone in her body. But she's just…you know…drifting without any direction."

Calla nodded. There were a lot of young people like that.

"I try to talk to her about college and the future and all the things that I'm working for," Nathan said. "I might as well be telling fairy tales. She doesn't see how any of it could ever apply to her."

"Well, it probably won't," Calla said. "If she can't stick it out in high school, then she'll never get a chance at college."

"But she could stick it out, Mom," Nathan said. "I know she could."

Calla wasn't so sure.

Saturday morning dawned sunny with a bright blue sky. Seated at the breakfast table in her robe, Calla lingered over her coffee. It was just laziness, she assured herself, and had nothing to do with the view outside her window. Her kitchen looked directly into Landry Sinclair's backyard, and the man himself was out there, clad in faded jeans and a sweatshirt that clung damply to his muscular torso. His sweat was well earned as he attacked the ground with a shovel and a hoe. He looked very different without his tailored suits. She'd always thought of him as tidy and professional. Not the kind of man to get his hands dirty.

He was certainly getting dirty this morning. And he looked really good doing it. Calla watched him as he worked, allowing herself the secret pleasure of lusting after a man who wasn't hers. She thought she'd left all that nonsense in the past. But somehow, from the moment Landry Sinclair moved into the neighborhood, she'd felt differently.

And she didn't like it one bit. Every woman on the block had already staked a claim. Calla hated to follow along with the crowd. And she despised the kind of mooning over men that a lot of women her age engaged in. It was one thing to be boy crazy at fourteen. It was downright undignified to be that way at forty.

Still, she could hardly take her eyes from the vision of Landry Sinclair sweating over a garden hoe.

A knock sounded at the front door. She glanced at

the clock. It was barely nine. She couldn't imagine who would be visiting so early. She went to peer through the peephole. The familiar figure standing on the porch was visible only in profile. Her long, thin legs and round backside were encased in tight jeans. Her skimpy jacket showed off her curves but wouldn't provide any protection if the weather turned colder. And her long dark hair was a flawless mix of braids and curls.

Her expression, however, even from the side, appeared wary and secretive.

Calla opened the door.

"Good morning, Jazleen."

The girl's suspicion toughened into something that looked like hostility.

"Where's Nathan?" she demanded with no other greeting.

"He's sleeping," Calla answered. "It's Saturday morning. That's what he does on Saturday mornings."

"We're going…someplace," Jazleen hedged. "He's supposed to be ready."

"He probably overslept. Come in and I'll wake him up."

"I'm okay on the porch," Jazleen said, her chin slightly in the air.

"Come in," Calla insisted, knowing the girl's hesitation to enter the house was because of her. Jazleen had been inside with Nathan many times.

Hesitantly she followed Calla. "I'll go wake him," Jazleen said.

"No!" Calla answered firmly. "You wait here, pour yourself a cup of coffee. I'll wake my son."

As she went up the stairs, Calla glanced back towards the girl. She stood in the doorway of the kitchen, her arms wrapped around her as if she were cold or protecting herself.

At the top of the stairs, Calla turned right and knocked on her son's door.

"Nathan? Nathan!"

An unintelligible rumbling was the only reply. Calla opened the door and peered into the shadows for an instant before crossing the darkened room and pulling up the shades. A wide shaft of sunlight revealed her son completely cocooned in a tangle of blankets.

He groaned.

"Better get up," Calla told him. "You've got company downstairs."

"Huh?" he asked, without bothering to poke his head out of the covers.

"Jazleen is here," she said. "Apparently you were going someplace together this morning."

Nathan moaned again and rolled over, flipping back the blankets to reveal his face and T-shirt clad torso.

"Oh yeah," he said. "I told her I would take her to Oak Street Beach. I couldn't believe she'd lived here all her life and never been."

Calla nodded.

With a sigh of determination, Nathan rolled out of bed. "Let me get a quick shower," he told his mother. "Tell her I'll be downstairs in fifteen minutes."

Calla left him to get ready and returned to the kitchen. Jazleen was still standing in the middle of the floor.

"Nathan says fifteen minutes," Calla told her. "Would you like a cup of coffee?"

"No," Jazleen answered too quickly.

"Are you sure?" Calla asked. "I'm going to have another cup."

Jazleen hesitated. "I don't mind," she said, finally.

It wasn't exactly "yes, please," but Calla decided it was the best excuse for manners that the girl could muster.

"Sit down," she told her as she set the cup on the table. "There's milk and sugar."

Jazleen reluctantly seated herself. Calla took the chair opposite her. The girl continued to eye her warily. The silence lengthened between them. Calla was racking her brain for a neutral subject and was just about to comment on the weather when Jazleen spoke.

"That man next door has got a shovel," she said. "I think he's burying something."

Calla glanced in the direction of the window. She couldn't see Landry Sinclair at this angle, but she could still perfectly recall the sight of the man.

"He's digging a garden," Calla said.

Jazleen's brow furrowed and she snorted in disbelief. "This time of year? Not likely. He's burying something."

So much for neutral conversation, Calla thought.

"Nathan said you two are headed for an outing to Oak Street Beach."

Jazleen didn't answer. She eyed Calla suspiciously and then sipped her coffee as if that gave her permission not to comment. Her eyes were widely set and a rich dark brown. She was wearing a bit too much make-up, but a cleft in her chin made her look vulnerable.

"We used to go to Oak Street Beach a lot when Nathan was a little boy," Calla told her. "Lots of fresh air and room to run around. On a crisp fall day it's absolutely the best. He would sit and just look at the boats on the water."

She paused, but again Jazleen said nothing.

"I'm sure that's what he wants to share with you,"

Calla continued. "Even if it does mean giving up a sleepy Saturday morning."

Calla was frustrated when the girl made no attempt to keep up her side of the conversation. She decided maybe questions and answers would be easier.

"Nathan says you watch a lot of TV?"

"Some."

"Have you seen anything good lately?"

She shook her head.

"I like those dancing shows," Calla told her. "But more often I prefer reading."

Jazleen sipped her coffee.

"Do you like to read?"

The girl shrugged.

"When I was your age, that was what I loved best."

Jazleen raised a brow. It wasn't exactly an eye roll, but Calla was fairly sure it had the same meaning.

"Do you know how to read?" Calla asked.

"Of course I do!" Jazleen snapped. "I'm not stupid."

"I didn't think that you were," Calla said. "But a lot of very smart people don't read, or don't read very well."

"I can read fine, thank you."

"Okay, good." Calla hesitated. "Nathan said you've dropped out of school."

"Maybe. I haven't decided."

"What does your aunt think about it?"

"I'd guess she'd think that it's none of her business," Jazleen declared. "And it's sure none of yours."

The young girl's expression was angry. Calla was not feeling very friendly herself.

"If you're seeing my son, then I make it my business," she answered.

"What? You trying to turn him into some mama's boy?"

"Every male on this earth is a mama's boy," Calla said. "He may love her or he may hate her, but there is nobody else in the world who can talk to a man the way his mama does."

Jazleen's jaw set tightly with anger.

"Nathan and I are very close," Calla told the girl quietly. "If you stay tight with him, you're going to have to deal with me. So maybe you should think about getting used to it."

After the teenagers left, Calla didn't even attempt to get back to lazy day musing. Saturdays were busy days with chores she put off all week, but she couldn't help thinking about Nathan and Jazleen. So it wasn't surprising that just after lunchtime, she headed across the street to have a chat with Gerty Cleveland.

The woman took her time getting to the door. The tiny apartment was crowded with furniture, but it was neat as a pin except for the area around the recliner that sported TV trays on either side loaded with food, drink, tissues, assorted junk and the remote control. As soon as Calla walked inside, Gerty returned to the chair and popped it into the raised position.

"I try to keep my feet up every minute that I'm home," she explained to Calla. "As it is, I'll be lucky to get five more years of work out of them."

It seemed to Calla it was probably already time for Gerty to stop working. Steel-gray hair covered her head, her hands shook and she didn't hear all that well.

"I wanted to talk to you about Jazleen."

"Say what?"

"I wanted to talk to you about Jazleen," she repeated a bit louder.

"Jazleen? She's a sweet girl," Gerty said. "I was real reluctant to take her. Her mama's no good. And my sister, her own grandma, gone to Jesus twenty years ago. She was living with my daughter, Val, for a month or two. But there was some kind of trouble with Val's man. So there was no one else and here she is. But she keeps the place tidied up, and when I get home from work, she's always got some kind of dinner for me. That's been nice, real nice."

"Did you know she's thinking of dropping out of school?"

"No, I didn't pay no attention to that. Guess if she's not going to school, she should get a job. That's what I did. I left school and got myself a job."

"Things were different back then," Calla told her. "Nowadays it's tough to find a job if you don't finish high school."

The old woman nodded absently. "That's likely true."

"You shouldn't let her drop out," Calla said.

"I hope she won't," Gerty said. "But truth to tell, as long as she don't get into no trouble, I'm tempted to just let her be."

Calla shook her head to disagree, but her neighbor forestalled her.

"You don't know the life that girl has lived," Gerty said. "She's had troubles like you and me have never seen. That doesn't happen to people and leave them unmarked. If she can find some happiness on her own, then I'm all for letting her have it."

Calla continued talking with Gerty for a half hour or more, but it was clear that the old woman had no plans for Jazleen's future and was only vaguely interested in the young woman's present.

"But you must be worried."

"The girl will be all right," Gerty assured her. "She'll find her way. I don't have the time or the energy to make sure she does this, that or the other. She's nearly grown, so she's on her own. Besides, she has that boy of yours to make do for her."

"What?"

"It was real smart of her to latch onto him," Gerty said. "He's got a lot of gumption and he's not afraid of hard work. He'll be like his daddy, a good family man. Jazleen is lucky in that."

"Nathan is off to college next year," Calla explained.

The older woman eyed her skeptically. "That's what you're hoping," she said. "But he seems mighty sweet on her."

Calla shook her head. "No, it's just a passing thing. It's not serious between them."

Gerty Cleveland didn't believe a word of that.

Calla left the woman's apartment and went straight to the supermarket to do her weekly shopping. The day had gotten significantly colder, but she found the chilly wind invigorated her.

It was too bad about Jazleen, she thought to herself. The girl might be stuck-up and rude, but she was still a girl. And someone Nathan seemed to think was special. But if she was pinning her hopes on snagging Calla's son, she was doomed to be disappointed. Jazleen would end up like a thousand other girls. Working at a menial job as she struggled to raise kids she could hardly support.

Calla decided it would be her goal to make sure that

none of those kids were on the way before she could get Nathan safely off to college.

By the time she'd made it home from the store and put the groceries away, she was tired. The house was cozy and warm. She settled herself on the couch with a book but hadn't read more than a half-dozen pages when her eyelids began to get heavy. She set her book open upside down on her chest and lay back on a throw pillow to catch a quick twenty winks. The glare from the reading lamp seemed to permeate her eyelids, so she switched it off and drifted into a comfortable nap.

Voices from the kitchen awakened her sometime later.

"Let me fix you something to warm you up."

"Just wrap me in your arms—that gets me about as warm as I need."

Nathan chuckled, a low masculine sound.

The ensuing silence spoke for itself. They both seemed a little breathless when the conversation resumed.

"What do you want to do?" Nathan asked.

"Uh…let's just sit together and talk," Jazleen replied.

He chuckled. "You haven't had enough talk from me already? I've been at it for hours."

"I love to hear you talk," she said.

"It's crazy how we never run out of things to say."

"Yeah, strange," she agreed. "But in a good way."

"That is, until I start talking about school, and then you just say nothing at all."

Jazleen hesitated. "It's a part of your life that I can't share."

"Of course you can," Nathan said. "We can share the fun of my senior year and graduation and me going off to college."

"I want to be happy for you," Jazleen said. "But the truth is, I don't want you to go off to college. If you go away, I won't have anybody."

"It's not like it's forever. And if I get into Northwestern, it's not that far away."

She made a huff of disagreement. "You might as well be going to the moon. If you really care about me like you say, you won't take one step off Canasta Street."

Calla couldn't keep listening. It was wrong to eavesdrop on Nathan, even by accident. She knew she wasn't supposed to hear any of what they'd said.

She reached up and turned the light back on. But instead of reading, she set her book on the coffee table and got up and left the room. She didn't speak to them or acknowledge that she'd heard them talking. But they knew.

It had been easy to walk away from the conversation. Less so to get it out of her head. And along with it came other voices.

"She's got your Nathan wrapped around her little finger."

"He's mighty sweet on that girl."

In the following weeks at work, Calla worried about it. Evenings at home, it colored her enthusiasm. College was what she and Nathan had worked for, waited for. Her son was going to graduate with honors. There was so much going on and Calla wanted to be celebrating. But she was worrying instead.

CHAPTER
❧ TWO ❧

Mid-October brought a blast of cold weather and two tickets for All-Academics Night. The local schools got together for one special evening to honor their top seniors. Nathan would be receiving a special citizenship award as well as his certificate as a National Merit Scholar.

"Two tickets?" Calla held them up in question.

"I've invited Jazzy," he told her. "Could you bring her with you? I'm afraid she won't show up if I just hand her a ticket and ask her to be there."

Calla selfishly didn't want to share this night with anyone. But if Nathan wanted the girl to go, Calla determined that she would.

She was less certain when Jazleen answered the door. Calla had on a conservatively cut wool suit in a chic coral color set off by a felt cloche hat with a matching ribbon.

Jazleen, on the other hand, was dressed in tight jeans, a low-cut blouse and a hoodie.

It was on the tip of Calla's tongue to suggest the girl find something else to wear, but she managed to keep the words from flying out of her mouth. She knew enough about teens to understand that criticizing hair or clothes was an open declaration of war.

The evening together could not have been called particularly congenial. Jazleen spoke when she was spoken to. And after three or four attempts at casual conversation, Calla decided that polite silence was probably better for the two of them anyway.

The auditorium was crowded with happy, optimistic families. The upbeat mood seemed to affect Jazleen adversely. Her jaw was set tightly with annoyance. Anyone who glanced in her direction was treated with suspicion.

What a charming girl! Calla thought sarcastically. Where was the smartness and sweetness that Nathan saw in her?

"Hey look, it's your neighbor," Jazleen said.

Calla glanced up to see Landry Sinclair coming up the aisle. He was dressed immaculately in a dark blue suit and blue-and-gold striped tie, a matching handkerchief peeking out of his breast pocket.

Jazleen snorted. "He looks like he's decked out for the prom."

Calla thought he looked just plain gorgeous. The opinion might have been mutual since the man stopped dead in his tracks when he caught sight of her. He stepped purposely in Calla's direction.

"Mrs. Middleton," he said. "How lovely you look tonight."

"Oh...thank you," Calla answered. She heard the silly breathlessness in her voice and chose words to counter it. "My son is receiving an award. So as a proud mama, I have to fix up enough not to embarrass him."

"You always look wonderful," the man told her. "It must be the sense of accomplishment that has you beaming." His gaze lingered on her just an instant longer than necessary, before he acknowledged Jazleen. "I don't believe we've met, but I've seen you in the neighborhood."

"Uh-huh," the girl offered lamely. She stared warily at his outstretched hand, then limply accepted the handshake.

"This is Jazleen," Calla offered as introduction when the teen said nothing."

The man's eyebrows went up. "Jazleen Coakley?"

The girl's jaw dropped. "Uh…yeah. How'd you know my name?"

"I know all my students," he answered. "Even the ones who don't show up at school."

"Your students?" Calla asked.

Landry Sinclair nodded. "I'm school principal at C.A."

"C.A.?"

"Cavitz Alternative," he answered. "We're a small high school, but we have our share of students winning awards."

Calla was genuinely surprised. "You're a school principal?"

He nodded.

The seats were filling up fast and someone wanted the one where Landry was standing.

"Perhaps I'll see you later," he said.

Calla didn't have time to answer, but she would have told him no. She had plans to spend the evening with her son. This was a big night for Nathan.

The evening was long as each student was allowed his or her moment in the sun. The teenagers thanked their parents, their teachers, their school counselors, their brothers and sisters and friends.

One young woman caught Calla's attention because she was from Landry Sinclair's Cavitz Alternative.

"I want to thank my teachers, who never gave up on

me," she said. "My baby boy, Keeton, whose sweet smile helps me stick to my priorities. And I want to thank my book group. It's so cool that you came to see me tonight. But then, that's what you're good at, being there for me. Sharing your lives and your hearts with me. Without you, I wouldn't be standing here."

As the audience politely applauded, a cluster of teenage girls rose to their feet whistling and cheering. Their enthusiasm rejuvenated the crowd.

Calla's long wait was worth it when it was finally Nathan's turn.

He looked so tall and so handsome in his suit. And so grown up.

When had that happened? Calla wondered to herself. When had her gangly teenage boy turned into such a young man? She had seen him every day, but now, looking up at him behind the podium, it was as if he were irrevocably changed.

She watched as his eyes scanned the crowd. When their gazes met, Nathan smiled.

"I stand here, happy and grateful for the future I see before me," he said. "And like my fellow students, I realize I didn't get here alone. I've worked hard. But the journey to this day didn't begin with me. It began with my mom and dad. Before I could speak my first word, they read to me and dreamed for me and planned for me to have opportunities that they never had. My father didn't live to see this night. But my mother is here and I dedicate this award to her as I say, 'Thanks, Mom, I won't let you down.'"

The crowd applauded as he stepped off the stage. Calla felt such a lift in her heart. She glanced toward Jazleen beside her. The girl was applauding, but what caught Calla's attention was the evidence of a tear in her eye. Somehow Calla couldn't imagine this angry, stubborn young woman to have a sentimental side. Then she realized that the emotion on the girl's face was not pride, but fear.

At the end of the long evening, Nathan caught up with the two of them in the crowded foyer. He was happy, excited. He offered Calla a dutiful kiss on the cheek. Then he whirled Jazleen in the air. Laughing, smiling, the girl was absolutely radiant. She bore no resemblance to the slouching, sullen young woman Calla had spent the evening beside. Nathan's presence had somehow transformed Jazleen. And when he clasped her in his arms and kissed her, it seemed as natural as if he'd done it a million times.

"Mom, some of the kids are going to make a party of it at Grace Church Coffee House," he said. "We won't be late."

He wasn't asking permission and it wasn't at all

what Calla had planned. But somehow she found herself smiling.

"Have a good time," she told them.

The two scampered off like the children they almost were. Calla headed to the door herself.

"Mrs. Middleton!" she heard a low-pitched voice call out behind her. She knew who it was before she turned. She took a deep breath and schooled her expression into casual unconcern.

"Mr. Sinclair," she said.

He was smiling. "Call me Landry," he suggested. "I get Mr. Sinclair all day long, and to be completely honest, I get tired of hearing it."

"All right…Landry," she agreed. "I'm Calla."

"I know," he answered quietly. "The most stately and elegant flower in the entire garden."

"Oh my goodness," she said, shaking her head. "That's a bit over the top, don't you think?"

"Is it?" he asked. "I apologize. I can only blame it on years of writing bad poetry as an undergraduate."

He was standing very close. Close enough that Calla felt enveloped in the clean masculine scent of him. It was exhilarating. Almost scarily so.

"May I see you home?"

"Oh no."

"No? You won't let me see you home?"

"Oh, I…"

"Please don't say that it's out of my way. I live right next door," he pointed out.

"I just…I just wouldn't want people to talk."

He grinned at her. "People always talk," he said. "Sometimes I feel it's almost my Christian duty to give them subject matter."

Calla laughed aloud. She couldn't help it.

"All right, Landry," she said. "Why don't you walk me home."

Calla felt self-conscious while they were inside the school building and in the lighted area of the lawn in front. But once they reached the anonymity of the sidewalk, she relaxed. She made no attempt, however, to take his arm when he offered it. It was better, she was certain, simply to walk beside him.

His hand brushed casually against her own. The idea that he might take it in his was enough to make her fold her arms across her chest.

"Are you cold?" he asked.

"No, no, I'm fine," she said. Hastily, she grasped at a neutral subject. "I noticed that you put in a garden."

He nodded and smiled. "I think it must be all the farming in my blood."

"You must be from Florida or someplace. Chicago winters are too harsh to grow things."

"Originally I'm from out west, but I've been here in Chicago ten years."

"Then you must know you can't grow a winter garden without a hothouse."

"Actually, I planted bulbs," he said. "I do it every autumn."

"What kind of bulbs?"

"They're a metaphor," he answered, and then he laughed. "They're daffodils, but I think of my fall planting as being like my students."

"In what way?"

"I plant them in the fall, and then all winter long when it's cold and miserable and every day is a challenge, I remember that just because I can't see any growth, my flowers are all still making progress, and by the time spring gets here, they will be beautiful. I expect the same to be true of my students."

Calla smiled at him. "That's a nice thought."

"Yes, it is," he agreed. "And in the day-to-day darkness of many of these young people's lives, a nice thought is sometimes the only thing there is to hang on to."

Calla knew that was probably true. There were teenagers in the neighborhood, guys and girls that Nathan had played games with as a child, who now seemed directionless and trapped in a dead-end existence. But Calla didn't want to talk about that tonight. The air was too crisp and the stars too bright to dwell on the sadness in the world. She changed the subject.

"So is this faith in springtime based on actual farming experience?" she asked. "Somehow it's hard to picture you in a straw hat, holding a pitchfork with a sprig of hay seed in the corner of your mouth."

Landry laughed.

"Did you grow up on a farm?" she asked.

"Me? No, I grew up in the high country—Flagstaff, Arizona."

"Arizona? I've never met anyone from there."

"Now you have," he answered. "My parents were both professors at Northern Arizona University. My parents, my brother and my sister still live there. But I did spend a lot of summers out at my grandparents' farm in Arkansas."

"Aha! So perhaps there *is* some mud on your boots. What kind of farm was it?"

"A pretty small one," he answered. "But they did harvest peaches and strawberries and almost every kind of greens you could think of. It was a great experience for a kid. Teaches you a lot of lessons about working hard and having patience and not giving up in the face of failure. Good things to know in life."

Calla nodded in agreement.

"What brought you to Chicago?" she asked.

Landry sighed dramatically. "The only thing that can ever jolt a man out of his comfortable little world—a beautiful woman." He chuckled.

"Oh?"

"I followed her here about ten years ago," he said. "Our romance didn't last six months, but my infatuation with this city just gets stronger every year."

On the sidewalk ahead of them, the light from Cal & Cecil's Café spilled out on the concrete.

"Let me buy you a cup of coffee," he said. "It will warm you up."

She shook her head. "It would just keep me awake all night."

"Decaf?" he suggested. "Or wait, there is nothing in this world more guaranteed to make you sleep than a big slice of Cecil's lemon meringue pie."

"I should probably get on home."

"Why? Your son won't be there and I doubt very seriously if you'll get one wink of sleep before he comes in. Coffee and pie, by way of a small celebration."

Calla was still protesting halfheartedly as he steered her into the small, well-frequented little diner.

They took a narrow booth some distance from the door. Landry ordered a couple of pieces of pie and coffee, decaf for her. The place was warm and cozy and friendly and she had a smart, good-looking man hanging on to her every word. It was hard for any woman not to appreciate that.

"So you know about me," Landry said. "Arizona boy who sought love in Chi-town and found a career instead. What about you?"

"Me? There's not that much to tell," Calla assured him. She spoke briefly about working for Dr. Walker.

"What about your husband?" he asked.

"Mark? He passed away five years ago."

Landry nodded. "I gathered that from Nathan's speech. What happened? Was he ill?"

"It was an accident," she told him. "He was a postman walking on Grand Avenue making his daily delivery. A woman's car skidded out of control and came flying up on the sidewalk."

"I'm so sorry."

Calla nodded as she had a million times before when sympathy was expressed. "He didn't suffer. The paramedics told me that he died instantly."

"And you've been on your own ever since."

"Yes," she admitted. "Making a living and raising a son keep me busy."

He nodded slowly. "Too busy to make time for a man in your life?"

His question was as direct as his gaze.

"I...uh... " Calla could feel herself blushing.

"Or maybe you've just been waiting for the right guy to come along," he suggested.

She wasn't sure how she should answer that. He saved her from having to by changing the subject.

"What did you think of All-Academics Night?" he asked.

"It was very long," she answered. "But I guess that's the good news. Lots of our young people are doing well."

He nodded agreement.

"Your son is a good public speaker," Landry said. "He was one of the most comfortable at the podium."

Calla nodded. "He's always been that way. My husband and I used to debate whether he was destined for politics or the preacher's pulpit."

"Which do you think?"

"Neither. These days all he talks about is business. I think he wants to be somebody's CEO before he's thirty."

Landry nodded encouragingly. "A smart, determined young guy with a good work ethic," he said. "We need all we can get of those."

It was a compliment of sorts and Calla smiled, accepting it as such.

"I noticed the young people from the alternative high school were not too shy in front of the microphone either," she said.

"It's a little intimidating for them to come back to a

turf where perhaps they didn't do so well," he said. "But we talked about it, set it as a challenge. I think they all did well."

"I was especially impressed by the girl who was inspired by her baby," Calla said. "And she thanked her book group. That was a surprise."

Landry nodded. "The book group is a great thing. It really adds a lot to their success both in and out of school."

"I love to read," Calla admitted. "I haven't been in a book club for years. But I always enjoyed it. It's fun hanging out with people who share your interest."

"This group is not exactly for young book lovers," he said. "Although most of the members probably are now. They sure didn't start out that way."

"Oh?"

"They're in a program called Literature for All of Us. It was started by a woman from Evanston," he said. "She spent a lot of years leading book clubs just like the ones you're thinking about. And then one day somebody suggested that she share her talents and her experience with at-risk young women. With all the challenges in their lives, reading a book and sitting down to discuss it is just not something that usually comes up."

"I guess not," Calla said.

"And it's more than just sharing stories and eating

cookies," he said. "It gives these young women, sometimes for the first time in their lives, a chance to get outside of their circumstances and approach the world from a new perspective. And to express themselves among their peers on a new level. I've been impressed with the outcome."

"Well, your well-spoken award winner was very impressive."

"She was, wasn't she," he said. "There are groups for boys now, too. It's a proven idea that really works. And there are side benefits like improved reading skills and better peer-to-peer communication. It's just a great program. I wish we could get all our students into groups."

The waiter arrived with their pie and the two of them ate congenially as they talked.

They discussed the weather, the neighborhood, the problems with the transit service. Calla told Landry about her job and its challenges. He related some of the problems in his own work. Eventually they got around to a book discussion themselves. Calla recommended a story she'd just read. Landry mentioned a movie that had just come out on a similar subject.

"I haven't been to the movies in…I don't know how long," she admitted.

"Really? Well, I'll just have to get you to go with me. I hate eating popcorn alone."

CHAPTER
❧THREE❧

Calla wasn't sure if Landry's suggestion was the same as asking her on a date. But she'd declined anyway, saying how busy the season had become. And it was true for the next two weeks, at least for Nathan. Senior year was proving to be full of tests and papers and deadlines of all types. And when he added to that parties, get-togethers and a girlfriend, he barely had time to spend with his mom.

Calla had grown accustomed to seeing a smile on her son's face, and when she noticed it wasn't there, she had to ask.

"What's wrong, Nathan?"

He shrugged and shook his head.

She figured it was just a bad mood. But when days went by and the dark cloud only lifted sporadically, she knew she had to say something. She waited up for him, yawning in front of the TV until he returned home from being out with Jazleen.

"Hi, Mom, you're still up?"

She shrugged. "I can't sleep a wink anyway until I hear you come in," she told him, remembering that Landry Sinclair had realized that about her immediately.

"Well, I'm home now," he said. "So you'd better get some sleep. The morning comes early."

It was a line she often said to him. But she made no move to go upstairs.

"Son, what's going on with you?" she asked him.

"Nothing."

"Something."

He shook his head. "Really, it's mostly nothing," he assured her. "It just feels like something."

"Are you having trouble at school?"

"Oh no, everything is going great," he said. "Senior year is the best."

"Are you getting worried about college? It's still too early to get an acceptance."

"No, I'm not worried. I'm excited. It's almost un-believable that it's really happening. I can hardly wait."

"Then what is it?"

Nathan hesitated. "Okay. But if I tell you, I don't want you giving me any advice or doing anything about it or butting into things."

"Is that what I do?"

"Sometimes," he answered. "When you think you need to. But this is one of those things that I need to deal with on my own."

"Okay," she said. "No advice. No meddling."

"It's Jazzy," he said.

Calla's heart caught in her throat. *Please don't let that girl be pregnant!* she prayed silently.

"You know I really like her a lot," Nathan said. "I like being with her and she's…she's special, Mama. I know you don't like her that much, but she's special to me."

Calla nodded, biting her tongue.

"But she's just not on board with my future," he continued. "She doesn't like me to even talk about it. And she's getting so…clingy or…jealous…or something. She calls me twenty times a day, and if I don't pick up or call right back at the next class change, she thinks I'm mad at her or I'm with some other girl or I want to break up. I can't pick up the phone every time she calls. I'm in school or I'm studying and I need to be doing that, not talking or texting."

He looked to his mother for agreement and got it.

"And when we're together it's like Jazzy can't decide

between starting a fight or crawling into my lap." Nathan sighed heavily. "I've told her a million times that I'm crazy about her. That I think she's the one for me. But…but not now. I'm not ready to be with her now."

Calla considered thoughtfully. "This is not advice," she said, prefacing her words. "But I would like to remind you what you were like just a few years ago. Remember when it was so hard to see past the next weekend or even the next day? You'd know for a month that you had a book report, and the day before it was due you'd just be sitting down to work on it."

Nathan chuckled. "Yeah, I was a kid. Kids are like that."

"They are," Calla agreed. "And although I think Jazleen is a very grown-up girl in a lot of ways, she's not looking five years in the future the way you are. She's looking at next fall and she sees you leaving her and it scares her."

"It's not like I'm going to the moon." Nathan spoke hastily, as if he'd said as much before.

"It might as well be the moon for her," Calla said. "Her world has gotten very, very small. It's shrunk down to little more than her great-aunt, Canasta Street and you. When you leave, that's a big chunk of her life gone missing."

"What am I going to do, Mom?" he asked. "I really…

I really…I think I…I love her." He made the confession with predictable hesitation. "I don't want to lose her. But I don't want to give up my dreams either."

"No, of course you can't give up your dreams," Calla said. They were her dreams, too. And she wasn't about to let them go. "You just have to try to understand what she's going through. And you've got to see if you can figure out a way to make her world bigger."

"How do I do that?"

"Well, she needs friends."

Nathan shrugged. "I don't think she wants any," he said. "I've introduced her to all the girls I know from my school. She's not interested in any of them and seems almost suspicious of most of them."

"Maybe you could ask one of them to include her in stuff they do," Calla said. "Once they get to know each other, they might find things in common."

"I can try," he said. "But I don't know. Jazzy never lets people see how sweet and funny she is. If people knew her, they'd like her. But she seems determined that nobody gets to know her."

Calla felt a wave of sympathy, but it was all for her son. "If you love her, you need to be there for her, son. But nobody can be everything to her."

"I just wish I could think of something to make it better."

"I'll try thinking too," Calla promised.

Over the next few days, Calla did try to think of something that might improve the situation, though if she was being honest about it, she would have admitted that a lot of her solutions involved Nathan finding another girlfriend. But she tried to keep that sort of wishful thinking at bay. It wasn't all that unusual for the mother of a young man not to be impressed with his choice of girlfriend. Mark's mama hadn't been all that crazy about her. But mamas could be wrong, and Calla was willing to trust Nathan's judgment over her own.

Friday afternoon, Calla walked from the bus stop down Canasta Street, thinking about the weekend ahead of her. There had been a nice break in the cold weather and everyone on the street seemed to be taking advantage of it.

She should invite Jazleen to have dinner with them on Sunday. She hated to give up her only guaranteed alone time with her son. It was the weekend and the girl would be stuck to him like glue. But the only way that Jazleen would ever feel comfortable with her was if they spent time together.

She interrupted her own musings to wave at old Mr. Whitten as he sat on his porch.

The Carnaby children were all running around like banshees, their coats flapping open in the afternoon sun.

When she saw Mrs. Gamble and Eunice sitting on their porch, she called out to them.

"Afternoon!"

She assumed they would invite her to sit with them for a few minutes on a gorgeous day, but surprisingly they did not. In fact, they both just stared at her as if she'd grown two heads.

Calla was puzzled. At least she was until she reached her own gate. Sitting on her porch steps, dressed in sport slacks, a dark cable-knit sweater and brown suede jacket, was Landry Sinclair. He looked good even dressed down. He had a book in his hands and glanced up from his reading as she approached the gate. His smile was heart-melting.

Oh my God, she thought to herself. *No wonder Eunice looked so peeved.*

"What are you doing here?" she asked him.

"Waiting for you."

Warily she entered the yard and walked up the sidewalk. "What's going on?" she asked.

"Nothing," he answered. "Of course you couldn't prove that by our neighbors. Every eye on the street has been focused on me since the minute I walked up to your porch. I can't decide if they think I'm going to rob the place or that I haven't realized my house is the one next door."

His grin was absolutely infectious. Calla couldn't help but smile back at him.

"Would you…would you like to come in?"

"No thanks, I've got some things to do over at my place, but I wanted to ask if tonight was good for that movie date we talked about?"

She was thrilled. And mentally berated herself for the feeling. She was no giddy teenager. She should remind him of that right now before he got the wrong idea about where this was going. He might be interesting to talk to, but she wasn't on the hunt for a new man.

"I'm not a movie person," she answered. "I haven't gone to see one in years."

"Why not?"

The question should have been expected, but wasn't. Calla was forced to answer without seriously thinking about it.

"Mark, my late husband—he couldn't sit still that long," she said. "He needed to be busy all the time. Spending a couple of hours in an uncomfortable chair watching a screen was near torture to him."

Landry listened and nodded. "That's why he didn't go. Why don't you?"

"I suppose I just got out of the habit," she answered finally.

"Then let's get you back in," he said. "They're showing the film version of a book I just read and I'm really interested in seeing it." He told her the title.

"Oh, I loved that book," Calla said, then hesitated. "Well, I don't know exactly how I can say I 'love' something that was so tragic. But it was certainly a story that stuck with me."

"Aren't you interested in seeing how a director would handle it?"

She shrugged. "Well, yes, I am curious. But I can always wait for the DVD."

Landry shook his head. "I'll pick you up at seven."

Left with no chance of refusal, Calla agreed. She made her way inside not quite believing the reality of her first date in over twenty years. She couldn't help smiling.

And that grin stayed on her face all through preparations for an eat-and-run dinner. She left more than enough for Nathan on the stove.

Up in her bedroom, Calla fretted over what exactly to wear. The first thing she put on looked way too dressy. It was fine for church, but people were very casual at the movies. She changed into slacks and a blouse, but she didn't like the way that looked either. The more clothes she tried on, the more nervous she got. And as she got nervous, she became almost resentful. She was a grown woman. She shouldn't have to get all dolled up for some silly man. She didn't want a man. She enjoyed being on her own. Her life was fine, just her and Nathan.

But none of those rationalizations kept her from trying on everything in her closet until she finally chose an outfit. Her hands shook as she hooked the latch on her necklace. Fight or flight reaction was zizzing through her bloodstream and there were butterflies in her stomach as she walked downstairs. She stepped into the living room and inadvertently caught Nathan and Jazleen on the couch in a passionate embrace.

Calla was more startled than shocked, but the noise that escaped her lips did sound scandalized. The young couple guiltily separated. Unsure of what to do, Calla left the room. In the safety of the kitchen, she paced. She could hear their furtive whispering and the distinct sound of nervous giggling.

She tidied up a counter that was already neat, until she heard her son's voice behind her.

"We were just kissing, Mom." Nathan's voice was defensive.

Calla turned and gave him what she hoped was a reassuring smile. "I know," she said. "I trust you." Then she lowered her voice to add, "Just remember she's only seventeen and you have four years of college ahead of you."

Calla turned away quickly, as if the counter desperately needed her attention. If Nathan was going to roll his eyes or make some other impatient response, she didn't want to see it. Her son was nearly a grown man. She wanted to treat him with the respect he deserved.

"So are you two staying in tonight?" she asked.

He nodded. "Yeah, we're going to watch the game."

Calla idly wondered if Jazleen was also a fan of the NBA or just interested in more snuggling on the couch.

"You look nice. Where are you off to? Is something happening at the church tonight or are you meeting up with the ladies from your office?"

"I'm going to the movies," Calla said.

Nathan's eyebrows went up. "The movies? I didn't think you liked movies."

"I don't even know, it's been so long since I've gone."

"Are you going by yourself?"

"No, with the next-door neighbor."

"Eunice?" Nathan snorted. "Voluntarily putting up with that woman for hours is not a night out, it's a path to sainthood."

"I'm not going with Eunice," Calla said. She was reluctant to say the words out loud. "I'm going with Landry Sinclair."

"Who?"

"Landry Sinclair, the guy that lives next door." Calla gestured toward the window.

Nathan stared at her wide-eyed. "Is this a date?"

Calla stumbled over her reply.

"It *is* a date," her son declared, incredulous.

"We're just two people who enjoy each other's company and want to see a movie."

Nathan frowned. "I don't know if this is a good idea," he said. "Who is this guy? What does he want from you?"

"He's our next-door neighbor," Calla answered. "And it seems as if he wants the pleasure of my company."

Nathan was shaking his head.

"I like him." The statement came from Jazleen in the doorway. Jazleen. Her typically sullen expression was now replaced with a more thoughtful one.

"What do you know about him?" Nathan asked her.

Jazleen shrugged. "I saw him at your awards thing. He's okay. He's got a good job. He treated your mama with respect. And he didn't pretend like I was invisible. So if your mama wants to date him, what's it to you?"

Nathan clearly did not appreciate his girlfriend chiming her two cents into the discussion. But he was saved from having to say so by a knock on the door. Because Jazleen was closest, she took it upon herself to answer.

"Oh hi," Calla heard Landry say. "Nice to see you again...Jazleen."

"Well, it's pretty nice getting a look at you, too," the girl answered. "You must be the hot date from next door."

Landry cleared his throat a bit self-consciously and gave a halfhearted chuckle.

Jazleen let him in and ushered him into the kitchen. His dark eyes met Calla's from across the room and she felt herself blushing like a schoolgirl.

Landry addressed her son as he offered his hand. "Nathan."

The manners instilled by his mother made it impossible for the teenager to do anything but accept the handshake. Landry then moved to stand beside Calla. He didn't touch her in any way, but his mere closeness seemed to say, "we are together."

The few minutes of polite chitchat were stilted. Only Jazleen seemed completely relaxed, as if she were grateful to have the focus on someone else.

When she and Landry finally made their goodbyes and were able to get out of the house, Calla was too relieved to even remember how nervous and jittery she'd been about going on this date.

Landry walked beside her as they talked about the

weather. The sunny afternoon had turned into a very chilly evening, but Calla enjoyed the warmth of male-female companionship. She hadn't realized how much she'd missed it.

They took the L, the elevated train, into a downtown neighborhood. The stop was only a few blocks from the movie theater and they got their tickets and were headed inside in plenty of time.

Landry bought a huge bucket of popcorn.

"Two human beings could never actually consume that much," Calla warned him.

He laughed and nodded in agreement. "The guy told me we get free refills on this one, so who knows."

In the darkness of the movie theater, they sat close together. As previews played, Landry leaned closer and asked her, "Should we see that one, too?"

"Okay," she replied.

"It's a date then," he said. "What about this one?"

The next trailer was even better than the previous.

"That looks good."

"Then it's a date," he said.

When the final preview came on, he leaned close once more. "Third time is a charm," he told her. "Why don't you agree to see this one with me, too."

"It's not showing until spring," she pointed out.

"I'm still going to be on Canasta Street next spring," he said. "Are you still going to be available?"

Fortunately the movie started and Calla turned her attention to it without answering.

The director had chosen not to deal with all of the abuse horrors that had been in the book. The ones he did address were shocking enough. Like the book, the movie was filled with wrenching emotions, anger and disgust. And yet the ending was somehow hopeful. The film grabbed the audience by the throat and refused to let go. Yet Calla didn't think the movie was as powerful as the author's written words had been, and she told Landry so as they filed out.

He took her hand in his own. "Our minds can capture a scene much more completely than the most sophisticated camera," he agreed. "But at least the movie was mostly true to the spirit of the book."

Outside the theater the night had a surprise waiting for them. The sky was filled with big, fluffy snowflakes that drifted lazily toward the sidewalk.

Calla fastened the top button of her coat. She wasn't cold, but when Landry wrapped a protective arm around her, she didn't pull away.

In the glistening darkness they walked slowly back to the train.

"Would you like to do something else?" he asked her.

"We could go to a club and listen to some music. Or we could find a place to do some dancing?"

"I don't really feel like a lot of noise," she said.

"Me neither," he admitted. "I just don't want to take you home. I enjoy talking to you."

Calla didn't answer, but felt much the same.

"How about we stop in here," he said.

She glanced at the glass-fronted building. "Ice cream? You want to stop for ice cream while it's snowing?"

He shrugged. "I know we'll have the place to ourselves. And it fits in perfectly with my evil plan of getting you alone." He added a melodramatic malevolent chuckle and feigned twirling a nonexistent mustache.

Calla laughed. "You're a lunatic."

"Yes, but one who will feed you ice cream."

She chose pistachio almond and Landry went for Rocky Road. They sat in a table near the window where they could watch the snow come down as they chatted and enjoyed their late-night snack.

"So Nathan didn't seem all that comfortable with the idea of you dating," he said.

Calla shrugged. "I think it caught him off guard. And…and things are challenging for him right now."

"How so?"

"His future is coming at him headlong," she said. "And breaking away from the old neighborhood is always hard.

Added to that, he's very stuck on his girlfriend and she doesn't want him going anywhere."

Landry nodded. "Relationships are tough for everybody. And the younger you are, the more complicated they seem."

"Yes, I suppose so," Calla agreed with a sigh. "They have hit a rough patch, and to be quite honest, my first thought was I hoped they would break up. But I can't bear to see Nathan hurt. He believes there is something special in this girl, something unique and worthwhile. So I'm trying to think that way, too."

"What's her story?" Landry asked.

Calla shook her head. "I don't really know," she said. "Just lots of rumors. Her mother's been bad news for a long time. I think Jazleen's been passed around among her relatives. And then a few months ago she came here to live with her great-aunt. The aunt is nice enough. I think she genuinely cares about the girl. But somehow not enough. I guess her plate of problems was already pretty full when she was forced to take Jazleen. Now I think she's just waiting for her to turn eighteen so she can turn her out."

Landry nodded. "There's a lot of that going on."

"Jazleen doesn't have any friends," Calla said. "She has no one she can count on, except Nathan."

"All that pressure on a teenage boyfriend—it never

works. No one person can be everything to somebody else."

Calla nodded. "I keep thinking about that young woman from your school, the one with the book group. I wish Jazleen had something like that."

"Well, she could have if she came back to school."

"She could?"

"Sure, we've got a new group just getting started. I could have a place made for her, but she has to come to school."

Calla shook her head. "She sure doesn't seem interested in school."

"Maybe the book group could spark her interest," he said.

"What would it be like?"

"Most of the girls are young moms who were out part of last year either having their babies or caring for them. This is their chance to get back into a school setting. A lot of these young women are as isolated as Jazleen is, no friends, not enough family support. They might be able to be there for each other."

"That would be great," Calla said. "But nobody can make the girl go back to school if she doesn't want to."

Landry nodded. "I guess that's going to be your job. I'll get a place for her in the group and you get her there."

"Me? I'm not the person to tell her what to do."

"I guess you'll have to," Landry told her. "Because nobody else is going to do it. If we want flowers in the spring, we have to get those bulbs in the ground right now."

CHAPTER
❧ FOUR ❧

C alla didn't know exactly how she was going to broach the subject of going back to school and getting involved in the book group. Her first plan involved the easy way out. She'd tell Nathan and he'd tell his girlfriend to go and she would.

Of course, nothing was ever easy.

"She doesn't like the idea of going to an alternative high school," Nathan said. "Jazzy says they're only for misfits and criminals. And she's not that big on reading. I don't think she'd be interested in a book club."

"It's not really a book club for people who already love reading," Calla explained. "It's more a book club for young women who haven't even thought about reading."

He shrugged. "Look, I don't think she'll go. But you can ask her."

"I was hoping that you would," Calla replied.

"Me?" Nathan looked up from his breakfast cereal. "Not a chance."

"Why not?"

"Things are just not that good between us," he said. "She's in this weird place. She wants to be with me every minute. But everything I say or do seems to annoy her. If I suggested it, she'd think I was trying to get rid of her or change her or...or something. I'm just laying low and letting things work out. Isn't that what you told me to do, Mom?"

It *had* been what she told him. And he was probably right about her reaction. Calla needed to be the one to convince her. She decided to try the direct approach, and if that didn't work, she'd play it by ear.

She made arrangements to leave work early the next Monday. She wanted to go by the Cleveland apartment before either Gerty or Nathan had gotten home.

She knocked on the door of 2B. She could hear the sounds of a game show on the television. A shadow momentarily passed across the peephole and then the door opened abruptly. Jazleen's eyes were wide with fright.

"Is Nathan all right?" she asked.

"Oh yes, yes, Nathan is fine," Calla answered. "I didn't come here about Nathan."

Jazleen sighed with relief, then immediately her expression turned puzzled.

"What are you doing here?"

"I wanted to talk to you about something."

Jazleen's gaze became wary. She leaned indolently against the doorjamb.

"What do you want to talk about?"

"May I come in?"

With a reluctant shrug, she invited Calla inside.

The place was neat as a pin, and from the tiny kitchen came the warm and homey smell of pinto beans boiling on the stove.

Jazleen flounced across the room and seated herself cross-legged on the couch. She glanced at Calla and then deliberately turned her attention to the game show, as if she intended to ignore the woman's presence completely.

Calla, giving herself maternal license, picked up the remote control and silenced the room.

"I was watching that."

"I want to talk to you about something," Calla said. "It shouldn't take long."

Jazleen's expression was tight-lipped and defiant. "I'm not your child," she pointed out. "Don't think you can boss me around the way you do Nathan. Nobody tells *me* what to do."

"I didn't come here to give any orders," Calla said as gently as she could manage. "I came to extend an invitation."

"An invitation?"

"Yes. Do you remember the girl at the All-Academics Night, the one from Cavitz Alternative High School?"

"Uh, yeah, sort of."

"Remember she had her book group there and they all stood up and cheered for her."

"Oh yeah, that was totally lame."

"It was? I thought it was pretty wonderful. All those girls supporting one another."

"Don't believe it. You can't trust a bunch of females. I know that for sure."

Calla was beginning to think Jazleen didn't trust anyone—except maybe Nathan. How sad was that?

"There's a new book group just starting up," Calla continued, undaunted. "I thought you might be interested in attending."

"A book group?" Jazleen's question was incredulous.

"Yes. It would be an hour and a half each week. You have to be attending Cavitz Alternative, but being in the book club would ease you into a new school situation. It would give you a ready-made group to be a part of, and I'm sure you'd make some new friends."

Calla was smiling. Jazleen was not.

"I don't want to go to Cavitz Alternative," she said. "I don't care anything about some book group. And I don't need any friends."

"I think it might be good for you," Calla said. "Nathan is so busy and I know he talks about what he's doing a lot. This would give you a chance to talk about what you're doing."

"It's none of your business what we talk about."

Calla felt her own temper rising. This girl *was* none of her business and she didn't know why she was even trying. Then she reminded herself that she was trying because of Nathan. She was trying because Nathan believed in Jazleen. She needed to believe in her, too. And she had to find a way to get through to her.

"It's very important to me that you start back to school," Calla said. "And this book club is a great chance for you. Landry Sinclair is making a special effort to get you placed in the group."

Jazleen's jaw dropped open and her expression changed. She eyed Calla in silence for one long minute and then she smiled.

"Wait a minute," she said. "Oh, I see what's going

on. I didn't get it, but, of course, now it makes perfect sense."

"What?" Calla asked.

"This book group…why you're asking me to do this?"

Calla stared at her. She had no idea what the teenager meant.

"This is for Landry Sinclair," Jazleen stated. "Your *boyfriend* wants me back in school, so you're doing this to impress him."

"No, of course not," Calla said quickly.

"Yes, absolutely yes," Jazleen said. "You can't fool me."

Jazleen was grinning. Calla didn't think she recalled her smiling at anybody except Nathan.

"You want a favor from me," Jazleen said. "That's what this is. You want something and you're trying to pretty it all up to make me think it's for me, but it's really for you. It's for you to show off to your man."

The girl found that delightfully funny.

Calla was about to deny it, but instinct stilled her tongue. She realized she had a better chance of convincing Jazleen when she was laughing than when she was defensive.

"Well, I do know that he wants you back in school," she said. "And it would make me look pretty good if I could get you to go."

"I knew it!"

"So what do you think?" Calla asked her. "Could you do this for me? It would really mean a lot."

Jazleen hesitated. "If I did, you would owe me, big time!"

Calla nodded. She sent a wordless appeal to heaven that the payback would be worth it.

"Okay, I'll try it," Jazleen told her. "But I'm not promising to stick it out for the whole school year."

Calla nodded calmly in agreement, but she felt a sense of elation. And she could hardly wait to share news of her success.

She went home and spent the rest of the afternoon taking care of household chores and glancing out the front window at every opportunity.

Finally she saw Landry going into his house. She hurriedly checked her hair and makeup and then walked over to his front door, as bold as brass. Maybe the whole neighborhood was watching, but she couldn't have cared less.

He ushered her inside immediately.

"Where is your coat? It's freezing out there."

"I was too excited to grab it," she admitted. "I had to come tell you. I planted a bulb today."

He raised his eyebrows in surprise and grinned broadly at her.

"That's great!"

"Jazleen has agreed to attend Cavitz Alternative and she's willing to be involved in the book group."

"Wow, you are a miracle worker," he said.

Calla laughed and feigned a curtsy.

"Sit down. Let me fix you some...coffee? Hot tea? Hot chocolate?"

Calla opted for the last, which suited her mood perfectly. She felt like a kid just in from the cold on a winter afternoon.

Landry's tiny kitchen was only big enough for one person to move around in. It was separated from the living room area by a narrow breakfast bar with two stools. Calla took a seat on one and watched him. The place was clean and neat, Spartan in the way that only a single man could be. His one concession to decoration was the pot of African violets growing underneath the fluorescent light above the counter.

Calla noticed that he prepared the chocolate the old-fashioned way, melting sugar and semisweet chunks into the milk. He stirred it carefully to heat it without allowing it to scorch.

"I always use instant," she admitted.

He nodded. "I used to, too. But it's so quick and easy, I was drinking more than my share." Landry patted his midriff. "Most guys get forgiven for a beer gut at a certain age. I'm not sure that a hot chocolate paunch is ever acceptable."

Calla smiled. In his shirtsleeves, Landry didn't look in any danger of putting on weight. He was lean and trim, not heavily muscled like a man who spent a lot of time in the gym. Instead he had the firm body of a man who kept busy and active.

A rich scent filled the little kitchen as he poured the steaming hot chocolate in the saucepan into heavy mugs. He set both on the counter and then came around to sit on the stool next to Calla.

She tasted her drink and made an almost involuntary sound of pleasure. "Mmmm."

Landry smiled.

"This is almost as good as the news that Jazleen is coming to school," he said.

Calla chuckled. "It is that good."

"Yes it is," he agreed.

She took a sip of her chocolate, pleased. "So my job is done," she said. "The rest is up to you and Literature for All of Us."

"What?" Landry asked. "You're thinking that your part is finished?"

"I've planted my bulb," she pointed out. "Now all I have to do is wait for the springtime."

He raised a skeptical eyebrow.

"I don't think it quite works that way," he told her.

"What do you mean?"

"Once you've got your bulb planted, you're going to have to guard the ground where you put it," he said. "You can't let the rain wash it out or the squirrels dig it up or somebody pave over it with a concrete parking lot."

Calla laughed. "I don't think there'll be any parking lots going up around Jazleen."

Landry shook his head. "For every person trying to do the right thing for these kids, there's another person who's working against them and two more who just don't care. You've gotten Jazleen this far. You have to be there for her until she can find her own way."

"How am I going to do that?"

"I've got some ideas."

"Okay, what?"

"Well, one thing that this program tries to do is to give these students the book club experience," Landry said. "It takes volunteers to do that."

"I can't lead a book club," Calla declared with certainty.

"That's not what we need. The Literature for All of Us program sends trained leaders for the session. What we need are volunteers to set the ambiance, to provide the refreshments, to make it feel like the special event that it is. You could do that."

"But I have a job," she said.

He nodded. "Lots of employers want their employees to put in volunteer hours."

"Dr. Walker isn't a big corporation," Calla insisted. "He has a small office. I'm not at all sure that I could get away."

"Well, you can try," Landry suggested.

"Yes," she admitted. "I could try."

"If you can turn Jazleen around, your boss ought to be easy by comparison."

Calla chuckled. "I guess so," she admitted.

"How did you convince Jazleen?" Landry asked.

Calla opened her mouth to reply and then hesitated.

"What?"

"It's a little embarrassing," she admitted. "She's doing it as a favor to me."

"A favor?"

She nodded. "Jazleen thinks I'm trying to impress you. So as a favor, she's helping."

"Oh, I see." His dark eyes crinkled with humor, but his tone was low and sexy. "Well, I *am* impressed."

Calla felt herself blushing. "Jazleen's just so young," she explained unnecessarily. "She doesn't understand how two grown-up people can just…just enjoy each other's company without any…any silly romance sort of stuff going on."

His expression grew slightly more serious. He walked his fingers slowly across the smooth surface until they reached her hand, which he clasped gently in his own.

"No, no of course," he whispered. "Two grown-up people like us. There would never be any silly romance stuff going on."

Calla's heart was beating so loudly she worried that he could hear it. Breathlessness was not a feeling to which she was accustomed.

Get a hold of yourself! she silently admonished. She wanted to move away from him. She could have easily freed her hand, but somehow she didn't want to relinquish the warmth, the connection that he offered.

"I don't... I don't have flings or...or affairs or whatever you call it," she told him.

Landry lowered his chin slightly. "I'm not sure I have a word for what I want to have with you. Whatever it is, it's kind of a new thing for me." He rose to his feet and took a step closer to her.

Calla stiffened her back.

"I don't want to scare you," he said. "I just want to kiss you."

She didn't know what she thought about that. Her brain seemed sluggish as her senses tightened into electric expectation.

Landry laid his palm across her jaw and raised her

face toward him. His movements were slow, deliberate, as if he were drawing out the anticipation. Finally, she could no longer wait and she met his lips with her own.

He tasted like chocolate and Calla couldn't get enough. She trembled in his arms. Landry wrapped her tightly in his embrace. She felt so safe, so cared for, so desired.

When their lips parted, he continued to hold her close. Calla buried her face into his neck and shoulder, taking in the wonderful masculine scent of him. Oh how she had missed this! She could no longer believe that she'd been willing to forego this, willing to say these feelings were only something from the past.

Landry stepped back and seated himself once more on the stool facing her. His expression was smoky with desire.

"Do you think I could get away with seducing you on Canasta Street in the middle of a Monday afternoon?"

"Uh...maybe," she answered.

He laughed. "I take that as a challenge."

CHAPTER
⟡ FIVE ⟡

Calla was genuinely surprised how easy her venture into school volunteering turned out to be. The book group was scheduled for Thursday mornings, which just happened to be Dr. Walker's weekly match at the handball court. The office staff used that time to clear up paperwork and the doctor was completely fine with Calla staying a half hour later each afternoon to make up her share.

Jazleen was as good as her word. Monday morning, she made her way to Cavitz Alternative High School and filled out the paperwork to officially become a student again. Calla didn't see any magical change in the girl. And when she asked, "How was school?" Jazleen's responses always centered around whether or not she'd seen Landry that day, which was apparently what she thought Calla wanted to know.

On the first day of the book club, Calla found herself almost as leery of going to school as Jazleen had been. The building did not have a gathering place for students, a statue of a long-dead community hero or a motto in Latin over the doorway.

Cavitz Alternative was located in a corner building in the shadow of a busy expressway. It had once housed a dry-goods emporium, the name of which was still visible in the tile of the lobby. Calla was loaded down with what she hoped were the perfect accoutrements for a book club. She must have looked as out of place as she felt because a young woman stopped to help her.

"I need to find the book group."

The woman nodded enthusiastically. "Second floor, study hall," she told Calla, pointing toward the wide stairway in the back.

Struggling with all she had to carry, Calla wandered around until she found the elevator. She took it up one flight and then, after asking more directions, found herself in front of a door with a sheet of white paper identifying the location.

She tapped politely a couple of times before turning the knob. The room was empty. Calla set her bags on a nearby table and surveyed it slowly. Dingy, aged glass block provided light from the upper half of the two outside walls. There was an old but comfy-looking couch in one corner and a couple of mismatched armchairs. The center of the room was dominated by a functional-looking library table surrounded by chairs.

Calla immediately set to work. She dragged the table to the wall and rearranged the chairs to form a conversation circle around the couch. What the space needed was a coffee table, but of course there was nothing like that. She allowed disappointment to spark innovation and borrowed the metal wastepaper basket by the door. Hanging on the wall above it was a small bulletin board that held only two notes. One was a schedule for the room's use, the other an admonition with exclamation points about cleaning up your own mess. Calla decided the room could do without both for a couple of hours. She set the bulletin board facedown across the top of the wastepaper basket to create an instant coffee table. From her bag she got out a table runner. It was too long, but it covered the width of the board perfectly. She folded it so that it hung down a few inches from the floor on either side. Calla liked the look. It was welcoming and cozy. She added a couple of candles for a centerpiece.

Her Sunday best tablecloth covered the big table next to the wall. She'd brought her nicest things. Most of them never got out of the cabinet except on Christmas. The Fosteria glass pitcher that had been her mother's was soon filled with raspberry tea. The tray Mark had bought for her on a trip to Washington displayed the fancy finger sandwiches she'd made. There was a plate of apples that she'd carefully cut into leaf patterns and brushed with lemon juice. And for something sweet, she'd made a pineapple upside-down cake with red maraschino cherries in the centers of the rings.

She'd just finished laying out the forks and napkins when the door opened. A stylish young woman, short and round and wearing black jeans and a bright pink sweater, came through the door. She pulled a rolling bag that looked more like an oversized briefcase than a piece of luggage.

"Hi, I'm Lyssa," she said. "I'm the group leader from Literature for All of Us."

The two shook hands. "Calla Middleton, volunteer," she said, by way of introduction.

"This looks lovely," Lyssa said.

Calla smiled, pleased. "Well, Landry...uh, Mr. Sinclair said that you wanted it to be like a ladies' book club. So, it seems you've got to have fancy food and nice tablecloths."

"You've outdone yourself," Lyssa said. "We usually

just have juice and chips. I hope we can count on you coming every week."

"I'll do my best."

"Typically the volunteers make themselves scarce during the meeting," Lyssa said.

Calla nodded. "I think that would be best. My son's girlfriend is in this group and I'm sure she'll settle in better without thinking I'm looking over her shoulder. I'll find someplace to bide my time and then I'll come back to clean up."

Perhaps five minute later the girls began arriving and Calla made her exit. She passed Jazleen in the hallway. The girl sidled over to her and spoke in a furtive whisper.

"I just saw him go into the teachers' lounge around the corner and all the way to the end of the hall." The girl added a thumbs-up sign for emphasis.

Calla could only shake her head. But she did follow those directions. As she approached the door, it opened and Landry walked out. If he was surprised to see her, he gave no indication, just a wide grin of pleasure at having run into her.

"Have I discovered the truth about you, Mr. Landry?" she asked. "Are you one of those principals that hang out in the teachers' lounge?"

"Not really. And none of my teachers get much lounging time."

"But you're here now."

"Looking for you," he admitted. "I thought you might be hanging out here while the book group is in session."

"Actually Jazleen sent me in this direction," Calla told him. "She saw you headed this way."

Landry grinned. "I like that girl more and more," he said, chuckling. "I wanted to give you a tour of our school."

"Great."

"The teachers' lounge here is about what you'd expect," he said, opening the door wide enough to peek in. "A coffeepot and a refrigerator. Not the complete comforts of home, but it works. And you are welcome to hang out here anytime."

"Thanks."

They began walking down the hallway. He kept his voice low so they wouldn't disturb any classes in session.

"We have eighty-six students currently enrolled," he said. "Ten teachers, six full-time and four part-time. We've got a staff of three, a few volunteers and a dozen trained mentors that are here on a regular basis."

"That seems like a lot of people for so few students."

"It's a ten-to-one ratio, which is much better than a typical school," Landry said. "But many of our students have been in our educational system for years without spending ten minutes with a teacher, so I figure it all evens out."

He showed her an empty classroom that had only a half-dozen desks.

"We do both day and night classes," he said. "We try to accommodate varied schedules, so all the classes are small."

Calla nodded.

"On the first floor we have our Family First program," he said. "Right now we're just providing child care for our students when they're in class. We're hoping to start up some regular parenting classes not only for our students and alumni, but for all the young parents in the neighborhood."

"Wow," Calla said.

"Our students face a lot of obstacles to education," Landry said. "We try to figure out what they are and deal with them as effectively as we can."

The tour included a tiny but up-to-date computer lab, the half-dozen shelves that made up the school's lending library, and a former loading dock that had been turned into an experimental theater.

"Our students are from a media generation. They write the plays, perform the plays, provide the music and even capture it all on film."

Calla couldn't help but be impressed. "Jazleen is going

to love it here," she said. "I'm beginning to think this is where Nathan should have gone."

Landry shook his head. "Nathan is a lucky guy. He's smart, motivated and he had parents that had an eye to the future. He was going to flourish no matter what the educational element. Our students need a little more help to get them onto a more level playing field."

In the stairwell, Landry took her hand. "Are you saving your Saturday night for me?"

She nodded.

"Good, can I have Friday night and all of Sunday, too?"

"You're going to get very tired of me," she warned.

He shook his head. "I can't help myself. You're like hard liquor, completely intoxicating and very addictive."

By the time he took his leave they were back on the second floor in front of the study hall. The ninety-minute book club meeting was ending. Calla waited for the first few girls to leave before she made her way inside.

She spotted Jazleen immediately. A large girl, heavily pregnant, was talking to her. Jazleen's face was completely blank, revealing nothing. When Jazleen caught sight of Calla, she immediately made an excuse to get away.

"So how was it?"

"I think that's the question I'm supposed to ask you," Calla said.

Jazleen shrugged.

It was a noncommittal gesture, but it wasn't negative. Calla took that as a good start.

"The real reason I'm here is to score you points with the principal."

Calla smiled. "Well, you're doing a great job. I just spent the whole time you were in the book group touring the school."

Jazleen raised an eyebrow.

"Did he show you the Lust Bin?"

"The Lust Bin?"

Jazleen laughed, her face lighting up as if from the inside. "It's really the janitor's closet, but sometimes couples sneak in there to steal some snug time."

Calla tutted and shook her head. "No, I missed the Lust Bin. I'll have to ask him about it next time."

"Don't have him *tell* you about it," she teased. "You've got to have him take you there."

The next few weeks passed almost like a checklist. Nathan's college paperwork in the mail. Check. Halloween candy. Check. Buy a turkey for Thanksgiving. Check. And every Thursday, Calla made her way to the book group. Coming up with interesting snacks to serve and decorating the table was quickly becoming an important and cherished part of her week. She had begun to know the girls now, and as they loosened up with each other, they also did with Calla. They didn't always express their appreciation directly, but she felt it and she liked it.

Missing the week's meeting for Thanksgiving was a bit of a letdown, but it spurred Calla to action. Since Mark's death, she and Nathan had shared the holidays alone. Their celebrations were quiet and at times bittersweet. A husband and father was most missed on family occasions, and becoming accustomed to not having him there did not make the loss any easier to bear.

"Jazleen, I want to invite you and your aunt for Thanksgiving dinner," Calla announced the weekend before the holiday.

The kids were on the couch. Jazleen was sitting up and Nathan had his head in her lap. Both were reading. Calla saw Jazleen's book was *Beloved* by Toni Morrison—the group's chosen title for the next meeting. They looked up at her comment.

"That's a great idea!" Nathan said.

Jazleen seemed hesitant. "I don't know if my aunt will come."

"Tell her I bake the best pumpkin pie she's ever tasted," Calla said. "And that I'm inviting Mrs. Gamble and Eunice."

Nathan frowned. "Do you think they'll come?"

"I know they will," Calla answered. "Landry Sinclair is going to be here."

Calla was right, of course. She never doubted for a minute that a gossip like Eunice wouldn't jump at the chance to spend time breaking bread with her current favorite subjects.

With Nathan's help, she moved some of the living room furniture upstairs and pushed the heavier pieces against the walls, then brought in the dining table, extending it as far as it would go. The linens, now staples of book group days, were already ironed, and Calla brought down her good dishes from the top cabinet over the sink.

In fact she was standing on a chair retrieving them when Jazleen showed up in the kitchen.

"You're going to kill yourself!" the girl predicted.

"Let me hand these down to you," Calla suggested.

Together they made quick work of the task. When all the plates and cups and saucers were safely on the counter, Jazleen spoke.

"I came to ask you a favor. No, I guess I came to collect on a favor. You *owe* me, remember."

Calla did remember. Jazleen's tone was so sharp and defensive, it was obvious that the girl was not at all accustomed to making requests

"Okay," Calla said, hoping fervently that she wasn't going to ask the impossible. The only way Jazleen would ever learn to ask for help was if she could anticipate that it would be provided.

"You know Darlada," she said.

Calla nodded. The heavyset, heavily pregnant young woman was one of the book group members.

"She's got nowhere to go on Thanksgiving, so I wanted to invite her here," Jazleen said. "Now, you got to know up front that she eats a lot. I can bring a dish of something, but you're still going to have to cook more than you thought."

"Of course she can come," Calla said, thrilled not only that it was such an easy request, but that Jazleen was the person to think of it. "We should have asked the entire book club."

"Everybody has a plan except Darlada," Jazleen said. "She's got...she's got nobody really, and I don't like the idea of her spending another holiday alone. She wrote a poem about eating potato chips last Christmas. That ought to be just a once-in-a-lifetime thing."

Calla agreed.

"By next year," Jazleen said, "she'll have her baby to be company. But until she gets born, it's really up to people she knows."

"Jazleen, you tell her that I'm delighted and excited to have her here to share our holiday," Calla said. "And she can eat as much as she wants. There is always way too much food."

The young woman seemed surprised at that last statement and Calla wondered how many holiday dinners she had been to.

Calla did recruit Jazleen to help her with the cooking. The girl was handy in the kitchen, but she had no experience with fancy cakes or pies and she knew nothing about basting a turkey. The two spent most of the day working together in the kitchen, Nathan coming in from time to time to check on their progress and sneak nibbles. It became a game between him and Jazleen. He would let her catch him at it and she would feign fury and chase him out of the room.

By the time the guests began to show up, everyone was in high spirits. Gerty Cleveland had dressed more attractively than Calla had seen her in twenty years.

"I can't let Eunice and Mrs. Gamble show me up," she explained.

There might have been some danger of that. Each woman had on her very best Sunday outfit. Eunice pretended that this was nothing out of the ordinary, but Mrs. Gamble was not so discreet.

"I'm so excited to have on this dress," she said. "I was beginning to think the next chance I'd get to wear it I'd be lying in my casket."

Nathan answered the door for Darlada and the girl hesitated on the porch. She had changed her mind and was making excuses why she couldn't stay, when Jazleen went out and dragged her in.

"I'm not in the right clothes," she whispered worriedly to Calla. "But I've got so big, I can't fit into anything else."

In jeans and a sweatshirt the size of a pup tent, she was under-dressed for the occasion, but Calla didn't care.

"When we're pregnant we always think we look worse than we do," she told the girl. "Once you get your figure back, everything will fit beautifully."

"I didn't have a good figure to begin with," she said. "I've always been fat."

"I think we now call it 'traditionally built'."

"Traditionally built? I like that."

"It's from *The No. 1 Ladies' Detective Agency*. Have you read it?"

Darlada shook her head. "I never even heard of it."

"I've got the first two books," Calla said. "I'll loan them to you."

The young woman seemed momentarily surprised and then happily agreed. "I guess that's what people who read stuff do," she said. "They loan books to each other."

Landry arrived looking both handsome and at home. He was charming to the ladies, including Darlada, whom he recognized from school. Eunice was giving him a down-the-nose eagle eye, but he made no attempt to disguise his feelings for Calla. In fact, he kissed her hello. It was just a peck but spoke volumes about their relationship.

"Jazleen said you were dating Miz Calla," Darlada said. "It's a good idea."

"I think so, too," Landry told her.

Calla wasn't sure that Eunice agreed, but at least as a guest in Calla's house, she kept her opinion to herself.

They took their places around the table, and Calla offered a prayer with a depth of thankfulness that she hadn't felt in years.

As the food was consumed and appreciated, the conversation gained momentum. Gerty Cleveland talked a little louder than necessary and frequently asked to have things repeated, but no one complained about it. She and Mrs. Gamble took turns telling Darlada about their childbirth experiences and both managed to entertain and enlighten without scaring the teenager.

Landry talked to Nathan about his college admissions and even dragged Jazleen into the conversation.

"It's not too early for you to be thinking about college."

She looked shocked. "Me? Go to college? I'll be lucky if I finish high school."

"It doesn't take luck," Landry assured her. "It just takes time and self-discipline. My impression is that you've got your share of both."

Jazleen didn't deny it. Calla saw that as hope.

The cranberries were passed. The gravy was ladled. The stuffing was served and the succotash spooned. When the last fork was laid down, Calla urged everyone to keep talking as she cleared the table.

Darlada followed her into the kitchen carrying a stack of dishes.

"You don't have to do that," Calla insisted. "You're a guest. Go enjoy yourself."

"I wanted to help clean up—as a kind of thank-you for inviting me."

"I was happy that you could come," Calla said. "And I'm so glad that Jazleen thought of it."

"She's good, you know," Darlada said. "I mean, I know being Nathan's mama and all, you probably worry about who a girl is. But I know Jazleen is good."

"Thank you," Calla said. "It's nice to hear that."

"When I read my potato chips poem," Darlada said, "our group leader was real supportive of it. I am the worst poetry writer in the book group and I know it. But Lyssa told me that what is important is what I have to say, not how well I say it. Jazleen—her poems are way better."

"You write poetry in the group?"

"Oh, yes, ma'am. We all do. That's what our journals are mostly full of. We read what other writers write and then we try to express our own feelings in our own words."

"That's a great thing," Calla said. "I wrote a poem or two when I was young. I still feel close to those words, even though that was a long time ago."

Darlada nodded. "You should ask Jazleen to read you her poems. She can express herself real good. Sometimes she seems all closed up. But when she writes, it's like a flower just opening right up."

"Maybe I will," Calla told her.

She sliced the pies and cake and allowed Darlada to help carry them to the table. After pouring cups of strong coffee for everybody, Calla gratefully settled back into the discussion around the table.

"Do you think you'll put in a garden in the springtime?" Mrs. Gamble asked Landry.

"I'm thinking about it," he said. "Nothing like snow on the ground and a cold wind blowing outside to put my mind to thoughts of fresh tomatoes and snap beans."

There was more talk about the weather, the neighborhood, the future. It was late by the time everyone was talked out. Gerty Cleveland, Mrs. Gamble and Eunice made their way home. Jazleen and Nathan decided to walk Darlada home and Landry stuck around to help with the cleanup.

"I think everything went well," she told him.

"It was the nicest Thanksgiving I remember in a very long time," he told her. "It was great that you included the Gambles. I know they've been spreading gossip about us, but I really did my best to charm them."

"If they weren't charmed, then they must be excellent actresses. Mrs. Gamble thinks you're the greatest thing since sliced bread. And Eunice, well, I'm afraid you missed your chance there. She had her eye on you."

"Really?"

"You never noticed?"

Landry shook his head dramatically. "Once I caught sight of you, I was blinded to all other women."

Calla slapped him with a dishtowel. He took it from her and began drying dishes.

"It was good meeting Jazleen's aunt," he said. "I really try to get to know the families of my students. Sometimes it's not possible."

"What about Darlada's family?" Calla asked.

"Nothing much to speak of," he answered. "She's living in a kind of halfway house for expectant mothers. She'll be able to stay there a few months after the baby is born, but ultimately she's going to have to find some different kind of arrangement."

Calla nodded. She told Landry what Jazleen had said about Darlada's poem.

Landry sighed heavily. "That's one of the realities of the lives of these girls. Often they do find themselves all alone in a very scary world. I think that's why the book group helps so much. They find out that their experience is not unique to them. And they can talk about it with other girls who have been in the same place."

"It's really interesting that they write poetry," Calla said. "I always thought that poetry was like a pipeline to the deepest interior of the soul."

Landry raised his dark eyebrows and grinned at her. "Now that's a very vivid image," he said, reaching over to snake an arm around her waist. "Is that how I get to the deepest interior of your soul?"

"You said you wrote poetry in school," she reminded him with a flirtatious grin. "You might have to hone your skills again."

Landry stood behind her at the kitchen sink and wrapped both arms around her tightly. He leaned down to bury his chin into the crook of her throat.

"I'm always willing to try," he said. "My Calla has a house on Canasta. Falling for her, I could not have done any faster..."

CHAPTER
∽SIX∽

I t felt as if the Thanksgiving dishes were barely put
away before the festive lights of the Christmas season started showing up in the neighborhood. Calla
had never been much of a holiday decorator, but this
year she found it fun to integrate the season into the
book group's refreshment table. And the girls seemed
to appreciate it, oohing and ahhing over little Santa Bear
cookies and candy canes. School, of course, would be
out for winter vacation. That meant three group meetings cancelled.

"I don't know if I can live without book club for three
weeks," she heard one girl comment after a session.

"I know what you mean," Calla heard Jazleen reply.

"Being here, being with all of you—I look forward to it all week long."

Inside her head, Calla was doing a goal line celebration. If Jazleen loved book group, she would not be dropping out to sit at home and watch daytime TV.

Nathan said as much one evening at dinner.

"Jazzy's really liking her classes and making friends and her grades are good for starting so late in the semester. I told her she could probably get Mr. Sinclair to give her a transfer back to high school with me."

"Really?"

Nathan nodded. "She wasn't interested. Jazzy says she likes the teachers and students where she is. It's going to take an extra year for her to graduate. And she said since I'm going to be gone off to college anyway, she thought it might be good for our relationship to have our own lives."

He said the last line with such incredulity that Calla couldn't help but chuckle. "I think your baby is growing up," she teased.

She may have been joking, but it was easy to see that for Jazleen, something had changed. The singular focus on Nathan and the raging jealousy had disappeared. And in her relationship with Calla, the anger was gone.

Calla decided to ask the girl about it.

"What made you decide that you weren't angry with

me?" she asked. "My involvement with the book club or dating Landry Sinclair?"

They were sitting in the warm kitchen on a blustery winter evening. Nathan had gone to a basketball game with a couple of friends. In the past, Jazleen would have tagged along, but she'd finally become secure enough to let the guys go without her.

"Nathan always talks about you like you're so perfect. I'm not so perfect." She shrugged. "I guess you wanting Mr. Sinclair, that made you more human."

"I am not perfect," Calla said with incredulity. "I can't imagine Nathan thinks that."

"Well, maybe he never used that word," Jazleen admitted. "But when he'd talk about you, even if he was complaining about something, it was obvious that he respected you and that he knew that everything you did, you did because you love him."

"Of course I do," Calla said. "He's my child."

"See, that's what made me mad."

"What?"

"That confidence that it's nothing unusual. That doing what's best for your child is what mothers do. That it's proof of loving their child."

Calla nodded.

"The backside of that for me was that my mother

didn't look out for me, she didn't do what was best. Does that mean she didn't love me?"

Calla didn't know what to say.

"I know the truth," Jazleen said. "I know that she did love me. At least at one time she did. And the way you are, it just…it just made me think that I might be wrong, or that you would say that I was wrong or…or I don't know exactly what, but comparing you to my mama, it just made me mad."

"I'm sorry you felt that way," Calla said.

Jazleen shrugged. "And the weird thing was, I wasn't really even aware of what was going on in my head all the time. It's like I didn't stop long enough to think about it and figure out what was going on there."

"That happens sometimes."

"Then I wrote a poem about my mama and how I felt about her and how angry I am at her," Jazleen said. "It just felt so good to say it. And once I could say it, it's like I finally know that I can handle it."

"That's wonderful, Jazleen."

"Would you like to hear it?"

"Your poem? Yes, I'd love to. Darlada says you're the best poet in the whole book club."

Jazleen waved off the compliment. "There's all kinds of different writers in the group. I have lots of vocabulary, more than a lot of the girls. But some of them have a richness or a deepness that I can't come close to."

"Still, I'd like to hear your poem."

Jazleen nodded and went to the living room where she'd left her book bag. A couple of minutes later she was back with her book group journal. She set it on the table in front of her and began leafing through it. Calla knew that she was being offered a trust that was rarely given. She silently vowed to always deserve it.

"Here it is," Jazleen said. "I call it *The Gift from God*."

She glanced up at Calla, who gave her a reassuring nod.

"I am the gift from God
That's what she told me.
I believed it.
I love you. I need you. I don't regret you.
That's what she told me.
I believed it.
Then the day the choice came
Between the dealer and the daughter.
It was the dealer who got deference
And the daughter who got done.
Damaged.
Damn you.
How could you?

I am the gift of God
Given to pay down
Debt on a dirty drug deal.
You better believe it.
Some gifts get tossed.
Even a gift from God.
But inside my mama, hidden
By the glaze from a needle,
Is the love she bears for me always.
I still believe it."

Calla didn't know what to say. She got up from her chair and went to kneel next to Jazleen. She took the young woman in her arms and held her tightly. Sometimes only words could express and sometimes words were unnecessary.

Spring finally came to Canasta Street. The Carnaby children played stickball in the street. Old Mr. Whitten snored in the sunshine on his front porch. And the dirty gray snow that had been part of the landscape for so long magically retreated for another year.

Nathan prepared to cross the stage as a high school graduate. Calla would be there as she'd always imagined, but she would not be alone. She'd have Landry on one side and Jazleen on the other. Nathan got a full-ride scholarship to Northwestern, which was everything they had hoped for. Jazleen, too, now had college as her goal, but it would take another year at least.

Darlada had her baby, a healthy little girl. Surprisingly she'd moved in with the Gambles. Mrs. Gamble had suffered a fall late in the winter and Eunice realized that she needed help. Bringing Darlada and the baby into their household was like a tonic to the older woman and a breath of freedom for Eunice.

Early one morning Landry came knocking at Calla's door. She was still in her bathrobe and her hair was in a towel.

"Come outside," he said.

"What?"

"I have something to show you."

"Let me get dressed."

"No time for clothes. You've got to come right now."

Calla followed him down the porch, out through the gate and around the fence to his backyard. There in the small plot of ground, just poking their little green shoots out of the brown earth, were the bulbs he had planted.

"It really happened," she said. "After all the cold, dark waiting, there are really going to be full-grown flowers here."

Landry nodded. "And I want us to be together when our daffodils all come into bloom."

He held her hand in his and pulled her closer. "Calla, you are the most stately flower in my garden. I don't think it would even be a garden for me without you. Do you understand my meaning? It's pretty muddy here, but I'll drop down on one knee if I have to."

Calla smiled. "I understand your meaning, Landry. And my answer is yes!"

* * * * *

Dear Reader,

Karen Thomson was not looking to change the world. A stay-at-home mom with a desire to do work she liked on her own schedule, Karen utilized her education and love of books by becoming a professional book-group leader. She loved her job and was having marvelous success. Her work was personally fulfilling and she was completely satisfied with the direction of her life.

Then one day a person in her group suggested that the power of the book club was such a wonderful thing, wouldn't it be great if they could find a way to share it with at-risk young women in the city's urban core?

Karen thought that was an interesting idea, but she didn't feel qualified. She wasn't a social worker. She wasn't a youth counselor. She wasn't a survivor of a depressed inner-city community. She wasn't young and she wasn't a minority. Surely she wasn't the person for the job.

For a year she went on with her day-to-day life as the idea percolated in the back of her mind, calling her, pushing her.

Finally she decided to do one group. Just one group, she assured herself, just to see if the concept was even feasible.

That first group was almost an homage to her own career. She remembered how she got started: how alone and isolated she'd been as a young mother, and how desperate to think about something besides babies and diapers and the cost of the light bill.

Her first group was made up entirely of teenage moms. Many, including Karen, worried that they might not have any interest at all in reading, writing or each other.

From that very first day, Literature for All of Us changed lives. To hear Karen talk about it is like listening to the witness of a miracle. Reading stories, responding to the themes presented and talking about how they pertained to their own lives had the power to alter the young people's perception of themselves and the world around them. "Their self-esteem and self-confidence went up." Using the literature they read as a model, Karen asked them to write poetry about themselves. "At a difficult time in their lives…they wrote the truth… and realized how much strength they had."

Today, in collaboration with alternative high schools, GED providers and after-school programs, the organization carries the book-group model to young men and women in underserved neighborhoods impacted by poverty, violence, gangs and drugs. More than half of their clients are pregnant or parenting teens. The program not only enriches their lives, but allows them to pass on the gift of family literacy to the next generation.

If you would like to share your love of reading and the magic of its impact on your life, please check out the website literatureforallofus.org or write to Literature for All of Us, 2010 Dewey Avenue, Evanston, IL 60201.

Volunteers, trained book-group leaders and financial donations all help to change lives. And changing lives is changing the world.

Pamela Morsi

#1 *New York Times* Bestselling Author

SUSAN WIGGS

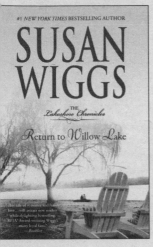

Sonnet Romano has the ideal career, the ideal boyfriend and has just been offered a prestigious fellowship. But when she learns her mother is unexpectedly expecting in a high-risk pregnancy, she puts everything on hold and heads home.

When her mother receives a devastating diagnosis, Sonnet must decide what really matters, even if that means staying in Avalon and taking a job that forces her to work alongside her biggest, and maybe her sweetest, mistake—award-winning filmmaker Zach Alger.

In a summer of laughter and tears, of old dreams and new possibilities, Sonnet may find the home of her heart.

Available wherever books are sold.

#1 *New York Times* Bestselling Author
ROBYN CARR

Virgin River became a safe haven for prosecutor Brie Sheridan after she nearly lost her life at the hands of a crazed criminal. Though she still has fears, she also has someone who wants to show her what it means to trust again.

A decorated marine, LAPD officer Mike Valenzuela was badly wounded in the line of duty. Twice divorced, he longs for the commitment and happiness his marine buddies have found.

Mike will do anything to help Brie free herself from painful memories. Passionate, strong and gentle, he vows to give back to her what she's so selflessly given him—her heart, and with it, a new beginning.

Available wherever books are sold.

**Sometimes the best man
is the one you least expect….**

New York Times **Bestselling Author**

KRISTAN HIGGINS

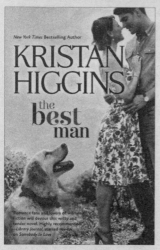

Faith Holland left her hometown after being jilted at the altar. Now a little older and wiser, she's ready to return to the Blue Heron Winery, her family's vineyard, to confront the ghosts of her past, and maybe enjoy a glass of red. After all, there's some great scenery there….

Like Levi Cooper, the local police chief—and best friend of her former fiancé. There's a lot about Levi that Faith never noticed, and it's not just those deep green eyes. The only catch is she's having a hard time forgetting that he helped ruin her wedding all those years ago. If she can find a minute amid all her family drama to stop and smell the rosé, she just might find a reason to stay at Blue Heron, and finish that walk down the aisle.

Available wherever books are sold!

Be sure to connect with us at:
Harlequin.com/Newsletters
Facebook.com/HarlequinBooks
Twitter.com/HarlequinBooks

HARLEQUIN® HQN™
www.Harlequin.com

REQUEST YOUR FREE BOOKS!

2 FREE NOVELS
FROM THE ROMANCE COLLECTION
PLUS 2 FREE GIFTS!

YES! Please send me 2 FREE novels from the Romance Collection and my 2 FREE gifts (gifts are worth about $10). After receiving them, if I don't wish to receive any more books, I can return the shipping statement marked "cancel." If I don't cancel, I will receive 4 brand-new novels every month and be billed just $5.99 per book in the U.S. or $6.49 per book in Canada. That's a savings of at least 25% off the cover price. It's quite a bargain! Shipping and handling is just 50¢ per book in the U.S. and 75¢ per book in Canada.* I understand that accepting the 2 free books and gifts places me under no obligation to buy anything. I can always return a shipment and cancel at any time. Even if I never buy another book, the two free books and gifts are mine to keep forever.

194/394 MDN FVU7

Name	(PLEASE PRINT)	

Address		Apt. #

City	State/Prov.	Zip/Postal Code

Signature (if under 18, a parent or guardian must sign)

Mail to the Harlequin® Reader Service:
IN U.S.A.: P.O. Box 1867, Buffalo, NY 14240-1867
IN CANADA: P.O. Box 609, Fort Erie, Ontario L2A 5X3

Want to try two free books from another line?
Call 1-800-873-8635 or visit www.ReaderService.com.

* Terms and prices subject to change without notice. Prices do not include applicable taxes. Sales tax applicable in N.Y. Canadian residents will be charged applicable taxes. Offer not valid in Quebec. This offer is limited to one order per household. Not valid for current subscribers to the Romance Collection or the Romance/Suspense Collection. All orders subject to credit approval. Credit or debit balances in a customer's account(s) may be offset by any other outstanding balance owed by or to the customer. Please allow 4 to 6 weeks for delivery. Offer available while quantities last.

Your Privacy—The Harlequin® Reader Service is committed to protecting your privacy. Our Privacy Policy is available online at www.ReaderService.com or upon request from the Harlequin Reader Service.

We make a portion of our mailing list available to reputable third parties that offer products we believe may interest you. If you prefer that we not exchange your name with third parties, or if you wish to clarify or modify your communication preferences, please visit us at www.ReaderService.com/consumerchoice or write to us at Harlequin Reader Service Preference Service, P.O. Box 9062, Buffalo, NY 14269. Include your complete name and address.

ROM13

#1 *New York Times* bestselling author

LINDA LAEL MILLER

presents the Stone Creek story that started it all...

When trouble strikes in Haven, Arizona Ranger Sam O'Ballivan is determined to sort it out. Badge and gun hidden, he arrives posing as the new schoolteacher, and discovers his first task: bringing the ranchers' children under control. So he starts with a call on Maddie Chancelor, the local postmistress and older sister of a boy in need of discipline.

But far from the spinster Sam expects, Maddie turns out to be a graceful woman whose prim-and-proper demeanor is belied by the fire in her eyes. Working undercover to capture rustlers and train robbers has always kept Sam isolated and his heart firmly in check—until now. But something about the spirited postmistress tempts him to start down a path he swore he'd never travel....

Available wherever books are sold!

Be sure to connect with us at:

Harlequin.com/Newsletters

Facebook.com/HarlequinBooks

Twitter.com/HarlequinBooks

HARLEQUIN® HQN™
www.Harlequin.com

PHLLM721